"So You Seek Combat?"

"Even with yourself!" said Coral Bud.

Rustad smiled. "Nay, it is not allowed a seasoned warrior to fight such as you. But combat you shall have."

He turned to the slaves and thundered: "Set up the battle ring—and uncage a burrow rat!"

In spite of herself, Coral Bud trembled. No one could survive in the battle ring against those fangs!

THE LIGHT-BEARER

SAM NICHOLSON

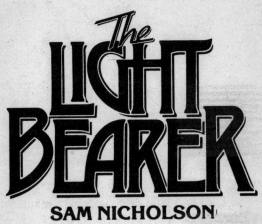

THE LIGHT BEARER

SAM NICHOLSON

BERKLEY BOOKS, NEW YORK

THE LIGHT-BEARER

A Berkley Book / published by arrangement with
the author

PRINTING HISTORY
Berkley edition / July 1980

For information address: Berkley Publishing Corporation,
200 Madison Avenue, New York, New York 10016.

ISBN: 0-425-04587-0

A BERKLEY BOOK® TM 757,375

PRINTED IN THE UNITED STATES OF AMERICA

The LIGHT BEARER

THE LIGHT-BEARER

"HO, BARGEMASTER! ATTEND YOUR PROW! What barge approaches Mus-al-ram, great mistress of the Desert Cities?"

The newly betrothed bride hidden within the splendid tent on the barge's midship platform sat up impatiently on her cushions, reflecting that the Gatemaster's question was just a stupid ceremony. *This* barge was known on all the canals from the Desert Cities to the Seacoast.

The ceremonious answer came, "The barge of Bulbul, Chief Eunuch to the Wizard Amfi, master of the parthogen bottles!"

The girl listened further. The barge was humming at a standstill. There was no rumble or clank of a bronze watergrid being raised. What were the awkward land crabs doing now?

Coral Bud, daughter of the sea king Hamar, master pirate of the planet, sprang to her feet and tossed her soft dark hair back from her shoulders. She put her hand to the tent fold—and drew back, feeling the immodest discomfort of her harem attire.

On her father's ships Coral Bud had worn the wool and leather of a seaman, a bright scarf binding up her hair, a sharp dagger sheathed at her waistband. But since her father had escorted her aboard Bulbul's barge, she had been shivering in flimsy gauze—

ankle-length pantaloons, short braided jacket, a nose veil that hung crookedly beneath her flashing dark eyes.

She could not show herself—and yet she was curious. She heard the watergrid rise in its grooves. The barge hummed into motion. Old fat Bulbul himself must be at the prow. She could hear his high, giggling "Make way!" as the barge arrogantly shoved and bumped other canal traffic.

Oof! That *was* a bump. They were at a standstill again. Bulbul suddenly called out in a mocking tone.

"Light-Bearer! Second seed-son of my gracious master! A word, I pray, young Lord Zeid!"

"Zeid ben Amfi!" breathed the girl. At last she could catch a glimpse of the young Lord Zeid—Moonship apprentice—messenger of the Space Givers—her future husband!

Drawing her flimsy jacket modestly over her high young breasts, Coral Bud opened the tent curtain a crack and peered out.

The scene was strange to the eyes of the pirate girl. The late-afternoon sun, its bright beams knifing through the parched air, was slipping toward the horizon of wind-swirled sand. In the great city of Mus-al-ram, the tightly packed mass of mud brick dwellings were throwing open their shutters to the oncoming night. From the surrounding oasis came the rattle of palm fronds against the rising breeze.

In the crowded bazaar along the main canal, the outcries of vendors were reaching a crescendo.

"Ai—ai—come hither, master buyer from the Marble Lands! Touch this carpet, woven from the silken floss of the Space Givers!... *see, abu Falat, how the fool bends like a barley sheaf with gold!*"

"Hoy—hoy—young man from the sea kingdoms! Buy beauty this day! Cross the stone bridge at the palace canal to the rose-and-lily doorpost, and find duplos fashioned within the parthogen bottles of the Wizard Amfi himself! Smooth-skinned, sleek-tressed, love-instructed duplos—!"

Woolen cloaks jostling embroidered satin robes—lurid colors—strident voices—the barbarous tumult of an illiterate planet.

Coral Bud gazed long at the bazaar before turning her attention to the barge itself and the fat, satin-clad eunuch standing on the command platform at the prow. Bulbul wore a green jacket over a white blouse, flaring pink pantaloons, gilt slippers. His turban was thick rolls of white silk, pinned by a gold brooch dangling with gems.

To whom had Bulbul called? The girl's glance followed the direction of his outstretched arm and pointing, bejeweled finger.

A lustrous-eyed, soft-bearded young man in a hooded white robe was walking slowly through the throng which hushed and gave way before him. Also a vendor, he carried his wares hanging on gold chains from his staff—globes of pure light, as many-colored as the stars now glowing forth in the darkening sky.

Zeid had paused at the eunuch's shout. His expressive eyes were glinting thoughts that boded ill for the insolence. He turned from the bazaar, walked to the canal edge, rested his staff on the stone blocks retaining the canal, and waited.

There was a silent duel that delighted the watching maiden. Bulbul was the loser. Having craved an audience, he perforce had to climb down from the command platform, with much wheezing and wobbling, and go across the cargo barge moored between his own barge and the waiting Zeid. He stumbled and waddled on the cargo, smearing his gilt slippers and pink pantaloons on bundles of black incense bark.

Finally he hauled his bloated flab to the stone retaining wall, and Coral Bud laughed to herself. Serve the bloated slave-tyrant right! How his gossip had bored her on the journey from the Seacoast!

But what was he saying to the Light-Bearer?

"AH, ZEID BEN AMFI!" he was complaining, as he straightened his turban. "Once too often will you make jest of your servant! And yet I hail you but to enrich you!"

"More likely to enrich yourself, Bulbul," smiled Zeid. He glanced at the bronze-shielded barge and the gold-bordered purple tent at midship. The veiled, dark-eyed face at the tent fold startled him. He demanded, "Who is the girl? Another chattering wife for my brother Rustad?"

Bulbul averted his head and watched the setting sun bring

3

sparkles to his jeweled fist. "Hasn't the Princess Serada told my lord Zeid of the girl?"

"My mother Serada is as close with her counsel as with her gold."

"Then it is not my humble place to reveal secrets."

Zeid laughed aloud. "A looser-tongued talebearer never existed! However, the girl is certainly no concern of mine! Why did you hail me? What traitorous scheme must be spoken here because it cannot be spoken within my father's walls?"

"Bulbul a traitor? Not so! But the Wizard's commands must sometimes be executed in stealth. Lord Zeid, look upon this glass! Have you seen better loveliness for the parthogen bottles?"

The eunuch drew a glass rectangle from inside his jacket. He rubbed his palm over the surface and handed the rectangle to Zeid.

The blank glass shimmered. A female figure lay there, as if floating in a silver sea. Her tresses were coppery waves—her eyes sea-green—her breasts high—her limbs fair.

"No coarse-pored, big-footed, hairy-limbed grape treader, that one!" giggled Bulbul. "With her seed in the parthogen bottles—"

Revulsion darkened Zeid's countenance. "What swine would sell such beauty to the parthogen bottles?"

"Well now, Zeid, if she could be sold, there would be no need for conniving. But she is Fire Lotus, free princess of the Marble Lands, and wishes to sell her seed but not herself."

"Wishes to sell her seed—?"

"No princess is so rich that she does not desire more. And who will pay better than the Wizard Amfi?"

"He will pay not a copper. He will entice the princess to the Seacoast and send Rustad to capture her."

"Yes. And how will *that* profit Fire Lotus—or poor Bulbul—or my Lord Zeid, whose mad whims need more gold than he earns from the Space Giver lamps?"

Zeid was gazing wistfully on the delicate features. "Surely no crass desires animate such tender eyes!"

"I don't know at what point desire for pearls, rubies, and emeralds becomes crass, my Lord Zeid. I only know that Fire Lotus demands gold, not slavery. She is daughter to the Prince of the Milk White Quarries, and her fortress would hurl even Rustad into the deep quarry lakes."

"And you would send me to bargain on her behalf with my father—to bear his greed and wrath?"

"To beard an old lion, one sends a young one."

Zeid sighed. "I can't believe—Fire Lotus doesn't know what she's doing—"

"But my Lord Zeid can speak to the Wizard? Keeping silent as to the paltry sum he and Bulbul have been promised by the princess?"

"I never could make such a contemptible bargain—yet I wish I could speak with the princess. I could pretend to my father—"

He lost himself in the beauty of the portrait. Bulbul glanced at the now closed purple tent, and he smiled a mean smile. He took the glass and slid it into the sleeve-slit of Zeid's robe. "Yes, young prince, speak cunningly to the Wizard."

Zeid came out of his dream and bethought himself of the evening's duties. He had completely forgotten the dark-eyed girl within the tent.

THE SKY WAS NOW overspread by myriads of low-hanging stars, whose colors filled the air with a mottled shifting light. Aiming the glow of his lamps ahead of him, Zeid hurried into a narrow street.

Rioting beggars were fighting before a closed door with a circle carved on the lintel above it. Each of the planet's lords, wizards, and merchants had an elaborate seal which they wax-stamped, carved, or painted as identification. Zeid, the Moonship apprentice, could read and write, and he believed a circle most clearly represented himself and his ideas.

The beggars—the crook-backed fighting and cursing the lamed—rushed him as he approached. "The hospice dog has barred us—and admitted others!" they whined.

"Begone, scum that would twist your own limbs rather than work!" raged Zeid, swinging his lamps at their heads. "Begone!"

The heavy door opened, and Zeid strode over the threshold.

The dimly lit inner chamber was thick-strewn with pallets and bodies. At the back of the chamber a large caldron was bubbling with spicy stew. Somewhere children wailed as if in pain.

"Full house tonight, as usual, Lord Zeid," said a sturdy man in white robe and leathern apron, "and not more than six honest souls. Didn't the Space Givers tell you how to separate sheep from goats?"

"They said it couldn't be done, good Jibbo. Why are the children crying?"

"Alas, my lord, a father maimed two babes and thrust them at the hospice door so that they could live on your bounty until they could beg."

"The babes we will keep and heal. Do you know the father? Tell the public executioner to slit his throat and display the body in the bazaar."

The sturdy man paled, then bowed and said, "It will be done, Lord Zeid."

For all his Moonship learning, Zeid, too, was a barbarian— and a lord.

HE WALKED THE LONG WAY around the Wizard's walls to the gate farthest from the canal grid and the turmoil Bulbul's arrival must be occasioning.

He paused before the massive bronze and spoke. "Open, O gate! Zeid the son commands!"

The gate swung smoothly aside. Zeid entered a quiet courtyard lit by larger globes. A group of young girls—identically fair, in gossamer trousers and jackets—ran laughing away from him into a colonnaded passage.

One girl remained, lying along the alabaster rim of the central fountain. She seemed to be asleep, but when Zeid walked over to her, he saw that she was dead.

He called angrily, "Aya!" and an old woman hobbled from the colonnade.

"So another must be thrown into the Wizard's lightning oven!" she grumbled in a cracked voice. "We were unlucky with that year's parthogen bottles and will hardly mature enough for a profit!"

Zeid left her with the dead duplo and walked up the broad steps into the pillared palace hall. At the far end was the harem door, a mirror on its gold paneling.

He recalled Bulbul, and his hand went briefly to the portrait glass in his sleeve. He hesitated while he extinguished the lamps hanging from his staff. Then he walked to the mirror, pressed an embossing on the rim, and said, "It's your son Zeid, O Wizard."

His own face was replaced by his father's harder, heavier, more darkly bearded countenance. "With important news, since you interrupt my pleasure?"

"Only behold."

Zeid drew out the portrait glass, rubbed it, and held it to the mirror. His father's eyes widened; his fleshy lips curved back from his teeth. "Who and where, most excellent son?"

"Fire Lotus, free princess of the Milk White Quarries. The rascal Bulbul would have had her by guile—but failed, and now would send me to bargain for some obscure reason, which, perhaps, your greater wits can understand."

Humor came into his father's eyes. "I understand it so well that I bid you discuss the journey's expenses with your mother, true daughter of Serad the Miserly. Bulbul would rather not bargain in that direction, either."

The mirror blanked in dismissal.

Zeid replaced the portrait in his robe, took up his lamps, and walked to his own quarters.

As boys, both Zeid and his elder brother Rustad had been carried aloft in the Space Giver's cloud to the giant Moonship. In a richly heaped bazaar they had been asked to choose a Gift which they could take back to their home.

Rustad had seized upon swords and battle axes—and had been returned with the trophies to the palace in Mus-al-ram. Zeid had been interested only in the glowing lights hung above the wares.

SAM NICHOLSON

"They're really not part of the Gifts," said the white-coveralled Givers, "but you may have one if you like."

"But then you might lack a lamp," said the observant boy. "You said I can have anything I want. I want to learn to make lamps. Keep your promise and teach me."

The Space Givers smiled and kept him aloft until manhood. When he returned to the Wizard's palace, a Space Magic workshop descended with him and was now an ell continuing from his palace rooms. Always locked because of danger to meddlers, it had barred skylights which opened automatically to let in the cool night air.

However, on this evening, Zeid did not enter the workshop. He left his staff at the workshop door, threw open the shutters of his dressing chamber, discarded his dusty robe—carefully setting aside the portrait—bathed in his mist-fountain, reclothed himself in princely gold-thread gauze and gold-braided turban, and ascended the staircase to his mother's apartments.

The eunuchs at the double doors bowed and admitted him. In the first chamber, the currently matured duplos were singing and dancing while slave-tutors instructed them. Short-lived, sterile, with no capacity for thought, the duplos cheerfully bestowed pleasure and died without really having lived.

Seated on gold cushions in the next chamber was the dark-eyed girl from the barge. She was clad in rainbow gauze and had a gold circlet holding back her heavy tresses. She was looking at a casket of jewels a slave girl was offering her.

So, thought Zeid, the maiden was to be Rustad's wife. She was not ill-looking. Slim-bodied, like a boy, with a direct, fearless gaze.

He bowed to her but did not speak, and approached his mother's audience chamber. At the threshold he paused. His mother was resting carelessly among her cushions, and his brother Rustad was seated cross-legged beside her.

When she saw Zeid, she smiled and waved him to enter.

Serada, daughter of Serad the Miserly, was still a beautiful woman with warm-toned flesh, cinnamon hair, and pearl-gray eyes.

Rustad sprang to his feet, a magnificent figure in the long,

8

scarlet-brocaded tunic and narrow trousers of a warrior and a cloth-of-gold turban.

"Brother Zeid comes to hear his good fortune," he sneered. His hand went to his jeweled dagger as he spoke, and Serada quickly rose to stand between her sons.

"Sweet Rustad, most beloved of first-born sons," she coaxed, "don't begrudge poor Zeid the cheap purchase Bulbul has fetched from the Sea Kingdoms. A wife Zeid must have, and a less costly one we could not find. Be content, dearest Rustad, with your wives and duplos—and leave the weary business of the palace to your doting mother."

"Your love ever commands me," returned Rustad. He kissed his mother's hand and left the chamber, after giving Zeid a murderous scowl.

"Come, sit down, my son who has all the family's wit," continued Serada, drawing Zeid down to the cushions. "What think you of the little Coral Bud?"

"Not much," said Zeid, "and less of any scheme to mate me. Rustad brooks no cousinly rivals to his own sons. Were I to wed, his knife would unman me at the bridal chamber."

"Nonsense. The Wizard would take a terrible revenge upon Rustad's flock."

"Which would not mend my sorry state. No, mother, let Rustad have the girl."

"His harem is a screeching torment already with the three wives he has. I will tolerate no more. But I had not yet sent for you, Zeid. Why have you come?"

"The Wizard bids me take a journey to the Marble Lands. I must have Bulbul's barge to the coastal river—"

"The trading barge is smaller and more convenient."

"—and ship passage across the Great Sea—"

"Feelafell the Space Bastard will give you passage to please the Moonship."

"—and a slave to prepare my meals and wash my clothes."

"A slave you may *not* have. You would only free him at the Seacoast. Take Moji, the hired Counting Master. You'll need Moji to seal for you anyhow."

Zeid had no intention of eating meals prepared by a bead-counter, but he kept silent.

Shrill, quarreling female voices erupted into the apartments and came toward them. Serada rose, but Zeid remained seated. Harem disputes were not his affair.

Three young women, stout and sleazy despite rich apparel, came into the chamber dragging Coral Bud after them.

"Mother Serada!" they chorused. "This hussy has caught Rustad's eye! Send her back to her father!"

"Loose me, fishwives!" cried the girl in a clear, strong voice. "I am to marry the Lord Zeid!"

"Not so!" retorted Zeid. "From whatever Seacoast harem you were fetched—"

"Seacoast harem, indeed! My father is the great Hamar, scourge of horde-ships and raiders alike!"

"Yes, dear Zeid," said Serada hastily. "Coral Bud is not a girl to be scorned."

Zeid got to his feet and bowed. "Coral Bud, my scorn is not for you but for arranged marriages. I'm not a battle beast to be mated with a chosen mare. And, what is more important, my heart is given to another."

Here was a bit of gossip to make the harem women forget all else! They gasped and stared wide-eyed.

In the stunned moment, Coral Bud wrenched free of her captors, sprang over the cushions, leapt upon an inlaid chest against the chamber's outer wall, seized a tapestry, and pulled herself up to the sill of the opened window high in the wall.

She knelt a moment on the sill, twisted her body, and slithered upward outside the window. Her gauze-trousered legs—shapely legs, Zeid had to admit—wriggled and disappeared aloft.

The sea rover's daughter was clambering like a finger-cat up the cornice-and-gargoyle façade of the palace.

Serada turned to her son. "Go after her!"

"Nay, mother, I do not want her," said Zeid mulishly.

"Then who is this girl who *does* have your heart?"

Zeid was silent.

Serada went on. "Since you returned from the Moonship, you have said you would have women quick of mind and wit. I've

10

never seen a cleverer girl than the she-pirate, and I would not let her escape me!"

"Send the eunuchs after her. She cannot scale the outer wall and will soon tire of the roof. I must hasten on my father's errand."

He kissed his mother's hand, bowed to his sisters-in-law, and left the apartments.

Zeid went quickly to the next floor in the palace where the hired artisans were quartered—craftsmen whose skills had bought freedom. Slave boys were playing at dice before the door to the quarters. They scrambled to their feet as Zeid approached.

He ignored the dice and smiled, "Is Moji the Counting Master within? Summon him."

A boy raced away and was soon back with a young man in wool blouse and trousers, carrying an abacus. Moji was from the rocky peaks that were the source of the great rivers nourishing the Desert Cities. His was an unbearded race with eyes like ripe olives and shiny black hair.

Zeid beckoned him onto a balcony beyond the hearing of the slaves. "Moji, my father the Wizard has sent me on a journey to the Marble Lands—and I must leave this night, if I'm to stay alive to leave at all."

Moji's eyes widened. "Who would harm the wise, gentle Light-Bearer? True, Prince Rustad is a fierce lion, but the lion does not harm the owl!"

"The lion and the owl are not brothers dividing the Wizard's inheritance," smiled Zeid. "Nor is the owl so gentle that he doesn't have claws and a sharp beak."

"Made sharper by Space Giver Magic," admitted Moji. "Many times has Rustad shown envy of the favors the Space Givers have granted you."

"As long as I was unwed and he knew I myself had no interest in challenging him, Rustad could let his ill will stop at envy. But my mother Serada has fetched Coral Bud, daughter of the pirate Hamar, to be my bride."

"And Hamar's grandsons might not be as indifferent as yourself to the inheritance," nodded the young Counting Master. "Rustad has cause to be rid of you, for his sons' sake, if not his own."

"He has no real cause. Never will I let my mother burden me

as Rustad is burdened—by duplo dolls and shrewish wives! However, his fears make the cause real enough. Bid the major-domo furnish and provision the palace trading barge at once."

Moji tucked his abacus under his arm and bowed slightly. "Does the Lord Zeid travel alone?"

"Of course! Am I Bulbul that I can demand purple tents and a retinue? But, in confidence, Moji, I'd like a slave who would serve us well in return for freedom. You perhaps know—?"

"I have long loved the slave Kalia, my prince. She was captured as a child and now serves the princess Serada. If it were possible—"

"What would be necessary for us to smuggle her aboard the barge?"

"My lord Zeid must remove the guard at the door to the captive quarters."

Zeid considered. "I'll raise the alarm for burrow rats and thus draw the guard away. Be swift, Moji! My blood pounds eagerly for the Marble Lands!"

Moji bowed and returned to the artisan quarters.

Zeid looked over the balcony rail. He had to get to the cellars—and one of Rustad's assassins could be hiding behind any door.

He thought of the sea rover's daughter and dropped from the balcony to a narrow parapet. Feeling his way from gargoyle to gargoyle, he edged around the palace until he could see the canal basin.

(Above him, a slight figure, flattened to invisibility on the outer ledge of the roof parapet, was watching.)

The wait seemed long, but the brightly colored stars had not wheeled far before the courtyard came to life with slaves hurrying to prepare the moored barge. Zeid dropped from the parapet to the roof of the great kitchens and thence to the ground.

Though it was evening, the cooks were still bustling about the ovens, adjusting the temperature rods. In a separate alcove, the door to the cellar storerooms was open, and Zeid slinked quietly down the stone stairs.

He descended in darkness. At intervals in the pitchblack cellar gleamed the hot red eyes of burrow rats entrapped for the planet's cruel blood sports. Zeid felt his way to the nearest cage, lifted it—with difficulty since it contained an adult rat—carried it up the stairs and released the furious animal.

In springing away from him, it sprang toward the cooks who yelled, jumped on tables, and banged their ladles against the baking pans.

Confident that the alarm would distract all the guards in the palace, Zeid threw down the cage and ran along the courtyards until he was in the quiet garden outside his own quarters. No assassins lurked. Probably they were stalking him within the passages, waiting outside the door they could not force.

The opened window of his chamber was far above his head. He took off his turban and unpinned and unwound the folds. He fastened the brooch near the end of the long strip and whirled the strip at the end of his arm, flinging it against a louvered shutter.

The brooch caught within a louver. The scarf hung. He ran at the wall and up it, clutching the scarf to lever himself onward.

The gauze ripped away—but the continuing motion boosted him to the window sill. He hung over it a moment, then slued his body, and dropped to the chamber floor.

(Above, the shadow that had slithered on the parapet ledge, following his progress, now began climbing down the cornices.)

He lit a roseate lamp, discarded his princely attire, and donned a short wool jacket, wool pantaloons, and leather boots. After he had wound a wool turban around his head, he hastened into his workshop for the weapons he had neglected.

CORAL BUD, HAVING COME safely down the palace façade, stepped softly onto the workshop roof and peered curiously through a barred skylight. Zeid seemed to be affixing jeweled studs onto an oddly metallic belt.

He paused, as if listening, and she drew back, crossed to his chamber roof, hung from the parapet, and swung through the window and into the chamber. She prowled, eager to know how desert housekeeping differed from sea customs and whether princes lived as snugly and shipshape as sea kings. She found the portrait glass and gave it a rub.

"Ha! A fine, blood-sucking bitch *you* are!" she told the floating beauty.

Motion at the window made her look up. A small iron grapple had bit its prongs into the sill.

Not all of Rustad's assassins were inside the palace, and the fragment of scarf flapping against the shutter had told its own story.

Coral Bud was a girl who knew how to repel boarders. She struck the edge of the portrait glass against the wall, making it a jagged-edged weapon, and hid behind the hangings at the entrance to the bath.

The iron hook bit deeper with the weight of a body. A scarf-bound head, knife blade between its teeth, rose over the sill followed by a bare, brawny, welt-scarred torso. The breech-clouted assassin paused at the sill to haul up the grapple rope and lower it inside the chamber.

He took the knife from his teeth and dropped to the floor—but Coral Bud had jumped from the hangings, and the jagged glass in her hand ripped his tough muscles from navel to throat.

He screamed as he writhed on the floor. Coral Bud darted at him again. She bent over to slash at the hand holding the knife—struck the wrist—seized the knife from the nerveless fingers.

She heard Zeid cry out, "Hold—stop!" But she plunged the sharp blade into the assassin's heart.

"Foolish wretch!" Zeid sternly reproached her.

She straightened up, knife in hand, and looked around. Zeid was now wearing the strange belt around his waistband. A thick-hilted poniard hung from it.

His eyes were angry. "Did no one ever teach you, sea urchin, that death is a means only when it is an end, a finish?"

"Yon assassin is finished, well?"

"But the force of his threat is increased. Had I disarmed the brute and sent him back to the ridicule of his fellows, I would have made only one new hate-enemy. Now the entire gang will come upon me for revenge."

Coral Bud flipped the knife. It jabbed quivering into a crevice between floor tiles. "Well, land crab, I've never heard that a shark devoured fewer seamen because one shark was spared. Let them come to *me* for revenge!"

"Why did you seek me in my chambers?"

"I was fetched to be wife to a prince who sold Space Giver lamps in the bazaar and took his meals with bargemen and vendors. I expected to wed you right away, as is the custom at the Seacoast, and we could set up shop in a barge and travel all the Desert Cities.

"What does it matter if you love somebody else? You need a wife to direct your business and servants. I saw at once that you had rejected me because of Space Giver nonsense, and I freed myself from the harem so that I could come and talk to you."

"It is not nonsense to love a wife truly and faithfully!"

"If a man has the wit to know when he loves truly—and his wife is clever enough to keep him faithful! You had better follow your father's example and have one wife and many loves. Only the Space Givers have enough Magic that all work does itself without servants, and men and women can fall in and out of love as they please!"

Before Zeid could reply, the girl went on, "What do you think of my idea to set up shop in a barge, where everything is cozy and to hand, and where we can seek out customers instead of waiting hungrily like a finger-cat on the limb of an empty wren tree?"

Zeid was taken with her idea, but put it aside. "Did you give so much thought to my affairs? Well, they have changed, and I must forget the bazaars for a time. My father sends me on an errand to Fire Lotus, princess of the Marble Lands."

He gestured to the dead assassin. "The journey makes it possible for me to aid your escape to the Seacoast, bloodthirsty Rover Bud. Drag your victim aside and do otherwise as I bid you."

He went into the workshop. Coral Bud sang:

> "The Seacoast, where the air is free,
> Will turn the gentle prince to me!"

She rolled and pushed her victim to the side of the chamber, rose from her task, and wiped her bloodstained hands on her gauze trousers.

From the workshop she heard the thin rush of wind, as of a dozen hizzing vipers.

A pallet floated into the chamber on a low wind-cloud. Zeid was guiding it, and he halted it in the middle of the chamber. He tore a hanging rug from the wall and threw it on the floor. He ordered,

"Wrap yourself as well as can be done—but perhaps I should first bind your mouth."

"Why?"

"Because the carpet's Magic can be what the Space Givers call voice-keyed, and an incautious word while your hands touched the keying pattern might send you into a den of burrow rats."

"Do you and the Space Givers bind your own mouths?"

"We know the Magic. And in truth, sea urchin, I doubt that even Space Givers dare let chattering girls upon the carpet."

"My father Hamar would long since have dashed my brains out had I been a chatterer!"

She lay down on the carpet and rolled herself loosely along a diagonal. He picked her up and put her on the pallet. From inside her cocoon she could hear hinges creak open and lids bang shut as he heaped apparel and coverlets over her.

The hissing of the dozen snakes became the rush of a whirl-wind. She felt the pallet rise up—and up—and glide forward. The warm, perfumed chamber air became the cool, garden-fresh night. The pallet halted and descended, and the whirlwind diminished. She heard the scrape of the grapple, the light thud of feet on the ground.

Once more the pallet glided forward. Zeid's voice exclaimed, "The portrait! T'was *that* the sea urchin had in her hand! Oh, my lovely princess—shattered and lost!"

Coral Bud grinned and snuggled into the deeply piled carpet.

ZEID GUIDED THE PALLET through the courtyards without meeting more assassins and arrived at the canal basin. Moji was waiting beside the palace's trading barge from which the slaves were now disembarking, their stowage finished.

"Is everything aboard?" asked Zeid.

Moji bowed. "Everything, my lord. I myself bore the reed-blossom bed aboard over my shoulder, lest it weigh down a slave too heavily."

So the captive maiden Kalia had been smuggled aboard. Zeid said, "Well done!" and guided the pallet from the canal bank into the plain brown tent upon the midship platform. He bade the pallet come to rest—and Coral Bud to remain hidden—and he returned to Moji.

Across the courtyard, within the kitchen area, shouts and the crashing of clubs told that the burrow rat was still trying to flee to its burrows under the palace.

At the canal edge, all was quiet. As he and Moji boarded the barge, Zeid said, "This is unnatural. Surely my brother Rustad would not let me leave in peace!"

Moji shook his head. "Prince Rustad whispers urgently to all, and says he will pay well for your death. His warriors can't attack you openly within the Wizard's walls."

"Stand at the prow, Moji, and guide the rods. My own tricks shall guard the stern."

Moji sprang to the prow. Zeid stood with his back against the panel of the grooming chamber beneath the poop.

Within the tent Coral Bud was wriggling and humping free of the cocoon. She could remain hidden without being buried! The clothes and coverlets slid aside. The rug thudded to the deck, and Coral Bud unrolled. She sat up and heard the barge hum into motion.

Was the Light-Bearer prepared for an ambuscade? She sprang to the tent's front fold. The play of star-mottle cast confusing shadows; but she decided a slave was at the prow. Was no other slave aboard?

The barge was circling the palace basin. It headed for the grid in the palace wall. A guard bade the spikes rise. The barge hummed beneath them. No attack?

The barge rippled along the approach canal. No ambush at the stone bridge. They swerved into the main canal. Revelry resounded from the trading barges moored alongside the deserted bazaar.

They slowed at the city wall. The gate began to lift—

Where was the ceremonious challenge? Had the Gatemaster been overpowered or slain?

Coral Bud stumbled over the pallet as she turned and hastened to the tent's aft opening. She parted the folds and stared. No one?

Yes, Zeid was hidden beneath the poop. He had drawn a poniard which gleamed in the starlight.

The midship was now gliding beyond the wall, under the upraised grid.

The assassins struck. Six bodies, crouched beyond the wall, now rose and leaped into the barge.

Six! And the land crab had only a poinard!

Coral Bud charged out of the tent and jumped from the platform onto the shoulders of the nearest man. Her fingernails dug into his eyes, and he screamed.

It was the only sound in the barge—except for the heavy crash of bodies falling onto the stowed chests. In the split second between when the scream stopped and the body beneath her went limp, she glanced up.

Zeid had not moved. He still stood with drawn poniard.

A shock turned her body to stone—she was falling—and her mind went black.

ZEID, TOO, HAD NOTED the absence of the usual challenge from the Gatemaster. He thumbed the controls of his Combi-shot to "stun." He could not guess who might jump from behind the city wall. Hatred might have brought Rustad himself to slay with his own hand. For his mother's sake, Zeid did not want to kill his brother.

Even while the first assassin was in midair, Zeid aimed the weapon and pressed the trigger. He let the beam sweep over the attackers—and could not slow his hand when he saw the slight, wiry figure charge from the tent and leap into the fray.

The bronze gate spikes fell into place with a vicious crash—

but the stern was clear, and Moji increased speed by drawing up the rods.

Zeid shouted, "Moji! All's well! Bid the barge hold course—and come here!"

He made his way to Coral Bud and slung her slight form over his shoulder.

The barge had resumed its normal hum. Moji appeared at the curtain of the crew cabin beneath the midship platform.

"Six assassins lie within the barge, Moji," said Zeid. "One moment—I will help you cast them over the side."

He carried Coral Bud up the ladder to the midship tent. He groped for the Space Giver lamp hanging from a tent pole, lit it, and lowered Coral Bud to the pallet. He felt her wrist and was reassured by the pulse beat.

He hurried down the ladder and helped Moji lift the stunned assassins to the rail and push them overboard. Moji observed,

"They breathe—and yet they sink like stones! Will they come up, Lord Zeid?"

"With time, I suppose. Since the Space Givers forbade the throwing of offal into the canals, the bottom feeders have been starved out."

When the last body was overboard, Zeid said, "Has the barge been program—been bidden, I mean—for the river sluice? Good. Release your love Kalia from the reed-blossom bed. I must see if the pirate girl yet stirs to life."

Moji bowed and went back to the crew cabin. Zeid once more climbed the midship ladder.

Coral Bud was sitting cross-legged on the pallet, her head in her hands. Zeid sat on the deck and said, "The faintness will wear off. I told you to remain hidden. If my weapon had been at full power—"

She lifted her head and regarded him groggily. "Could I stand aside when I thought you held a simple poniard? Yet I deserve your wrath. I saw that your strange belt was of Space metal—I should have known you were Space-armed.

"Not that the weapon is aught to boast of," she added. "My father's fist hits a foe harder."

"I lamed the weapon, I tell you! I feared killing my brother!"

"You would be wiser to fear your brother killing *you*. What of the assassins? Are they swimming back to the ridicule of their fellows?"

"They can swim or sink. I don't care," shrugged Zeid. "Revenge compounded upon revenge can kill me only once."

"Now here's a pretty grading of battle tactics!" scoffed Coral Bud. "Few ships would be taken, if the attacking commanders had to ponder 'To kill—or not to kill!'"

Zeid burst out laughing. Coral Bud scowled, "Why does that amuse you?"

"Because I know Space Giver lore—and your words would strike laughter from all Space Givers. Don't ask *why*!" he added hastily. "The night is now far gone, and we'll arrive at the river sluice at dawn. This trading barge has but cramped space. The tent and everything within are yours. I'll withdraw to the poop with my rug and apparel."

"The apparel I must share," she retorted, indicating her battle-stained harem gauze. "No shameless naked red-haired hussy, I!"

"Hold your tongue! Fire Lotus is like a princess from the Spirit Lands!"

"An indolent flesh-trap, who can neither splice rope nor tie knots nor rig a sail! I can think how it would have gone, land crab, if Fire Lotus had been surprised by the chamber assassin!"

"Fire Lotus is a woman to be loved and cherished. What can a fierce sea urchin know of being a woman?"

He rose, seized his rug, and withdrew. Coral Bud pushed the pallet to one side, busily arranged cushions and coverlets, and began rummaging through the apparel. "I know enough, sweet handsome Light-Bearer!"

IN THE CREW CHAMBER beneath the midship platform, Moji and the captive girl Kalia, lying together within the reed-blossom bed, had been listening to the quarrel above their heads. Kalia asked,

"What does their talk mean, Moji? Who is the lady?"

"No one that Zeid intended to take along. I think she must be the pirate girl who arrived this evening aboard Bulbul's barge.

The eunuchs were searching for her, even as I was bearing you to the barge—and I trembled lest they prod the reed-blossom bed."

"Do you know what the Lord Zeid seeks on this journey?"

"No—but it's plain that Hamar's daughter will not let him seek alone."

"How long will he be gone from Mus-al-ram? Will he forget Jibbo and the hospice—and the captives and slaves?"

"Could a man forget such ceaseless labors?"

"A woman can make a man forget all else—and it seems as if Lord Zeid has *two* women to divert his wits."

"Well, we shall see—we shall see—"

ZEID WAS AN ANGRY young man as the trading barge whisked him smoothly along the night-blurred canal. He sat on the wide boards of the poop, his rug rolled beside him, and watched the ghostly desert stretch endlessly on either side of the canal. The sterile white sands, flood-caked near the canal banks, were a curtain upon which the low-hanging stars threw shimmering color.

Almost hypnotic, the night-enchanted desert.

IT WAS THE PLANET'S distinctly-banded colors that had attracted the Space Givers. The sand-white of the southern hemisphere, slashed by black mountains that stopped and channeled the rain. The intense blue of the great equatorial seas. The green of the northern forests, pockmarked by outcroppings of granite and marble.

The space expedition had come with fine purposes. It would educate the illiterate, civilize the barbarians, raise the living standard, and (incidentally) bring the planet into the mainstream of space commerce.

The first Space Givers had made a terrible mistake. Finding a half-nomadic, Early Bronze Age planet, they sent teachers and technicians. Like city slickers elsewhere in the universe, these routine-dulled bureaucrats were robbed blind by the cunning rubes. Appalled—helpless to intervene except by force which they were forbidden to use—the civilizers watched their space technology become Magic subverted to barbaric uses.

Troubleshooters supplanted the bureaucrats. They could not unscramble the omelet, but they did not break any more eggs. They withdrew or altered machines that could be converted into weapons. Whenever their satellite monitors detected a system breakdown, they descended and repaired the system. Thus they forestalled the slaughter that would have resulted from a struggle to possess increasingly scarce technology.

Having discovered that no catalyst will mature a civilization, the Space Givers waited out the generations, teaching only the agriculture and crafts that Bronze Age men could handle. They surveyed and tested the children, bringing them up to the satellite—rowdy, unwashed batches from the Desert bazaars—or the Seacoast alleys—or from the mines of the northern forest. The children would reflect the planet's natural ripening pace.

They dealt more particularly with the offspring of the planet's lords and wizards. In the random nature of the maturing process, a wider understanding could appear anywhere, but astuteness in a position of power could hasten civilization by law and example.

Gold—jewels—weapons—simple tools—through weary years the same Gifts were snatched by savage, illiterate children.

Until Zeid ben Amfi, who asked only for knowledge. . . .

WHEN HIS EYES FELT dazed by the desert's shadow colors, Zeid looked to the midship tent—and frowned at the glow of light within the fabric.

Was he not master? Why should he huddle on the poop while a little she-pirate—a fierce, unwanted bride—rested comfortably on his robes and cushions?

The curtains of the crew cabin parted, and Moji emerged. Zeid thought, *He and Kalia have heard our quarreling voices and wish to know why a lady is suddenly ruling my tent.*

Moji climbed over the sea chests and strongboxes, came up the stern ladder, and knelt beside the seated Zeid.

"Light-Bearer, it is not fitting that the master lies on bare boards while his servant Moji and his slave Kalia enjoy a reed-blossom bed within the cabin."

Zeid smiled, "Moji, if I lack the courage to seize my own tent, I should not dispossess my Counting Master and cook."

"Is the tent-lady the same girl the eunuchs were seeking?"

"Yes, she is Coral Bud, daughter of the pirate Hamar, and we'll be rid of her at the Seacoast. And how my mother could imagine such a girl would make an acceptable seed-wife—!"

"The lady Serada was ever one to recognize true value. Has it chanced you to speak much in confidence with the lady Coral Bud?"

"Speak! I had scarce met the sea urchin in my mother's apartments, when she fought off my brother Rustad's three wives, sprang out the high window, climbed the palace cornices like a finger-cat, and went stalking me—"

"She would naturally hasten to your protection."

"Protection! She lowered herself into my chambers, found an assassin—ripped him apart from belly to throat—plunged his own knife into his heart—and boasted she would do the same to his fellows!"

"Perhaps she should have been allowed to do so. You owe the lady a favor, Lord Zeid."

"She has my tent. What more does she want?"

Moji laughed at his young master. "A great deal more, if all I hear of she-pirates be true!"

"You jest, Moji, but my heart and feelings burn for another. Fire Lotus, princess of the Milk White Quarries. Tresses like waves of copper—jewel-green eyes—sweet body—"

"Is the princess offering herself to you?"

"Nay," sighed Zeid, "she is offering to sell her seed to my father's parthogen bottles. Poor innocent girl! The rascal Bulbul tempted her with gold, no doubt about it—as greedy as he is for commissions and bribes!

"So my father is sending me to her as his agent, but I won't bargain with her, Moji. I intend to enlighten her—to love her. I'd show you her portrait glass," he went on, "but the sea urchin shattered it, to slice the assassin like a cook slicing the pulp-root!"

"Perhaps the lady had no other weapon, Light-Bearer."

"Call me not Light-Bearer! To hurry the bloodthirsty maiden away from the assassin brotherhood, I forgot even my lamps!"

Moji eyed the wide metallic belt. "You have Gifts, perhaps, to recover Gifts?"

Zeid laid his hand on the rug beside him. "I could return to the palace, yes. But something might delay my journey. So eagerly do I seek the Marble Lands that I would not risk delay to recover pretty toys."

"Or to make your hospice secure? When the hospice host Jibbo wakes to find you gone—"

"The hospice! The vexatious Rover Bud has even made me forget the hospice!"

"Or is a young heart dreaming of a copper-haired princess?"

"Between the pair of them—! You do well, Moji, to bring back my wits. Return to your slumbers with Kalia. I won't need you before the river sluice at dawn."

Moji bowed and left the poop.

The tent fabric had gone dark. Apparently the wild she-pirate had known how to extinguish the Space Giver lamp.

Zeid unrolled the rug athwart the poop and laid down on it as if to sleep. But his hands rested on patterned arabesques, and he concentrated on the portation codes. After a moment's thought he repeated the rhyme,

"Would I were where work is done!
  For-to-see if-I've-won!"

The rug's micro-sensors began programming, 4—2—C—

CORAL BUD HAD PUZZLED over the glowing globe of roseate light. On the Seacoast, Feelafell the Space Bastard had similar lamps, but they obeyed only his spoken commands. Feelafell had been angry with his Moonship kin for letting the Wizard's son make Space lamps and sell them to anyone who had the gold to pay for them.

However, thought Coral Bud, if anyone could use the lamps, there could be no Magic words to remember. She looked closer at the globe and found a glittering gemstone at the base. She prodded, pulled, twisted—and the lamp went dark.

Immediately she wriggled through the cushions to the aft folds of the tent and peeked out. She saw Moji leave the poop—and Zeid lie down on the rug.

He seemed to become a shadow. He blended into the wavering starlight. He was no more.

Coral Bud pulled away her harem veil, swept her dark tresses from her face, and stared. Was there a form in the shifting light? She parted the tent folds, sprang from the platform to a great provision chest, leaped from box to box, and climbed the ladder to the poop.

The boards were empty. She bent and touched them. The Light-Bearer was gone!

She faced the midship and cried shrilly, "Ho! Slaves! Awake! The master is gone!"

Moji, who had just lain down, emerged again from the lower cabin. Adjusting blouse and trousers, he stumbled barefoot over the stowed boxes and once more climbed the stern ladder.

Coral Bud demanded, "Where has Zeid's Magic taken him? Tell me, slave!"

Moji bowed, "Honored lady, I am not a slave, but Moji the Counting Master. I know not where the Lord Zeid has gone."

"That's the trouble with freemen," complained the girl. "They're too busy with their own lives to care about their masters. Is no slave aboard?"

"Only Kalia the cook, whom the Light-Bearer will free at the Seacoast."

"And she knows even less than you, I daresay." Coral Bud paced a step and exclaimed, "Zeid has flown to the portrait princess! Even now he may be in the Marble Lands!"

"Nay, lady," smiled Moji. "Magic can take the Lord Zeid whither he will, but he needs provisions and servants when he arrives, and the garments due his rank. Can he appear at a princely gate in plain wool and the leathern boots of an apprentice?"

"My father Hamar has appeared at princely gates in wool and leather—and has broken the gates asunder!" retorted the pirate girl. "But in truth, he came not courting," she added.

"I would guess, Lady, the Light-Bearer returns only to the palace and his hospice."

"I know not what a hospice may be, but death awaits him in the palace. When Zeid expects his brother to kill him, he lames his weapon—and he won't long survive such folly. What is their fight about?"

"The prince Rustad fears his younger brother will take over the Wizard's realm."

"As stupid a thought as would come from a prince who has been unlucky in three wives and yet would take a fourth as soon as she set foot in the courtyard! If Zeid had wanted the Wizard's realm, he would have seized it as soon as he descended from the Moonship! So indifferent to power is your master, Moji, that he had not even put together his Space weapons until this night! Turn the barge—or send it backwards!"

"Alas, lady, the barges go only forward, and turn only in the proper basins. My lord Zeid told me the Space Givers lamed the operating rods so that the barges could not become battle beasts— to wheel and charge and retreat."

"Yes, thus have they lamed the ships of Feelafell, and he must send them out in hordes lest swiftly darting pirates seize them. And no basin until the river sluices! But look down the canal, Moji! A cargo barge is coming toward us along the opposite bank! Turn the rudder so that we run past hull-to-hull!"

"Nay, lady, I dare not!"

"A freeman ought to dare anything! Besides, Zeid would only thank you if I disappeared from his tent!"

"But he might not thank me if the honored lady appeared within the city."

The girl turned from him, jumped from the poop into the hold, leaped from box to box, and sprang onto the tent platform.

Moji leaped awkwardly after her, hoping to restrain her before she reached the command platform at the prow.

She was not interested in the operating rods. She stopped on the midship platform, thrust aside the tent folds, and jerked the high center pole from its deck socket. The tent roof collapsed, and Coral Bud plunged out of the opposite entrance, carrying the lithe, smooth pole.

She jammed one end into the deeply carved design of a sea chest below the platform near the outer hull.

Moji struggled around the sagging tent—but now the approaching barge was nearly up to them, across the canal.

Coral Bud backed up a few steps, ran, seized the pole, and vaulted over the water.

She seemed to fly like a bird—but hung in the air too long before descending. The cargo barge was passing beneath her. She fell past the poop—but clutched the after rail and dangled by one arm.

Almost too fast for Moji to see—as the distance between them increased—she swung her other arm to the rail, hoisted her body until her knees pressed against the lower frame of the poop, and pushed herself safely over.

Her body tumbled to the boards—and Moji could distinguish no more.

He became aware of a night-robed figure beside him. Kalia had come to the platform and was anxiously wrapping her night-cloth around her. Her pale face and golden hair seemed bleached by the starlight.

She asked softly, "Oh, Moji, what shall we do?"

"Nothing, Kalia love. The barge must hold a steady speed, or the Light-Bearer will splash down in the canal."

"But the lady goes unarmed into the city!"

"Fortunately. Else the city would know a new mistress," said Moji wryly.

Coral Bud sat against the aft rail of the cargo barge, hugged her knees to her chin, and laughed to herself. Hearty snores came from the midship tent and lower cabin. The barge crew, feeling safe from attack along the inaccessible desert, would sleep until the Master at the city's watergrid cursed them awake.

Her sea-practiced eye surveyed the cargo. In the confusing light she judged it to be loosely woven net sacks of mealy root from the northern forests. Surely the sacks would proceed first to the palace basin where the Wizard's steward would buy the finest roots, leaving the rest for the city marketplace.

She had only to restow enough sacks at the stern of the barge to make a little cave. She squeezed into the pocket and waited.

Soon the barge slowed, bumped a grid barrier. A hoarse voice challenged, "Ho, bargemaster! Awake! Man your command platform if you would be admitted!"

The hidden girl heard an indistinct reply and the rumbling of sacks as the crew emerged from their cabin. The voice continued, "Is it you, Sejput?"

"Are you wine-fuddled, Gatemaster," was the jovial reply, "that you can't see the blazon on my prow?"

"Fuddled by a nasty blow to my skull! A band of Rustad's assassins forced us from the grid! Six leaped into the palace's trading barge—and came not again.

"Word from the palace says that young prince Zeid was in the barge—and Moji—and Hamar's daughter Coral Bud—and a missing slave Kalia. It is also said that an assassin has been found slain in Zeid's chamber."

"Slain by Moonship Magic?"

"Nay, by his own knife, if rumor be true, and fiercely slashed besides, in pirate fashion. Rustad says the work was done by Hamar's daughter, who has done nothing but thwart and confound him since she arrived this night. I doubt you find much cheer in the Wizard's basin, Sejput!"

"But much news to bring to the Seacoast!" laughed Sejput. "The news bearer always dines well!"

The barge resumed course under the raised bronze spikes of the grid and proceeded along the main canal. Sacks tumbled over Coral Bud's cave at the turn into the palace canal. There was a second challenge at the palace grid, and the barge slowly drew into the basin.

A milder bump—a sudden immobility as the underwater walls of a landing slot extended to block the lower keel at bow and stern. The barge was moored.

The girl began to clear the sacks from her cave opening. She froze when she heard a high, arrogant voice address the Bargemaster. It was Bulbul!

"Sejput! Have you snored since the river sluice?"

"How else to spend the hot afternoon? And what else to see at night except the maddening star-haze?"

"You might have seen the palace trading barge—or bodies in

the canal! Zeid had the Wizard's leave to take Moji the Counting Master on a voyage to the Marble Lands—and has escaped Rustad's assassins!"

"With a pirate girl, I hear," gossiped Sejput.

"Yes—after he had declared he would have nothing to do with her! And truly, Sejput, Mother Serada's parsimony provided but tough, stringy meat for a gentle young appetite—"

The voices died away. Sejput and Bulbul were ambling from the barge. Coral Bud shivered indignantly. Tough, stringy meat, indeed! Was she not as tender and soft as any slothful harem beauty? Her face was mayhap burned from sun and salt—her hands made strong and hard by ship chores—her limbs agile. But could she not be as warm and yielding as the copper-haired man-trap?

Hoping she would be given the chance to slice Bulbul's flabby fat off him, measure by measure, she thrust the sacks aside and crawled in the darkness of the hold to the crew cabin. The crewmen, ashore as soon as the barge was moored, must have clean apparel neatly set aside, to display themselves in the bazaar when their trading was done and the barge stowed with cargo for the return to the coast.

Feeling her way in the darkness, she came upon a pallet, followed the edge to a small sea chest. Locked, of course. But beyond the chest was a mound of fabric—soft textured, clean-smelling.

Quickly she tore off her dirty harem gauze and donned pantaloons and a wide shawl. The clothing was so large that she knotted the gauze together and used it as a sash to bind the extra fabric around her waist.

She fumbled a wool cap from her find, twisted up her hair, and pulled the cap around her head.

She listened, heard no nearby voices, mounted the midship ladder, and slipped ashore. The center of the courtyard was lit by Zeid's lamps strung overhead. She kept to the shadows and looked around.

The warrior prince Rustad, still in his gold-cloth turban and scarlet-and-gold attire, was in the midst of a small crowd. Before him bowed the enormously fat, satin-and-gem-clad Bulbul, bringing the Bargemaster Sejput and a crewman to Rustad's recollection.

Rustad greeted the bargemen's bows with a coarse, loud welcome. Little will he learn from such hearty snores, thought the girl.

She paused only a moment—then faded into the garden so she could circle around to the palace façade.

In the shadows of a fern bush she came upon an embracing pair. A little servant girl gasped and ran away. The man laughed and turned as if to speak.

Then he jumped at Coral Bud, seized her, and shouted, "Ho, Sejput! Am I meeting myself through the Wizard's Magic—or have I caught a stowaway and the thief of my new quilted robe?"

Coral Bud glanced first at the shawl. Even in the shadows, the red-pink-green-blue squares shrieked at her. She should have chanced a lamp in the cabin!

Intent upon the shawl, she forgot to run. The man picked her up and carried her before him like a child to the grinning group. The bargemaster exclaimed, "Now has Tyr won a slave according to the law that says a thief must become slave to the man he has robbed!"

Tyr set his captive down hard before Rustad. "Won fair, Lord Rustad? Though the lad is but a puny thief!"

The girl saw Rustad's glance go to the small gilt harem slippers under the sagging pantaloons. He looked into her eyes, and she knew he had recognized her. He reached into a brocaded pocket, drew out two gold coins and said,

"I'm buying your slave, stout Tyr. A goldpiece for the beardless boy—and a gold piece for the stolen attire!"

Tyr bowed low and accepted the gold, well-pleased by the quick profit.

Coral Bud said, "I cannot be your slave, Prince Rustad. You know I belong to your brother Zeid."

"Who has deprived me of one hireling tonight—and perhaps six more—and owes me a return."

"It was *my* stab that found the assassin's heart, O jealous prince! And willingly would I seek combat with the brotherhood!"

The men laughed at this boastful young liar. Assuredly he was a poor half-wit of such as the mad Lord Zeid sheltered.

Rustad smiled, "So you seek combat?"

"Even with yourself!"

"Nay, it is not allowed a seasoned warrior to fight such as you. But combat you shall have!" He turned to the slaves and thundered, "Set up the battle ring—*and uncage a burrow rat*!"

A burrow rat! No man had a chance in the battle ring with those ripping fangs.

But Coral Bud cried out, "I will fight the rat—and claim the usual boon if I win! But I am no murderer doomed to a playful execution. I claim the right to a simple stick or club!"

Rustad hesitated. The men murmured among themselves. Finally Sejput spoke up, "Why, yes, Lord Rustad, let the lad have the club."

"May so much be permitted a thief?"

"Well, worthy prince, without a club there will be no sport. The rat will tear out his throat in an instant."

"What think you, Bulbul?" asked Rustad slyly.

Bulbul, too, looked into her eyes. She could not mistake his glee. He was remembering her contempt on the journey from the Seacoast. He smiled, "Give the boy the club, my prince—and be wary about wagering on the rat."

THE PORTATION RUG HAD shimmered Zeid to visibility on the floor of his workshop at the palace. He quickly rose and entered his dressing chamber. The body of the assassin killed by Coral Bud had been removed—apparently through the window by which he had entered since the chamber door could not be forced.

No possessions had been disturbed. From a strongbox Zeid took a pouch of gold coins and thrust it behind his wide belt.

Since he was believed to be on the trading barge, he feared no lurking assassins. He hurried from his chamber through the inner corridors and halls to the quiet courtyard farthest from the canal basin.

The central fountain sparkled under the lamps, but the courtyard was empty. The immature duplos were sleeping beyond the colonnaded passage.

The bronze gate opened once more at his voice-key, and he strode through the back alleys of the city. Deserted, they echoed like a hollow water gourd. The slaves and the poorer freemen were sleeping off the day's exhaustion.

Nearer the more prosperous revelry of the main canal, he stopped at the heavy door that had a circle in the lintel above it.

The hospice also slept. He called softly to the opened window above the lintel, "Oh, Jibbo!"

A night-clothed figure was a white blur at the window. "Lord Zeid! One moment!"

The figure disappeared. A pause. The heavy door opened. Now the large room was quiet, the sleeping bodies lit by dimmed lamps.

Jibbo, seeming sturdier at close hand, said, "The public executioner has gone to do your will. Tomorrow the severed head will hang in the bazaar as a warning to child mutilators."

Zeid had completely forgotten. He now said quickly, "How are the two babes?"

"Sleeping within the Space Giver balm leaves. The mother is also here. The husband was a brute—but without him she also is a beggar."

"Not if she thinks and acts otherwise."

"Will you teach her and find honest work for her?"

"You know the lessons I teach, Jibbo, and for a while you must teach without me. My father the Wizard sends me to the Marble Lands. I've brought you gold for sustenance."

He drew out the pouch and handed it to his hospice host, who weighed it thoughtfully in his hand. "Not a great sum, Lord."

"Then it must not be allowed to diminish. Increase the sum as if it were your own."

"If the sum were my own, I wouldn't be feeding beggars with it! No, no, young prince. I live well by maintaining your hospice, but I must bar the door when the last gold piece is devoured."

"I wonder," smiled Zeid. "More than your belly has been nourished by your hospice work."

Jibbo seemed interested but puzzled. "I don't notice that any other lack has been filled—but perhaps I'll do so when the gold is gone."

"Yes—as you would notice thirst only after the well runs dry. Don't be lazy, Jibbo. Take thought while the purse is full of gold, for gold breeds gold, and you can feed the hospice on the calvings."

"I'd rather continue as before and let my lord Zeid breed the gold."

"Why?"

Jibbo rubbed his touseled head. "Well, I'm lazy, for one thing. And for another, I fear I wouldn't be shrewd enough in placing money with the merchants, and the hospice would have to close. Not that I would mind kicking out the rascals—but, all the same, the thought makes me uneasy."

"You're far shrewder than I, Jibbo. If you were the Wizard's son, you'd have more gold than is in the purse—and yet the purse is my only store."

"Now *that's* true enough, young prince!" said Jibbo. "You've no head for business, whatever else you learned on the Moonship. If I were you—" He weighed the pouch again. "Well, since you wish it, I *am* you, since I have your gold. But as what to do with it—"

"Think about closing the hospice—and you'll know what to do."

Jibbo rubbed his head again. Zeid retraced his path through the alleys.

As he entered the palace grounds at the gate by which he had left, Zeid reflected that Rustad might take out his spite on the hospice, if he happened to remember it existed. Who would restrain him? Their mother Serada and their father the Wizard were merely amused by a madness that fostered beggars instead of paying goldsmiths and craftsmen.

However, perhaps Bulbul could be persuaded that if the hospice were harrassed, its patron would refuse to deal with Fire Lotus, and Bulbul would lose his bribe for securing her seed for the parthogen bottles.

It was, thought Zeid, a threat worth a try—but where was he

to find Bulbul? He dared not reveal his presence in the palace by summoning a slave.

He considered the habits of the powerful eunuch. Almost a lord, he did as he pleased. He played at games of chance with Rustad's warriors. He collected gossip as avariciously as he ammassed gold—and for the same reason: the power it bestowed.

After this day of palace conflict, thought Zeid, Bulbul most certainly was within Rustad's wing of the palace. A quick look would do no harm. He approached the palace steps, pressed a shiny stud on his wide belt, and voice-keyed the Space Giver code,

> "One half my weight—and one half more—
> The best to climb—but not to soar."

He felt his body become lighter. Effortlessly he bounded up the steps. He pressed his palm against a pillar—and rose to the entablature. From cornice to ledge—from ledge to gargoyle—up—up—until he sprang over the roof parapet and stood on the tiles.

He went to the edge of the building and looked over the parapet, into the barracks courtyard. Lamps glowed, but there were no roistering voices.

At last he bounded to the façade overlooking the canal basin. Yes, there was restless movement in the canal courtyard. Rustad and his courtiers—the fat, green-and-pink Bulbul—and the palace purveyor Sejput, a good-natured old rascal. What sport were they devising for the battle ring?

With a shock Zeid realized they were executing a thief. But surely the figure in the cumbersome wad of multi-colored clothing was only a lad!

To kill a young thief in so cruel a manner—! Yet, as the satellite tutors had warned, the planet's laws recognized neither forgiveness nor compassion.

Sick at heart—but restricted by the satellite's policy of non-interference in the law codes—Zeid drifted over the parapet, straddled a convenient gargoyle, and observed the scene.

Warriors brought a wooden club, handed it to the boy, and

tumbled him roughly over the wire. A slave activated the Magic, and the waist-high, bluish wall enclosed the circle.

The boy picked himself up and tested the weight of the club. Zeid wondered why he did not strip down to his loincloth. The bulky shawl and pantaloons would impede his movement and would be no armor against rat fangs.

Now two slaves came from the cellars, carrying a cage with an enormous rat. Even from his roof gargoyle, Zeid could see the red hot eyes and yellow fangs.

The spectators crowded around the bluish wall. The slaves held the cage above the wire, tilted downwards to spill the rat into the circle.

The boy approached the cage! Taunts showered upon him, but he stood calmly.

Rustad signaled, and the cage end snapped up. The boy made a lightning jab at the falling rat—and pinned it against the hazy blue wall.

With a scream of agony and rage, the rat writhed free and rushed. The boy stabbed the end of the club at the ground, and flung his body upwards, balanced in the air. The rat plunged beneath him, past the club. When the maddened beast turned and would charge, the boy was again on his feet and swept upwards with the club, flinging the rat against the wire of the far barrier.

The spectators jumped aside. Zeid straightened on his perch and shouted, "Oh, well done! Oh, finish him off, most excellent boy!"

The rat fell back into the ring. Twice numbed by the haze-band, it could not regain its feet. The boy brought the club down on its skull which split with a crack audible to the roofs.

In triumph the young victor swiped at the dead rat with a two-handed swing that sent the limp body flying over the rail and into the crowd.

A slave shut off the Magic, and the blue haze cleared.

The boy opened the ring and stood before Rustad. Zeid wondered what he was demanding. Rustad would have to grant any reasonable request or lose esteem.

Obviously the request displeased him. Zeid could see the arrogant turn of his head and wondered if the boy had asked for too

much gold. Rustad had inherited more than a little of his mother's
parsimony.

The courtiers were silent—a reproving silence unendurable to
the vain prince. He gave a sign of assent and was again the center
of praise.

Bulbul and the lad began walking to the palace—not toward
the visitors hall but to the entrance for females and eunuchs.

Eunuchs—! Surely the boy was not willingly joining the cas-
trates!

Zeid slithered down the facade even faster than he had climbed.
At the lowest cornice he again pressed the belt stud and said,

> "Increase the measure, make me all,
> In weight to rise, in air to fall."

His body grew heavy. He dropped from the cornice, plummeted
to the ground, and barred the palace entrance to the approaching
pair.

"My Lord Zeid!" exclaimed Bulbul, turban gemstones flashing.
"How came you here?"

"No matter. The boy must not join your wretches! So much
can I forbid."

"A fine time to use a lord's power, land crab," said the boy
in an all-too-familiar voice. He pulled off his cap, and heavy dark
tresses fell to his shoulders. "I saw you on the roof cheering the
bloody sport."

"The sea urchin!" exclaimed Zeid. "I might have known that
only a she-pirate could best a burrow rat. How came you with
Sejput? And why?"

"I came to save you from your brother—and, with good luck,
have done so!"

Zeid stared. Bulbul explained. "As boon of Prince Rustad, the
lady demanded safety for you unto the third ring—yourself, your
kinsmen, your servants."

Zeid remarked, "What means a boon-promise to a prince who
would slay his brother—and would pit a girl against a burrow
rat?"

"It means time gained for your servants," retorted the girl, "and for us until we can return to the barge."

"We?" Zeid sighed. "Yes, I suppose I must take you again as burden."

"Burden? What burden have I been? I, who twice today have risked my life to save yours!"

"But I don't need to be saved! I—" Zeid became mindful of Bulbul's eager presence. He dismissed the eunuch and began to escort Coral Bud through the shadowy gardens.

"You did a very foolish thing, risking your life for me," he began. "I have Gifts—and, I hope, courage. You clutter my path, striking here and there—battling for me—even thinking for me—"

"Because you don't seem able to think for yourself."

"Do you imagine I'm not thinking, just because I don't confide every thought to you? Come now, sea urchin," he said, taking her arm, "You've done a brave deed—but I think you must have been doing it for a boast of your own skills because you really weren't appreciating my wits or considering my feelings.

"Did you think I had returned empty-headed to the palace?" he went on. "By no means. I intended to let Bulbul's greed restrain Rustad's envy. It is Bulbul who allots my father's gold among the palace departments. He would tie Rustad up in his purse strings. Did it never occur to you that I must have had some such plan?"

Coral Bud said in a small voice, "The Sea Kingdoms are not ruled in that manner."

"No. So you must not think you know everything in the Desert. And what about my feelings, Rover Bud?" he said, giving her arm a little shake. "Suppose the rat fangs had ripped your veins apart. Your death would have been a shadow on my life—a reproach— a sorrow. Prince Zeid had let a girl die, fighting his battles for him!"

"Oh, no! It was not meant thus!" protested the girl. "It was as if one shipmate would help another!"

"The other having a weak sword arm and no brain?" teased Zeid.

"An *unwilling* sword arm," laughed the girl, "and a brain more at home with Moonship ideas."

They continued arm-in-arm through the palace halls to his own chambers. "Now I must beg for apparel," she said, squeezing her lurid, bulging garments. "I must move twice to take one step."

"There must be robe lengths left in the clothing chests," he said. "Find something while I prepare the portation rug."

His long staff, with lamps hanging on gold chains, was still leaning beside his workshop entrance. Quickly he strung more lamps from his workbench until they hung to the floor.

He twined the lamps closely and laid the staff down the center of the rug.

A fragrance of rose water came to his nostrils, and Coral Bud followed the fragrance into the workshop. She had bathed in his mist-fountain and wrapped a silken night-cloth around her in womanly fashion. Her waist seemed tiny, outlined by the sash folds. Under the white head scarf, her dark ringlets seemed soft and touchable. Her face was rosy and alert.

Zeid was surprised at her sweetness, but he chose to regard it as unfair tactics since she knew his heart belonged to Fire Lotus. He said severely, "What kind of apparel do you call *that*?"

"Night apparel. This is the hour of sleep, isn't it? Why should I dress in heavy day attire now when Magic will bring me to the tent pallet in half a breath? I came to ask how much attire I can take."

"The rug has room for only a small bundle."

She slipped into his chamber again and returned with the bundled clothes.

He said, "We must lie within the rug, and yet my hand must touch the border beneath you."

She tossed the bundle to one end of the rug. "It can be a pillow. All would be easy if the Light-Bearer could stow his lamps otherwise. However, land crab, place yourself where you must, and I can then come aboard."

He lay on one side of the lamps and stretched an arm across the rug. Immediately she snuggled beside him, her head on his shoulder and her body seeking his. The lamps were somehow on top of them both.

Quickly—lest his head start whirling—Zeid recited,

> "Return to same—yet same does move
> At speed the same—in same straight groove."

The workshop vanished, and they were lying under the shifting starlight on the poop of the palace barge.

The girl rolled off the rug with a clash of lamp chains, sat up, and said, "There! A Counting Master is good for nothing but reckoning beads."

Zeid lifted away the lamps, sat up, and looked at the midship platform. The tent roof sagged—the center pole angled over the barge rail.

"So you vaulted the canal!"

"You reproach me yet again?"

"No, sea urchin. Your father gave you hard lessons, else you wouldn't have survived the pirate life. I can't love you as I love my beautiful Fire Lotus, but I can be a kind, instructive brother and perhaps make your fierce nature milder."

Coral Bud hid her smile behind her scarf.

Zeid continued earnestly, "When I've raised the tent, I'll keep it as master. But I owe you the favor of the boon-promise that will keep Rustad from attacking my hospice. Therefore I will hang the veil that will give you a sister's corner."

He rose and leaped along the sea chests.

Coral Bud sang,

> "A corner nest is all I need
> To save you from the Fire Girl's greed,
> O handsome Light-Bearer!"

The Space-programmed barge hummed quietly to itself as it sped toward the river sluice and the Seacoast.

IF ZEID WAS CONSCIOUS of the girl sleeping beyond the dividing veil, it was only as an embarrassment to his plans. At the Seacoast he would have to return her speedily tò her father. He could hardly woo Fire Lotus while he was accompanied by a "sister". . . .

He awoke at dawn and thrust his sleepy face out the tent's forward entrance. Ahead stretched the pink-and-gold-touched canal. In the night-shaded west loomed the black, cloud-topped peaks of the Sky Chutes. The dawn glistened on the streaming wet cols and crevasses.

Soon the barge would be at the sluice that controlled the canal system.

Zeid turned, rose from his cushions and ambled to the tent's aft fold. The inner veil had been lifted aside. Coral Bud had already left the tent. Zeid, still night-clothed, emerged onto the platform.

Moji was seated on a provision chest in the hold. When he saw Zeid, he rose and climbed the midship ladder.

"The lady and Kalia are in the mist-chamber, Lord Zeid," he said, gesturing to the stern compartment.

"I knew I should have insisted on Bulbul's barge," grumbled Zeid. "We are too many—that is, we have one too many. We must leave the she-pirate at the Seacoast."

"How will Hamar regard your rejection of his daughter?" smiled Moji. "It's an affront no father would overlook, implying as it does a flaw in the maiden."

"Moji, I could keep you here all morning, recounting the sea urchin's flaws—yet she is a brave girl and, in truth, I doubt that any man has come closer than a sword's length." He stroked his downy beard and went on, "Can't Hamar and I simply agree that my mother acted too hastily?"

Moji replied, "Don't *you* be too hasty, young prince. A good companion is more comfort than a beautiful woman."

Zeid smiled, "Easy for you to say, Moji, when Kalia is both. Have the girls left any towels, oil, and clothing for ourselves?"

After his mist-bath Zeid returned to the tent. Both entrance folds had been flung back, and the cushions were tidied. At the front entrance sat Coral Bud with two short-legged food trays.

Zeid sat beside her and looked at his tray. It held honeycake and small round wine-fruits. But he raised his eyebrows at a dish of gruel.

Coral Bud waved her hand at the western mountains. "Soon we will feel the chill of rain-cold rock. Eat a porridge that will warm your bones. The day will be tedious and wearing."

"Tedious? Presently I will mirror-speak with Feelafell and order my ship."

"What! Would you give the Space Bastard advance notice of a lamb he can shear? It's enough to come upon him by surprise and let him find a trick at the moment!"

"Don't name the man 'Bastard' as if berating him for a parentage he can't help."

"Look you, Light-Bearer, a fang-snake can't help being a fang-snake, but the prudent man avoids him. The Space Givers themselves forbid mixing the seeds of different worlds."

"The Space Givers are concerned with government and prerogative. All worlds are seeded alike."

"Then you don't know what happened when the Great Wizard seeded his mountain."

"Fortunately, I was taken to the Moonship before I had heard the old men's legends."

The girl looked at him gravely. "Very well. Learn for yourself. But don't forewarn Feelafell."

She finished her meal without speaking further and left the tent platform. Zeid watched her spring lightly over the sea chests and climb to the command platform at the prow. She flung back her long hair and raised her face into the wind as if scenting the sea.

The wind was now chill. Zeid quickly ate the gruel—thinking of Jibbo and the beggars—and went into the tent for his cloak.

A small sending mirror was in the grooming box the slaves had stowed in the tent. Zeid hesitated, then took the mirror from the box. He would disregard Coral Bud's warning about Feelafell; a she-pirate would naturally feel antagonism toward the shipowner of the horde-fleet.

Every receiving mirror—and such mirrors were reserved for lords and wizards—was name-coded to the owner. Zeid lifted the small sender, let his image fall on it, pressed an embossing, and said, "I call the horde-merchant Feelafell."

A female doll-face replaced his own image. A duplo had been set to tend the mirror. She smiled, "Who calls the Lord Feelafell?"

"Zeid ben Amfi."

"Am summoning. Will you hear a song while you wait?"

"If the song is of your own creating."

"Song has been created in me. Would you bid a lark find a new tune? Or a finch sing like a nightingale?"

Before Zeid could think of an answer, the girl's face dissolved into the mirror, and another face appeared.

It was a Space Giver face—a broader, smoother forehead than those of the planet's natives—a smaller chin—a male baldness that had seemed strange to Zeid until he had got used to it. Space Givers were taller but less well-proportioned. They were soft-spoken in manner, fluent in language, patient in teaching, ready with humor. For a moment, as the face appeared in the mirror, Zeid felt respect and affection.

Then the eyes measured him—bold, mocking, unfriendly eyes with as bitter envy in them as he had seen in Rustad's.

Zeid realized Coral Bud had been right. Feelafell was a random mix of species which strove against each other.

Feelafell began, "Welcome, Zeid ben Amfi! Perhaps you bring greetings to me from my kin on the Moonship?"

"You joke unkindly, Feelafell. You know I was but a savage schoolboy, not likely to be used as messenger between Space Givers," said Zeid. He could see his humble words pleased Fee-lafell, and he continued, "I wouldn't presume to address you at all, except at the bidding of my father the Wizard, who sends me on an errand to the Marble Lands."

Feelafell laughed. "I'll wager it was your mother Serada who would have a ship passage to even the score of trade between Amfi and myself! Where does your barge now approach?"

Zeid would rather not have answered, but he could only say, "We come now to the river sluice."

"Then you can join the horde-ship that will be leaving two days hence. A place will be waiting for your barge in my basin. Farewell!"

The mirror blanked, and Zeid stared discontentedly at his own face.

He put the mirror away and emerged from the forward fold of the tent. He saw that the barge was at the sluice gate.

Coral Bud was an imperious little commander at the prow. "Pay heed with your steadying poles, Sluice Master!" she scolded. "We want no further gouge marks on our rail."

The sluice gate opened. As the barge slid into the sluice, the steadying track alongside extended the first jointed pole and swung it slowly to catch the barge at a groove in the bow's railing.

Usually the pole was allowed to slide along the rail and fall in place, but Coral Bud sprang to guide it into the groove. "Dolt! I wonder you can find your mouth with your spoon! Treat our midship more gently, or I'll remember I am Hamar's daughter!"

"Never could you be so rough of tongue, my lady," laughed the Sluice Master.

"But just as quick to douse you in the canal, lazybones," she retorted.

The Master laughed again, but the midship pole hooked accurately into its midship groove.

When the stern pole was also in place, the barge's hum ceased, and the poles guided the barge along the sluice, elongating at their joints as the water level sank.

Beyond the sluice was a large, busy, turning basin with landing places for cargo. Barges were moored close together along the basin. Crewmen and slaves toiled with trans-shipments. Not all the Desert barges continued to the Seacoast.

The basin led to three riverways—west toward the Sky Chutes—north toward the sea—and east toward the Weavers Lands.

Coral Bud expertly guided the barge through the basin traffic— and swung into the broad eastbound channel.

Zeid shouted, "Hoy!" and leaped from the tent platform.

By the time he had made his way forward over the stowed chests and climbed to the prow, the barge was well into the channel with no turning until the next basin.

"What mischief are you now devising?" he demanded.

She looked up at him innocently. "Did you want to continue without your servants?"

He stared at her, and she went on, "Here you are so foolish as to carry slaves out of the Desert and set them free—and expect them to serve you as before."

"Why do you constantly wrong me, Rover Bud?" he complained. "I always meant to pay Kalia well for the journey."

"And her anxiety about her parents? If you had troubled to speak to the girl, you would have found that she knows nothing of their fate. Were they killed by Rustad's warriors? If you go straight to the Seacoast, she will leave you and rush home to her village in the Weavers Lands—and Moji will rush after her."

"Has she said she will leave?"

"Of course not! The girl must keep silent until she is free. But anyone could guess her first thought would be to go home. I tell you, Light-Bearer, you will not spread much comfort until you think as other people.

"But, in justice to yourself," she added, "you know nothing of parents who encourage anxiety about their well-being."

Reflecting on the supreme self-assurance of his mother and father, Zeid had to smile. Then he remembered Feelafell.

The girl asked, "What causes your face to darken?"

"Feelafell has reserved me a place in the ship-horde, two days hence."

"What! After I had warned you away from him?"

"He's the horde agent for this stretch of coast. I don't see what harm he can do."

"The harm he would do *you*, Light-Bearer, is beyond reckoning. His Space Giver kin, while allowing him wealth, confine him to the planet. And yet they welcome you to the Moonship and teach you their secrets."

"Their knowledge," smiled Zeid, "of which I comprehend very little."

"Whereas Feelafell inherited a mind that could understand all, if he were admitted to the mysteries. But his father's kin know him too well—his heart is as savage as any of Rustad's warriors."

"Nevertheless, the reservation for the ship-horde has been made—and now must be unmade."

"No. Let him await us," advised Coral Bud. "When we don't arrive, he'll think you're being sly and maybe will be more wary about plucking you like a chicken."

"Rover Bud, you'll leave little for anyone else to pluck."

"What a thing to say, when I'm making sure you won't be

stripped of your servants. Aren't they worth a few days delay in the Weavers Lands? When you set Kalia free among her own people—when you are generous with gifts and praise—can she and Moji refuse to finish this one journey before they begin their own lives?"

Zeid thought the matter over. "Yes, I would keep Moji, if I could. Perhaps you're right, sea urchin."

"Of course I'm right. And now, since the barge will not need tending before the Weavers Basin, how shall we amuse ourselves?"

"To sit beneath the tent canopy and watch new lands unfold would please me best."

"Good. And Kalia will instruct us about what we are seeing. Well, now I can almost feel at home. There is nothing more pleasant than a merry ship's company. An hour in a Desert harem was near to wearying me to death."

ZEID HAD TO ADMIT it was pleasant. They sat in a semicircle of cushions at the forward tent opening—Zeid, Coral Bud, Kalia, Moji. Coral Bud had rigged a sun canopy over their heads so they could sit comfortably in the shade and watch the lush, sunlit fields on either side of the river.

A basket of fruit lay within everyone's reach. It held hard-peel purple apples, small red crunch-berries, yellow-pink juice wedges.

Bright-feathered birds flew out from the riverbank to catch fruit bits that were tossed to them. They were free and seemed more beautiful than the captive twitterers of the Desert gardens.

Kalia's cheeks grew bright with the happiness of recognizing her own land. Fields of silvery flax were bounded by yarn-puff trees. Broad-leafed hedges enclosed farm villages.

Occasionally fire-stunted hedges enclosed charred ruins.

Kalia sighed, "Alas, Rustad is not the only Desert raider. Our villages have no wealth except slaves. How is the loot worth the striving?"

Zeid remarked, "The striving and violence seem to be their own rewards. To send war barges—or to brave the Desert—and then to slash and burn fertile lands, to have the most horrors to boast of—"

"You speak as if all raiding were done against peaceful villages," retorted Coral Bud, "but I tell you, Light-Bearer, there's great joy in cutting down scoundrels. Kalia's villages would not be so poor if the merchant lords did not buy in copper and sell in gold. I would sooner *attack* a merchant ship-horde than sail with it."

"You would sooner have strife than peace, in any case," smiled Zeid. "As a child, what did you choose, when the Space Givers lifted you to the Moonship?"

"I? Do you think Hamar would give his child up to Space strangers? Oh, what a fine battle we had," cried Coral Bud leaping up. "The Space Cloud came down upon the sea as we were tacking close-hauled. Fools that they were, the Spacemen came down ahead and to leeward. We had only to shift our steering oar, let our sails take more wind, bear down upon them—and *ram!*"

The bowl of fruit went flying.

"But your ship must have been crushed," objected Zeid.

"The ramming timbers might have been crushed, true, but the Space Givers wished to board us, so they opened the Cloud. We had already backed sail to stop our speed, so the Cloud captured only our bow—and there we sat, like a bird with his beak in a fruit wedge.

"My father and our fighters ran to the Cloud, ready to board. Their weapons crumbled to dust in the Space Magic, but when the Cloud opened again, they rushed the enemy with their bare fists—and what a drubbing the Space fools took before they cried for a parley. I had crept after my father so as not to miss the fight—"

"Naturally," murmured Zeid.

"—and when the Space Givers said they wanted to take me to the Moonship, I sprang out and sank my teeth into the nearest enemy arm. 'Twas then they yielded completely, freed our ship, and lifted away.

"So I was given place of honor at the supper board," finished Coral Bud proudly, "and since then, I've won full booty sharing with the crew."

"An honor you can't expect potential victims like ourselves to appreciate," said Zeid.

"O Lord Zeid, the lady is a brave warrior," said Kalia.

Zeid smiled at the admiration in Kalia's blue eyes. "Would you rather have battle spoils than Moji?"

"Why should the choice be *either-or*?" demanded Coral Bud. "Kalia could just as easily capture Moji's heart as a pirate, and a Counting Master is reckoned a valuable prize."

"I dare not ask how a prince is reckoned," said Zeid, "but would you really rate seed-partners according to prize lists?"

"Well, marriage is a kind of bondage," mused Coral Bud, "and it must be more bearable if each spouse has useful value."

Zeid thought of his beautiful Fire Lotus. Was any value higher than beauty? Of course, he reflected, he was thinking as a man. A pirate girl would hardly understand his love for Fire Lotus.

IN THE EVENING IT RAINED. The Desert Prince Zeid did not know what rain was. He had not seen it as a child, and the Moonship had been far above the skies.

When the huddling stars disappeared into the clouds, Moji and Kalia spread the tarpaulins over the holds before they retired to the crew cabin.

Zeid and Coral Bud entered the tent, drew the tent folds together, and lit the roseate lamp. Coral Bud did not withdraw behind the "sister's veil." She plumped herself down on a cushion.

"A ship's cabin is coziest when the weather is bad. How the rain drums on the tent roof! At sea, the waves slap against the hull, and one's warm dry cabin is a womb the elements can't enter."

Zeid also sat on a cushion. "How do you spend the rainy hours aboard ship?"

"With talking and music, if one is lucky enough to have a string-thrummer or horn-blower aboard. Except for a sailor's chanty, I'm no musician."

"So you must be a talker," smiled Zeid.

"A listener—since a listener learns more."

"And is more able to retell." Zeid hesitated. "Today, when we were arguing facts, I didn't want to hear how the Great Wizard seeded his mountain, but now I think I would be interested in the legend."

"Oh, very well, though it is not a legend but as true as true can be," said Coral Bud. She sat up, crossed her trousered legs and began, "Know you that before this world existed, there was a world where the Great Wizard had made every perfect thing. But he also had children, and, as you know, there is always one child who is envious of the others.

"When the Wizard's eldest daughter was to marry the king of a far country, the Wizard feared she would be lonely and homesick, and he decided to seed a mountain for her and remove it to her new kingdom.

"But her youngest brother, who was named Discord, was very jealous. He thought, 'If I can steal a few of the seeds, I can have my own world and remove it whither I will.'

"So he dug a cave into the Wizard's mountain and waited. The first day, the Wizard came and threw the seeds of light. The whole inside of the mountain became light, except Discord's dark cave.

"Discord saw the light and came out of his cave and snatched the last of the seeds—but he did not snatch enough, so the stolen light was half-darkness.

"The next day the Wizard came and threw the seeds of earth, and all of the light-filled mountain became good land. As before, Discord came out of his cave and could snatch only the last seeds. So he had only bits and pieces.

"On the next day the Wizard seeded all the animals his daughter wanted to take to her new kingdom to play with and enjoy. Discord caught only the last of these seeds too—and so the stolen animals were misshapen, some with long trunks or tall necks or horns on their noses, and some were angry and fierce.

"Discord was determined to get the first of the next seeds, which would be Mankind. But he snatched too soon and got only a half handful. So his cave held Mankind who were physically very handsome, but their minds were as warped as the bodies of the beasts.

"Lastly the Wizard spread the seeds of self-sustaining life— and these did not get into the cave at all, because Discord was so harried by his crooked creation that he forgot to look for the

Wizard. So his creatures could live only by devouring each other. The plants fought and choked each other for the land, and the beasts devoured the plants, and Mankind ate the beasts.

"Meantime the Wizard's mountain was finished, and all the wedding guests came and admired it, never noticing Discord's dark cave because everything else was so beautiful. The Wizard's daughter and her new husband went into the mountain, and the Wizard removed it to their far kingdom.

"But when the Wizard's part of the mountain was gone, there was nothing to hold Discord's cave together, and it swelled up and began floating away. The water and sky separated from the land, and the stars separated from the sky and took bits of seed with them. Everything was disconnected, and the creatures of different stars began to change according to the way Discord had snatched the seeds. The faraway beasts became very different in appearance but kept the same minds, whereas the people kept the same appearance but changed within their thoughts.

"And this is why, O Light-Bearer, the cattle of the Space Givers do not mix seed with our cattle but remain a separate animal—and why the Space Givers can mix bodies with us, but it is an evil thing because of the difference of our thoughts."

Zeid pondered. "How came Feelafell's Space Giver father to forget the law against mixing seeds?"

"His mother was very beautiful. I forgot to say," added Coral Bud, "that beauty in Discord's world became a snare because it seemed like the beauty of the Wizard's real mountain and yet was often very false."

She smiled at Zeid, rose and withdrew to her own part of the tent, letting the veil fall shut.

The rain hammered all night, and Zeid awoke to a water-smeared sunrise. He rose, wrapped a warm robe about him and opened the forward fold of the tent. The air smelt fresh like newly sliced melon. The fields gleamed like silver where the rain-flattened flax lay in sheets and swirls.

A rainbow arched between Zeid and the pale sun. He had seen rainbows arching in the palace fountains, but this vast color vault overwhelmed him.

As before, Coral Bud had arisen earlier. Barefoot, trouser legs rolled up, she was sweeping the puddles off the tarpaulins covering the forward hold. Already the sun was fading the wet shine from the swept fabric.

When she saw Zeid, she smiled, threw down her broom, and climbed the ladder to the tent platform. "Good morning, Light-Bearer. Would you like to know why the Great Wizard called the colors together?"

"No, sea urchin," smiled Zeid. "I know a rainbow is but the scattering of light through water."

"And *I* know otherwise. But believe what you will. Soon Kalia will have freshly baked rice cakes ready for breakfast. She has been working since the light, to have her tasks done before we arrive at the Weavers Basin."

"Can we really keep Kalia and Moji from leaving us?"

"Why, yes—unless the Light-Bearer behaves foolishly."

"As he usually does?" smiled Zeid.

Coral Bud took time to consider. She rolled down her trouser legs, standing first on one foot and then on the other. Zeid noticed the loveliness of her little bare feet.

Finally she said, "Well, a man undoubtedly is too busy to run a household. I don't like to think how my poor father is faring, now that I've gone."

"He has no seed-wife?"

"He has never found my mother's equal as sometimes happens when a beloved young wife dies. So now he seeks his ease with duplos and is doubtless eating burnt meat and cold porridge."

"He should have kept you with him."

"Indeed, had he not been in debt to your father for the newest duplo, the subject never would have arisen. Bulbul disdained his gold, on orders from the princess Serada, who would have me as barter. And, truly, sensible seed-wives can scarcely be bought at any price in the Desert Cities. Just see the giggling harem idiots that have been foisted on your brother Rustad."

"I'm sorry your father sold you to no purpose."

"Oh, the purpose was served since he is rid of an irksome debt. I was not unwilling to marry the young prince whom Bulbul described since I thought I could make something of him."

"Pray don't attempt the impossible," said Zeid hastily. "I want to be loved, not improved."

"Well, all I can say is, the wife who leaves you as you are doesn't love you very much. Now do change your slothful robe for attire such as Weavers expect of princes, else Kalia and Moji will be too ashamed to continue service with you."

Zeid cocked his head at Coral Bud's makeshift clothing. "You're no fine-dressed lady yourself."

"A lack you can remedy with the Weavers."

"But I left all my gold with Jibbo to feed the hospice!"

"And a ravenous animal a hospice must be! Well, you can begin by cutting up your gold lamp chains. The lamps can hang as well from twine."

Zeid groaned—and yet was pleased to have had the gold chains brought to his attention. He would need every scrap of wealth to meet Fire Lotus in a princely fashion.

THE WEAVERS TOWN LAY in a broad, fair plain. Timbered, peaked roof houses stood apart, each in a garden. Larger buildings housed looms, and a constant thump-a-thump shook the breeze.

By the time the barge had approached the basin grid, Zeid had arrayed himself to Coral Bud's satisfaction. From the Gatemaster to the town markets went the news that a richly clad prince had arrived.

It was Moji who stood on the command prow and moored the barge, and then stepped ashore with Kalia. Her village lay a league south of the riverway, but she had kin in the town.

From the tent platform Zeid and Coral Bud watched as Kalia looked around uncertainly like a stranger. Then she gave a cry and ran. "Uncle! Oh, Uncle!"

A man clad in the box-jacket and wide trousers of a Weaver stood like a statue. "Kalia!" He opened his arms, and she ran into them. "We believed you dead, like your dear parents!"

Kalia gave a cry and went limp against his shoulder.

Zeid said to Coral Bud, "I must proclaim Kalia free before witnesses."

"Since the whole town is running to the landing place, you can just as well step ashore and do it now," said Coral Bud. "Accept what hospitality the uncle offers, but make my excuses."

"Why?"

"I don't have suitable clothing."

"Women's garments can be quickly fetched."

"And won't fit—or look right—or feel comfortable. Later I'll go ashore and choose carefully."

"Rover Bud, why won't you tell me your reason for staying aboard the barge?"

"Because we'll only quarrel. You don't like me to warn you against Feelafell. When we didn't arrive at the Seacoast yestereve, he certainly questioned the barges that followed us out of the sluice basin and found out we had turned eastwards."

"I know he hasn't forgotten us, sea urchin. I've already regretted mirror-speaking him. Yes, you judge Seacoast matters better than I. But I think you might trust me."

"How can I trust you when you hoard your thoughts?" cried Coral Bud. "You should have told me that the mirror-speaking revealed Feelafell's base nature to you. When perils threaten, why can't we talk them over like shipmates?"

"Because a closeness might result that would be very unfair to you. Soon we must go our separate ways. I would not want you to deceive yourself into imagining that a betrothal would have been possible or desirable. Anyway," he added, "I don't know why you would want to wed a man whose way of life—whose habits of thought—are so very different from what you have been used to."

"Perhaps I want to wed you for the same reason you want to wed Fire Lotus."

Zeid looked startled. "Such feelings would be most unfortunate."

"In that case, let's both renounce them," smiled Coral Bud.

She entered the tent. Zeid, wishing Coral Bud would not persist in misunderstanding him, stepped ashore from the midship platform.

By now the landing place was thronged. Zeid felt keenly that he was among strangers. It was not that the physical scene was more fertile—more open—but that the people were dressed differently and seemed freer, more at ease.

The more temperate climate of the Weavers Lands allowed the outdoor use of linen and finespun tree-yarn. The terrible heat of the Desert Cities had made necessary the outer robes of sheep's wool to turn back the white-hot sun and the inner garments of gauze or gossamer. The Weavers Lands, though but a short distance north of the desert, were cooled by rain and flourishing plants. The people could wear many-colored open-weave yarns of interesting variety.

The styles showed that personal taste and not rigidly-defined rank determined what a person wore. The town had servants and apprentices, but Zeid saw none of the servility—or arrogance— of his father's palace.

He also felt keenly how open the town lay to attack. In this instance Zeid was not thinking of his brother Rustad, but of Feelafell the Space Bastard. He was not so certain that Feelafell's space hardware was harmless. From conversations he had overheard on the satellite, Zeid knew that the liaison between Feelafell's father and the planet beauty had gone undetected for years. Who could tell what hardware had been smuggled to the planet or what knowledge had been confided?

To turn eastwards had been a mistake. Feelafell would interpret it as a deliberate lie, a derisive slap. However, he would wait at the Seacoast, knowing the prince he hated would be arriving, or so Zeid reasoned.

Thus he shook off his fears, as he stepped forward to meet Kalia's uncle. He was far more anxious about the pirate tricks the confounded Rover Bud might be thinking up!

Kalia was still sobbing against her uncle's shoulder. The hush of the crowd at his approach caused her to gulp back her tears and look around. For an instant her glance was wild, almost hateful, but Moji's touch on her arm calmed her. She made a trembling curtsey and stammered,

"My lord Zeid, may I present my Uncle Tind, Master of the Weavers Guild?"

Tind, clean-shaven with close-clipped brown hair, was still on the youthful side of middle age. Nothing except a certain gravity of demeanor proclaimed his Master's rank. He bowed and said,

"Pray accept our many thanks, Lord Zeid, for bringing Kalia back to us."

"Thank rather the random chance that permitted me to do so," replied Zeid. "And as is established by the laws of the free lands, I now pronounce Kalia once more free. All of you are witnesses— she is free."

Kalia trembled even more, grew pale, and almost collapsed into Moji's arms. The bystanders seemed choked by emotion. Zeid had expected joyful cheers instead of unendurable relief. Did they think he would bring Kalia this far and refuse to release her? Of course, they had no reason to trust any of his family.

Master Tind now bowed again and said, "We hope the compassionate prince and his lady will accompany us to my humble abode and join in our feasting."

"I'd like nothing better, Master Tind," smiled Zeid, "but as Kalia and Moji will tell you, we left the palace in haste. My lady must find attire, and I have much to do aboard the barge."

Kalia immediately looked conscience-stricken and said, "Oh, Uncle! Moji and I can't feast all day while our kind friends work alone on the barge!"

Zeid knew Coral Bud wanted the barge to herself. He said, "Don't trouble yourselves—"

But Kalia skipped past him and jumped aboard the barge. "Lady! The lord Zeid says you have work to do! Can we help?"

Coral Bud stepped out of the tent. "Why, the fact is, Kalia, if you could spare Moji for an hour, when the sun is midway towards noon, he could help us very much! Otherwise, there is nothing."

The crowd's mood lightened as if everyone was pleased by Coral Bud's frankness. Kalia rejoined Moji and Master Tind. They slowly left the landing place, stopping now and then to receive the congratulations of the townspeople.

Zeid stepped to the tent platform and confronted Coral Bud. In an exasperated voice he asked, "What possible use have you for Moji?"

"None. And now I must find a use before he returns. Why

didn't you go with the uncle, as I instructed you, instead of making Kalia believe we were heavy-burdened with chores?"

"I don't dare go anywhere, as long as you see Feelafell in every shadow. Even supposing him my enemy, what would bring him so far from the Seacoast?"

"The guess that you have Magic weapons, O unwary prince. Where have you hidden them?"

Zeid stroked his beard uneasily. "I rolled them within the rug."

"Thus doing the thief's work for him. Find the weapons and hide them under your robes. Then you can help me search the barge for a suitable wedding gift."

"Wedding gift?"

"Why should Kalia and Moji wait longer to be wed? And Uncle would just as soon have today's feast serve two purposes. Welcoming a niece back from the dead is a costly business."

"But what can I give Kalia? A length of gold chain?"

"Chains are indeed a tactful gift for a newly freed slave."

"A Space Giver lamp?"

"A lamp is what you give Uncle, who will thereupon advise Kalia to continue with such a munificent master. Now is not the time to stint. What treasure does the barge contain?"

"Why, none that I know of. Unless the grooming cases within the tent—"

Coral Bud entered the tent and knelt down to look at the ornate caskets stowed along the sides. "Nothing much here," she said of the first. "Gloves and turban strips."

At the second casket she gave a cry of delight. She held up a circlet for the head with a dangling ruby, and two gold-and-ruby bracelets.

"Duplo jewelry!" exclaimed Zeid. "The barge was stowed in such haste that the slaves seized a wrong box. Apparently the barge was last used for delivering a new duplo, and the same boxes were re-stowed.

"Kalia would recognize duplo jewelry," he added. "We can't insult her by giving it to her."

"Fine rubies are no insult."

"Very true, sea urchin. I could remove the gems and have them reset for Fire Lotus."

"And I could let you make such a glaring mistake, but I'll be a kind sister and tell you that rubies are no gift for a redhead since the one red fights the other."

"Why, that's true—and very helpful, Coral Bud."

"I've been trying to help all along. See how we could devise a necklace for Kalia," she went on. "We could clasp one bracelet into the other and bring the ends forward—"

"The links wouldn't lie flat," said Zeid critically. "Wait!"

He sought his portation rug and unrolled the weapons. He drew out the Combi-shot and began twisting the end of the barrel. It elongated and became smaller and smaller until it narrowed to a needle point.

He laid one bracelet on top of a casket and knelt before it, sitting back on his heels. He adjusted the grip of the weapon, pointed the needle at the wide wrist band, and pressed the grip.

Lines seemed to sketch themselves in the gold. The lines became a design, and the design suddenly became a beautiful filagree.

Coral Bud, who had knelt beside Zeid, exclaimed in admiration, "Why, you are a Magic goldsmith. Are such skills what they teach on the Moonship?"

"Yes, but not for making jewelry," smiled Zeid. "My hand was trained for microcircuitry. Moonship people don't bother much with jewelry, or with decoration of any kind. Everything is efficient, functional."

"Whatever that may be. It sounds very unpleasant. But they must decorate their shutters—and their barge prows—and seal-marks."

"The houses have no windows, but are of blank glass. Moonship people write their language down in combinations of seal-marks that never vary. Individual designs are our written language, which is why every house has a different design on its shutters. The Space Givers merely put a small seal-mark beside the door."

"How poor and desolate."

"Yes. I was happy on the Moonship, but I thirsted for the polished grain of living wood—for hand-sculpted mosaics—for beauty."

"I see," murmured Coral Bud. "Oh, yes, now I see. But thirst can be fatal. Many a seaman has died because sea water has seemed like pure spring water to him."

Zeid was frowning over the bracelet. "Matching parts should be done together." He got up to fetch the second bracelet.

Coral Bud picked up the Combi-shot he had laid aside. It would be fun to carve a line into the top of the chest. She aimed the needle and pressed the grip.

With a loud crack, the chest split open. Coral Bud gasped and stared. Zeid leaped to take the weapon from her hand.

"Wretch!" fumed Zeid. "Did Hamar allow you to play with his darts and knives?"

"But it looked to be only a stylus to make little grooves!" protested Coral Bud.

Zeid wrenched open the split cover. The sending mirror lay in splinters. Zeid groaned, "Coral Bud, you're the most vexatious sister who ever shared a tent."

Coral Bud said in a tired voice, "You could have explained what you knew I didn't understand. Even the great Hamar has time to say to an apprentice, 'The halyard is thus, and the sheet must not be made fast.'"

"Well, sea urchin, anger mends nothing," sighed Zeid. "It was careless of me to use the chest as a workbench. But please carry the chest away and dispose of the splinters carefully."

"You'll finish Kalia's necklace?"

"If clumsy she-pirates will cease plaguing me."

Coral Bud rose meekly and carried the broken casket from the tent.

Zeid dragged a larger chest to the center of the deck. He adjusted the Combi-shot again, and muttered, "If only she would stop trying to be useful to me. I'm lucky she didn't put laser holes in me or the barge."

WHEN MOJI ARRIVED AT the appointed hour, Coral Bud leaped nimbly ashore and joined him. She had put on her scuffed harem slippers but otherwise was her badly bundled self.

"We need a Counting Master because we are spending lamp chains, Moji."

"Does the lady have a gold chain with her?"

"No—because Zeid is working within the tent, and I would rather not disturb him. I suppose you can promise gold for what we buy?"

Moji's ripe-olive eyes looked amused. "If the purchase is within reason for a modest young prince whose expenditures must stand scrutiny by the Princess Serada."

"Well, even the Princess Serada would grant I can't tramp around like a banquet clown. But I want very plain attire, Moji."

"Not to worry, Lady. The prince's credit is good for gossamers and gold thread."

"And what is my father Hamar to think if I come aboard like a bride?"

Moji smiled, "Why, that you *are* a bride, lady."

"Yes—and when he finds my lord Zeid treating me like a sister, I'll own a prince who is a head short. No, Moji, the rejection must seem to come from me."

"For what reason would you reject the prince and still live in his tent?"

"Now there I had a knot that took me all of a quarter-hour to untie. Zeid is such a dear lamb, Moji."

"Don't be misled by his gentle ways, Lady. A sword at rest seems a fine piece of artwork—but the edge can kill."

"O indeed, Moji. I doubt that even Rustad dares strike a slave in Zeid's presence—or wherever Zeid would hear about it, for that matter. But by nature Zeid is such a dear that I couldn't imagine a woman who would reject him—except the greedy red-head he's lovesick for.

"And in a flash I saw how I could pretend the same greed. My father knows well how tightfisted the mother Serada is. I will come aboard meanly clad and denying to take Zeid as my husband until he has secured a princess's wife-portion for me."

"Lady, I think *meanly* goes too far if you wish Hamar to feel kindly toward the prince."

"Yes, you're right," agreed Coral Bud. "My father must be led to feel sorry for Zeid and think me unreasonable. And now, Moji, I trust this matter will remain confidential between us."

Moji smiled again. "Lady, I did not rise from slave boy to Counting Master by being indiscreet, I assure you."

"True enough. Well, then, let's seek out the apparel houses and spend as befits a couple of seamen on shore leave."

After Moji had seal-marked the apparel merchant's tapestry, Coral Bud sent him to rejoin Master Tind's guests. She walked back to the barge alone, wearing new attire and carrying a linen sack of her other purchases.

Zeid was waiting for her within the tent, and he nodded approval at her modest linen tunic and trousers, and her woolen cloak. As she tossed the sack behind the veil he remarked,

"You've been kind to my small hoard of gold."

"For myself, yes. But of course I had to buy Moji and Kalia their wedding clothes."

"What!"

"Well, my dear prince, even your mother Serada awards wedding clothes when her servants marry. I don't know what the Space Givers were thinking of to let you come home with your head full of nonsense about rainbows, but no idea at all about the duties of a prince.

"Today it is your duty to be generous—and decorative. The townspeople already have seen the robes you arrived in. Change them for something more magnificent."

"I don't have anything more magnificent."

"Exactly as I supposed. So I bought you a new turban strip of shining gold cloth, instead of the flimsy gauze, and a rare white warbler plume for the brooch."

"But you'll leave me no gold for my journey."

"How can you be so unfair? It was your mother who left you no gold for the journey. And it was I who thought of the lamp chains. I've increased your hoard, and now I'm doing everything in my power to retain your servants for you. I really don't know what more I could do."

Zeid suddenly laughed. "*I* really don't know, either. I wish I did."

"Why must we keep circling each other like village boys feinting with barrel staves? Your Moonship lessons taught nothing of the planet's snares—and yet when I would help you, I must be as wary as a woodsman trying to help a thorn bear out of a trap."

"Well, then," smiled Zeid, "tell me what you mean to do while I'm at the wedding feast."

"Oh, I'm coming with you. Moji says he will send two of Uncle Tind's apprentices to watch over the barge. So change into different robes to please the townspeople."

"Where's your own finery?"

"I don't need finery. I can go as myself—Hamar's daughter," said the girl proudly.

IN UNITING TO HONOR the wedding feast, Zeid and Coral Bud also showed their best qualities to each other. Zeid was a true prince— kind, thoughtful, putting even the most awestruck child at ease. His gift to Kalia—the duplo jewelry Magically transformed into a ruby-studded gold filagree necklace—was worthy of a princess. As Coral Bud watched him, all kinds of love throbbed within her—mother-love, sister-love, and wife-love that made her brave pirate heart ache with desire.

Zeid, though intent on the festive ceremonies, could not help noticing the loveliness of Coral Bud's shining dark eyes and soft, heavy, dark hair. She was graceful and unself-conscious, full of good spirits but not bold. He realized that if she had asked for recruits to Hamar's fleet, every male in the Guildhall would have enlisted under her colors.

He was pleased by her company and less perplexed and angered at his mother Serada. Coral Bud did not have the exquisite beauty or bewitching appeal of Fire Lotus, but Serada had chosen a girl worthy of princely rank.

They left the Guildhall early in the feasting. Zeid knew that princes tend to dampen village exuberance. Only after he had departed would the celebration take its untrammeled course.

Happy and feeling comfortable with each other, they boarded the barge, dismissed the young guards, and separated to change from their feast clothes.

When they met again, they looked like apprentices in woolen shirts and trousers and leather boots. They opened both tent entrances, so they could look ahead and astern, and sat on cushions in the middle of the tent.

Zeid smiled, "You would have been a fine young brother, Rover Bud."

"No—because Fire Lotus might like me better than you. I'm certainly livelier—but also poorer."

"Fire Lotus will forget wealth when her heart is melted."

"I would sooner try to melt granite in warm butter. However, we are as yet far from the Marble Lands—"

A boy's voice hailed them from the landing place. Coral Bud rose and went out of the tent. She came back with a platter of cakes and fruit.

"See, Kalia has sent our dessert after all." She set the platter down and resumed her cushion. "How artfully the cakes have been iced, with layerings from the Space Giver sweet-reed."

"They are indeed pleasant to the eye," smiled Zeid, "but can you stuff more food into yourself, little pirate?"

"If you could fetch us wine from the provisions—"

Zeid laughed. "Woe betide us if our servants don't come back. There will be constant quarreling about who is the wine fetcher—and who is the plate washer—"

"I will be the navigator," grinned Coral Bud, "and the porridge-maker. And wrestle you for freedom from the disputed tasks."

They settled back on their cushions, too comfortable with each other to move.

A wasp whined into the tent and circled the cake-piled platter. Coral Bud sat up. "A raider for our dessert. We must take the first bites ourselves."

"Now, Coral Bud, you know a woman doesn't make up her mind faster than a wasp. You have no idea what cake you want."

"Well, I can decide quickly," said Coral Bud as the wasp circled lower. "If I only knew which was the light bubble-cake—"

The wasp settled on a cake, and Coral Bud snatched another and laughed, "An even race—though you sought to distract me."

She lifted the cake toward her mouth—and Zeid's body rose from his cushions like a fish surging upwards from the sea. His hand closed around her wrist and forced it away from her face.

"Drop it! *Drop* it!"

She was not used to taking sharp orders, and her first impulse was to resist indignantly. The strength of his grip paralyzed her fingers. The cake fell away.

He sat heavily beside her. His arm held her back from the platter. "O that I had answered the boy's hail!" he exclaimed. "Look at the wasp."

She looked. The wasp lay upon a cake, already curled in death.

"The boy said Kalia sent the cakes," she faltered.

"Because someone had told him so." Zeid released her. "Go wash the poison from your hand. O that I had *thought*—!"

Coral Bud took a scarf from her pocket and rubbed her fingers clean. "Yes, we were foolish. Poison is not a seaman's weapon, but—"

"But it *is* a palace weapon. I should have suspected—and yet Rustad is a warrior, not a poisoner."

"Rustad is too fond of gory violence to be a poisoner," said Coral Bud. "Besides, how would he know where to find us? Search out the boy—he'll tell you Feelafell gave him the cakes."

"The poor boy is dead by now. I warrant he received a cake as part of his wages. And for that I will never forgive Feelafell. You were right, Coral Bud," added Zeid. "When we didn't appear at the Seacoast, Feelafell traced us here."

"But where is he hiding? How did he know about the feast? Can he listen?"

Zeid stroked his beard and considered. "My mind swings like a pendulum between what Feelafell's father *could* bring to the planet and what he *did* bring. He could have brought very advanced Magic, but Moonship Security is so effective that he probably brought nothing."

"Except knowledge."

"But it's knowledge that needs metals and crystals not mined on this planet—it needs tools we don't have. Feelafell may know how to listen to far conversations, but he can't build the tools. I think he came here with a native agent who spied out the land for him."

"If he came so quickly, he must have come by Magic."

"Yes—and that puzzles me, though I can explain it in many

ways that would be simple for a Space Giver and possible with the hardware already on the planet. But listening? I think not."

"Well, then, what do we do? His spy saw the cakes delivered and must believe we are dead. If we wait patiently until dark, we can catch Feelafell entering the tent to take your Space weapons."

"But you should go to the mist chamber and wash your hand."

"I touched only the sides of the cake, and I think the poison was dusted only over the top. Besides, I wiped the icing away, and if I'm not dead by now, I never will be. Soon it will be dusk, and Feelafell will come sneaking aboard from a boat or raft."

"How can he launch a raft unseen in a busy basin? He'll come from the land."

"Never," said Coral Bud. "At any moment we could have visitors from land. Feelafell is a shipowner—he thinks in sea terms—he will board from the water like any pirate. You may know the ways of Space Givers, Light-Bearer, but I know the ways of the Seacoast scoundrels."

"Very true, Rover Bud," smiled Zeid. "We will do nothing until dark when we can move freely within the tent without being seen."

Coral Bud sighed. "Waiting irks my nature. I would do more than sit here and look at a dead wasp."

"You can tell me the legend you were speaking of—about why the Great Wizard called the colors together."

"So you wish to know the truth about the rainbow? Very well. Be sure you tell the Space Givers how wrong they were." Coral Bud propped herself on the cushions and began,

"Now, Discord's cave swelled and swelled, and all the seeds separated, and the whole dark false creation came to the Great Wizard's notice. He hardly knew what he ought to do. He could have waved his hand and destroyed the cave—but that meant destroying the good that originally had been in each seed, and good really cannot be destroyed even by the Great Wizard.

"However, there was much misery in the cave—not only because of the strife and devourings, or the separation of the land and waters, but because there was no beauty. The whole cave and animals and people were gray—or not even gray, which has a kind of color, but no color at all.

"The Great Wizard realized the seeds of color had floated so far from each other that they could not combine to make anything beautiful. You know very well that when the sky and air are gray, the sea also is gray and the fishes lose their markings, and even the trees and grass are dull.

"So the Great Wizard ordered Discord to gather up all the wandering color seeds and put them back where they belonged. Discord tried, but he didn't have the skill of the Great Wizard, which is why animals have stripes or spots, and a parrot can be green, red, and yellow all at once, and people can be golden-haired like Kalia or dark-haired like me or neither the one nor the other.

"But because color itself is beautiful, even the mixed-up patterns were also beautiful, although Discord being a man, made all the male creatures splendid first and hence didn't have enough color to decorate all the females. That is why the male ducks have feathers as bright as gems while their seed-wives are as drab as mud.

"At last Discord was finished. The flowers were really most beautiful, because he had started with them, but nothing at all was ugly anymore, not even a burrow rat.

"The trouble was, Discord found the sky much too big for him because it kept swelling—and is swelling to this day—and whenever it rained, the colors dissolved out of the earth and flowers and people, and floated away, so everything soon was almost as gray as before.

"The Great Wizard was angry, but Discord complained, 'The sky has become too vast for me.'

"'Very well,' said the Great Wizard, 'I will gather the colors together after the rain has dissolved them, and lay them in correct order across the sky, and you may take them and return them to your world.'

"That is why, after a rainstorm, you see the colors laid neatly in an arch in the same order. And Discord takes the colors from the sky and puts them back into the world. The sky and sea turn blue, and the grass is greener than before, and all eyes sparkle, no matter what color they are.

"Of course, colors dissolve into the sunbeams too so that many things fade and wither, but Discord does not worry about it because he knows the Great Wizard will gather the colors together again after the next rainstorm.

"Thus many sun-faded things—like grass and plants—regain their color after the next rainstorm, but because Discord is lazy he lets the unimportant things stay as they are. So there is no use hoping that Discord will renew a faded cloak. You must take it to the dyers, who borrow color seeds from Discord's plants and make up for his laziness.

"So now, Light-Bearer, I hope you understand about the colors and can see how foolish the Space Givers are when they say a rainbow is merely light scattered by water."

"I certainly will look at a rainbow differently," smiled Zeid, "and I thank you for making the dusk come before I could notice it."

IT WAS NOW THE star-mottled twilight. Coral Bud said, "Let's lift the tent hem on the water side of the barge so that we can see a small boat or raft."

"I can make better spy-slits, little pirate. Move yonder caskets so we can sit against the tent fabric."

Coral Bud slithered to the side of the tent and moved the small boxes noiselessly. Zeid again made a needle point of the Combi-shot and traced a half-circle on the tent fabric at the height of Coral Bud's eyes.

When she pressed the curve with her fingers, the cloth opened. She murmured, "Oh, what a lovely spy-slit," and peered out. Zeid moved a short distance from her and made a half-circle for himself. Between them, they shared a view of the entire water rail.

The night became dark. Oil lamps flared along the landing place and flickered from the moored barges. The basin itself was a chaos of shadows.

Coral Bud's sea-trained eyes were the first to note a dark bulk rising from the star-flecked water. "Look—a monster!" she whispered.

"Great Cosmos! The bastard has a minisub," blurted Zeid. He explained hurriedly, "Feelafell has come up the riverway in an underwater boat."

The ovoid approached and disappeared below their range of vision as it nudged alongside. A grapple *clunked* and fastened upon the rail. A black shadow rose up—clutched the rail with one hand—then the other—

The indistinct body shuddered and almost fell back. Drunkenly it grabbed the grappling hook with one hand and spread the other hand to the starlight. Slivers glinted in the palm.

The raider seemed to shrink down. The watchers in the tent could hear a writhing body thud into a hatch. A Space lamp glowed briefly.

There was an angry cry, and the hatch banged shut. The underwater ovoid scraped the barge and made surface ripples as it turned in the basin to retrace its course.

"Rover Bud! What sea trick—?" demanded Zeid.

"Well, you know, barge rails are painted black so that grime does not show so easily and marks can be daubed away without trouble. While you were making Kalia's necklace, I fetched a keg of pitch from the repair chest, laid a stripe of pitch on the water rail, and strewed it with splinters from the broken mirror. I dabbed the glass with pitch so it wouldn't shine. Feelafell grasped the rail firmly—and won't be able to hold as much as a spoon for a long, long time.

"I didn't like leaving the apprentices aboard with such a sharp trap set, but before I followed you to the wedding I warned them the rail was newly painted, and they did not touch it.

"And now, let's feed the poisoned food to the barge, which makes nothingness of offal, and wash the platter so it can be returned to its owner tomorrow. Either Feelafell or his spy certainly stole the platter from the Guildhall serving pantry, and the cooks and waiters will be exchanging words about its absence."

Zeid objected, "Again, sea urchin, you took the matter out of my hands and left me nothing to do. Therefore, I propose to do nothing. If I had captured Feelafell, I would have had to take him to the Moonship, and my journey to Fire Lotus would have been delayed yet again.

"However, you stopped Feelafell from boarding. He sped away—and I propose to ignore him. But perhaps his spy is still in the town. To spend a quiet night, let's continue to remain hidden in the tent and hope he assumes we are dead."

"With me, it will be only half a pretense, because I'm very weary and will now retire to my corner."

In the darkness Zeid felt more than saw her lift the veil and disappear.

On the morrow Coral Bud once more was dressed and at work before Zeid. She carried the dessert platter to the offal whirlpool, rinsed away the poisoned food, and washed the platter thoroughly.

After scrubbing her hands once more, she cooked porridge and baked grain bars. The sun was rising over the distant hills when she carried the breakfast trays to the tent platform.

Zeid had bathed and dressed while she had prepared breakfast. As he sat down to his tray, he teased, "I've been working this morning, but I wager you can't find what I've done."

"You haven't shaken a cushion or folded a robe, at any rate," said Coral Bud, letting her eyes inspect the tent. "Nor have you moved the boxes—"

She remembered the spy-slits. They were no longer in the fabric. She sprang to look closer. She could detect only a faint smooth scar.

She returned to the breakfast trays, sat down, and commented, "Your poniard is very clever, Light-Bearer. It also weaves."

"It mixes the torn edges so fast that they don't remember where they belong. The threads jump into each other and bind the cut more firmly than before." He sampled a grain bar. "The food is delicious, little pirate. If you put your mind to it, you could be a fine cook."

"I have only so much mind, and must put it to so many things."

"Such as?"

"Scraping the pitch and glass from our rail. It would be a fine joke to make the rail the same as before. Feelafell would look at it and think he had mistaken another barge for ours. He could not have seen clearly from his underwater boat."

"He has Space guiders in his craft," said Zeid, "and Space air-makers, and other Gifts which could not possibly be smuggled from the Moonship."

"Is he making them himself?"

"He must be tearing apart old, discarded Magic. But that, too, is impossible. Each power system is registered and tracked. Broken Magic is repaired or brought back to the Moonship. No Magic is left inoperative on the planet."

"Oh, yes it is," crowed Coral Bud. "The sea floor is strewn with the wreckage of storm-crushed horde-ships. The Space Givers don't waste time going beneath the sea to fetch up old Magic. I myself have watched my father's men trying to grapple up wrecks, but the water is always too deep or the current too swift."

Zeid thought for a while. "Abandoned wrecks . . . yes, perhaps. But how could reactivation be shielded from Moonship sensors?"

The breakfasting pair heard feet lightly jumping into the barge, and Kalia's voice calling, "Lord Zeid? Lady?"

"Come—and welcome!" shouted Zeid.

Kalia and Moji entered the tent. They were clad in their working garb, just as if they never had worn wedding finery. They bowed, and Moji said, "You bade us come and talk, Lord Zeid."

"And glad I am to see you. Sit down. I hope you will continue with me."

They knelt and sank back on their heels. Kalia began, "We've thought over what you told us, Lord Zeid. We knew you spoke only to our profit since you can hire servants anywhere."

"None such as you," replied Zeid. "What have you decided?"

"Well, it is true that I can claim my parents' farm, which my Uncle Tind inherited, but the land would not bring me joy. Some people love their acres all the more for having fought and suffered for them, but I would live in sorrow and constant fear.

"Moreover, Moji would earn more as a Counting Master among the merchant lords of the Seacoast and would be happier than in a village.

"Thirdly, we both would like to see the Marble Lands, a far journey that would give us much pleasure to look back upon when we finally are settled on the Seacoast.

"So I'm letting Uncle Tind keep the land, for which he will

pay gold towards Moji's own Counting office, and we've come back to serve you and the Lady Coral Bud as before."

"Well done. But it won't be *quite* as before, since the lady will be leaving us at the Seacoast."

The lady said promptly, "I'm glad you both have returned, but I won't say 'Well done' until I hear how much gold Uncle Tind is paying. However, we can leave immediately."

"Not so fast," smiled Zeid. "Moji must count our town debts and cut enough gold chain to pay them."

"True. And Kalia must return the cake platter that was so kindly delivered to us yester eve."

"Cake platter, lady?" wondered Kalia. "Did the Guildhall send dessert aboard? How thoughtful."

"Yes, we appreciated the thought." She cocked her head at Kalia. "Where are your rubies? If you let Uncle Tind have the use of *them* also—"

Moji laughed, and Kalia grew pink. "In truth, Uncle Tind wanted to hold them in safekeeping, but—" she put her hand on the bosom of her smock "—I pleaded I was a poor vain girl who wanted to wear them, even though hidden under servant's cloth."

"Now, that *was* well done," laughed Coral Bud. "Let's finish our errands, say farewell to the town, and be off to the Seacoast."

They were not so easily to forget Feelafell. While Moji and Kalia were in the town, Zeid and Coral Bud noticed a woman running anxiously from barge to barge around the basin. They watched her approach. She hesitated before their own barge.

Zeid stepped ashore and said, "May we help you?"

Her cheeks were red from weeping, her voice was husky. "Oh, prince, you haven't perchance a little stowaway aboard? My dear boy has always been so eager for adventure—and was so excited by your arrival yesterday—and didn't come home last night!"

"No, we have no stowaway. If he boarded a barge yesterday, he is well on his way to adventure. I can understand your sorrow," Zeid went on, "but I can also understand the boy's forgetfulness. When I joined the Moonship crew, I gave no thought to my parents, and I now know that my mother was very hurt and lonely."

"Yes, indeed she would be, kind prince," said the woman with a tremulous smile.

"Please—remember your boy with affection, but don't grieve. Perhaps in later years he will, like me, return."

"Grieve I must, for a little while," sobbed the woman, "but I know your words will comfort me when I'm more used to his absence."

She turned and left the landing place. Zeid went back aboard the barge. Coral Bud had been listening from the tent platform.

"Her son must have been the boy who brought the platter. He now lies rotting at the bottom of the river. You should have told the woman so."

"Well, Coral Bud, we don't know that the boy was her son—or that he was slain. Why not let her be comforted by the thought that he is alive in a far land?"

"I think I would be more comforted by the assurance that he was dead and could not suffer any more. However, as you say, we don't know. Life is very strange, not least in the completeness of its end."

TWO HOURS LATER THE barge was freed outward from the mooring. With Moji on the command prow, she circled the basin, hummed past the watergrid and headed westward.

Zeid and Coral Bud sat under the tent canopy. Zeid said, "Have you given thought as to how you will return to your father?"

Coral Bud stared at him. "What a question. Have you squandered so much gold on your hospice that you can't afford to hire ship?"

"Be reasonable, little pirate," exclaimed Zeid. "How can I engage passage to the Marble Lands and at the same time hire ship and crew for yourself?"

"Why, one ship can go two places—and what more crew do we need than Moji and Kalia? How else am I to seek my father? Do you think his fleet sails in and out of the Seacoast fortress?"

"How did he deliver you to Bulbul?"

"By a sea meeting arranged through agents—and many weeks it took. Surely a brother doesn't let his sister wait alone many weeks in a strange hostelry."

"But I can't delay my journey to wait with you."

"Then I see no other course than to hire a small, sturdy sailing vessel we can sail without further crew. We must sail, you know, because the horde-ships are lamed to follow only one course across the sea, like barges confined to a canal, while the pirate ships roam freely with the winds."

"And if we meet an unfriendly pirate?"

"We must fight and escape, of course. However, the pirates prey upon the ship-hordes, as wolves follow forest beasts and spring upon the laggards, and the ship-horde to the Marble Lands already has sailed."

"Then how can we find your father?"

"Oh, he'll be resting his fleet among our islands, preparing to assault the laden pirate ships as they return. He's the lion who charges out and forces the wolves to give up their prey."

"A sorry life, Rover Bud."

"Why, it isn't sorry at all. It's a wonderful life on the boundless sea. I pity the poor folk who can't stray from their villages—or even the rich folk so bound by their riches that they must travel on pokey sea-going barges escorted by soldier craft like felons under guard.

"But why are we talking? We have much work to do, sorting our sea chests, taking what we most need, so we can board ship quickly and set sail to my father's kingdom."

"I don't know how it is," grumbled Zeid, "but the faster I move, the more slowly I seem to come to Fire Lotus."

"Well, that's no fault of *mine*," said Coral Bud.

THE SEACOAST SETTLEMENTS GIRDLED the planet, but the greatest port was where the Desert's canal-and-river system flowed into a delta where a string of offshore islands protected a long sound. Between the islands and the mainland were turning basins, landing places, a whole mart of commerce. The port was named Tenfold because it had so many safe anchorages.

The approaches to Tenfold were well-guarded by land and by sea. Because of the intricacies of the turning basins, pilots boarded the barges at the river grid. Certain pilots were attached to trading companies—others were sent out by the private basins.

Coral Bud had taken the command prow at the grid. She was not surprised when a pilot sprang aboard and said, "Prince Zeid's delay has lost him the ship-horde—but otherwise all is in readiness at Feelafell's basin."

"Hah! I daresay," huffed Coral Bud. "However, we will not await the next ship-horde at Feelafell's miserable hostelry."

"It was thus the Princess Serada ordered, Lady."

"And we all know the Princess Serada. My Lord Zeid has gold and will reside at the Travelers Palace."

"But the barge is to moor at Feelafell's basin."

"Moor? The barge was to be returned to Mus-al-ram two days since. Or did the palace neglect to send a bargeman to fetch it?"

"Nay, lady, the bargeman awaits."

"Then there can be no talk of mooring. As soon as we are ashore, the barge must travel back to Mus-al-ram. We'll discuss our further journey when it pleases my Lord Zeid."

"I'm only a pilot, lady."

"Then pilot us to the Travelers Palace and tell Feelafell we'll summon him when we need him."

The pilot muttered, "*We*! As between Serad's daughter and Hamar's daughter—"

"You spoke?"

"I said, as you will, lady."

The Travelers Palace was on the mainland side of the sound. Set back from its turning basin were storage warehouses and a two-story arcade of small private suites. On ten acres of garden behind the basin were larger suites for lords traveling with harems and retinues.

The pilot moored the barge in front of the storage warehouse and called out to the guard, "Prince Zeid ben Amfi wishes to tarry here! Summon the porters and clerks!"

The chief guard blew on a reed whistle, and linen-clad figures hurried from a lower room in the arcade.

Zeid stepped ashore from the tent platform. Coral Bud sprang from the command prow and joined him.

"What we want is a small arcade suite," she told him. "Be sure the porters take all the boxes we marked, especially the nails and hemp and other ship stores."

She began winding her hair on top of her head. Zeid asked, "What is the little pirate intending to do now?"

She took a wool cap from her jacket and pulled it over her coiled hair. "Why, you and Moji will be hours, seal-marking the boxes! Both Moji and the warehouse clerk must stamp Counting seals on the barge rail for each box we remove, so the palace major-domo doesn't accuse the bargeman of theft.

"Meanwhile I will hie to the shipowner Knarb, who trades by sailing ship among the lesser towns along the Seacoast."

"How do you know of Knarb, Rover Bud?"

"Many's the time he carried me aloft to the crow's nest when I was a babe! My father set him up in business here. Look you, Lord Zeid, there is more to being a pirate than learning to cut and thrust. Tenfold's merchants pay much gold to hire Knarb's escorting vessels, little realizing their effective escort is Hamar's pirates in different guise."

"Does escorting pay better than seizing outright?"

"Why, let us say a glass merchant will send a fine cargo along the Seacoast. If his ship is attacked by coastal ruffians, his cargo can be smashed, his clerks sold into slavery. He has much to lose.

"But what has the great Hamar to gain by attacking such craftsmen? Broken glass? The nuisance of selling slaves at paltry sums? It's much more profitable to pocket good gold for driving off the lesser raiders. And if a raiding ship is captured, there can be extra shares to the escorting crews, who therefore are zealous on behalf of the merchant who hires them."

"I begin to feel like a dove between opposing hawks," remarked Zeid.

"Say rather, a swallow darting away from clumsy vultures. But Moji impatiently awaits your commands. I return within the hour."

She waved a cheerful farewell, skipped like a boy along the landing place, ran over an arched stone bridge, and disappeared into the crowded bazaar that bordered the turning basins.

Zeid wished she had chosen a less costly inn. It was true that they could not have stayed at Feelafell's hostelry—but there were others. The gold chains would not last long at this magnificent abode.

RUNNING, DODGING, ALWAYS SWIFTLY on the move—for errand boys also were snatched up by slave agents—Coral Bud made her way into the city to a corner building that dominated a cobbled square. The Seacoast was pleasant with fresh sea breezes, and the shutters were thrown back from the iron-barred windows.

A doorman stood squarely at the narrow entrance to the building. Coral Bud panted to a halt in front of him and recited,

> "A messenger from sea to land,
> And swift must Knarb now give command."

The doorkeeper scanned her face. His eyes widened. He bowed and stepped aside.

She entered a great dark chamber of ship stores, smelling cooly of hempen rope, oiled woods, linen sails. A tall, slanting ladder led to a trapdoor in the ceiling. She climbed the ladder nimbly and banged her fist on the hatch.

A panel slid aside, and an eye peered down at her. She said, "Tell Knarb the seabird has left her new nest."

The panel closed. After a short wait the trapdoor folded back on its hinges, and Coral Bud scrambled into the room.

As soon as she was clear of the opening, the hatch slammed shut. She leaped to her feet and smiled at the grizzled, crop-haired, craggy-faced old pirate who was sliding the hatch bar shut.

Knarb was clad like a merchant in fine woolen pantaloons, embroidered woolen shirt, and heavy felt slippers. His office had no desks. The walls were hung with tapestries to which clusters of Counting seals were affixed. Each cluster represented a shipping transaction and described cargo, tonnage, value, owner, and agreement all in symbolic designs.

Beneath each tapestry was a cushion and a box containing the materials for this beautiful hieroglyphic shorthand. Knarb gestured to the boxes and said, "I sent the clerks away, little sea bird. Sit down and tell me why the nest doesn't fit."

"Well, Uncle, it could not be hoped that a sea bird could be caged in a harem—or a Moonship apprentice could last long in a palace," said Coral Bud, plumping herself down on a cushion.

Knarb lowered himself more slowly. "I told your father he should have thought twice about Serada—and the cruel Rustad—"

"And a ravenous beast that devours all our gold. What is a hospice, Uncle?"

"A lodging for beggars," laughed Knarb, "and ravenous it is! Jibbo is in Tenfold, seeking the best investment for a purseful of gold."

"Now, why couldn't Zeid have told me what a hospice was when I misspoke myself?"

"He probably thought your lively wits were making a joke of it. Why are you at the Seacoast?"

"The Wizard Amfi is sending Zeid to Fire Lotus, princess of the Milk White Quarries. Zeid has not disclosed the errand to me, but our servants Kalia and Moji say the princess wishes to sell her seed but could not come to an agreement with Bulbul. I doubt that Zeid can do better."

"The Light-Bearer is a handsome young persuader," smiled Knarb. "I can understand why the task does not please his bride."

"Oh, I have no fear of Fire Lotus," said Coral Bud loudly. "My worry is because Zeid has been so foolish as to alert Feelafell who envies him and would steal his Space Giver Magic.

"So, dear Uncle, you must find us a swift little sailcraft. We'll seek out my father and procure escort across the great sea from his fleet."

"Seabird, I myself can outfit you and escort you to the Marble Lands."

"Yes, but Zeid wants to—to meet—the great Hamar."

"Young husbands usually are not so eager to meet fathers-in-law."

"Well, Zeid *is* mad, in some ways."

"Also mad in love?" laughed Knarb.

"Yes, even that," sighed Coral Bud, feeling momentarily very low in spirits.

Knarb consulted his tapestry accounts and determined that he had a small, fast sloop—the *Whizzard*—available at an outer sea pier. Coral Bud was delighted with the name which seemed a lucky coincidence.

The *Whizzard* could be made ready to sail on the following morning's ebb tide before the day's heat sucked the breeze toward the land.

Coral Bud thanked Knarb and ran back to the Travelers Palace. As she approached the arcade, a door opened in the lower storey, and Moji called to her.

She entered an unfurnished chamber similar to Knarb's warehouse, but more fully lighted by windows high in the wall. It was much more elegant also with a black-veined white marble floor, marble pillars, and a curving marble stairway to the upper floor. For a lord with business to transact, the chamber would be an anteroom where visitors would wait until they were summoned.

While Moji barred the lower door, Coral Bud ran up the stairs and entered a hallway of pierced alabaster screens. The wealth of the soft carpets, satin cushions, and low tables gave Coral Bud a pang for Zeid's sake. She *was* wasting his gold unmercifully!

Kalia was waiting to bow her into the front chamber where the whole front wall from floor to ceiling was a window barred by wrought iron. The shutters had been thrown back, and light sea breezes puffed into the room.

Zeid was sitting among cushions, looking out over the busy basin and wide sound with the island fortresses beyond.

Coral Bud sat beside him, pulled off her cap, and shook down her long dark hair. "We board Knarb's sloop *Whizzard* at dawn tomorrow and sail on the ebb."

"And soon you'll be back with your father to await a more willing suitor."

"Why, as to that, we must wait and see if my father takes me back. A bargain is a bargain."

"Not when the party of the second part hasn't been consulted. I'm glad you came to terms with Knarb so quickly. Now I can inform Fire Lotus of my arrival."

"Oh? By what messenger?"

"I told Moji that as soon as he had admitted you, he was to

76

ask the hostelry's owner for the loan of a sending mirror. It's fortunate, after all, that you chose a hostelry of this wealth since they have been granted extra sending mirrors for their guests."

"Then the Moonship deals most unfairly!"

"Not at all, Rover Bud. The planet's lords are entitled to the same Magic while traveling as at home. The Moonship maintains the planet's customs in all areas—and equality is not known among us."

"But fairness and equality are not the same," protested Coral Bud. "It's possible to treat everyone fairly—and impossible to treat them equally."

Zeid looked surprised. "Very true, Coral Bud. More perceptibly true on the planet than on the Moonship where people are treated fairly *and* equally."

"I fear many customs are different on the Moonship, and you will appear foolish if you don't remember the difference." She paused a moment. "So you would mirror-speak Fire Lotus. On the Moonship would you thus speak directly to a woman you wanted to win?"

"Yes, of course. That is," he amended, "you would not call her at her place of work. But when she was at leisure, in her dwelling—"

"How different the matter is already. On the planet, princes and princesses are always at leisure. And I know the Moonship has no slaves except Magic, so the lady would answer the mirror herself."

"Yes. If she were absent or busy, the viewer would record the call, and she would call back later."

"We are even into another language! But whatever vyu'ors and reh-kords may be, the lady would not lose dignity or esteem by speaking to you at once?"

Zeid stroked his beard thoughtfully. "Say on, little pirate."

"Well, if you reflect a moment on the customs of the Wizard's palace, you know a princess never answers a mirror herself. Therefore, you must not call her. If you do, you'll get a mirror-slave—and then a clerk—or perhaps the chief eunuch, if your princely rank seems impressive enough. All will laugh at your blunder, and ridicule is not the best highway to a princess's heart."

"Again, very true," Zeid admitted.

"Moonship prince, you know I mistrust the shameless redhead and doubt she would ever make you happy, but your heart is set on her, and it would grieve me to see you scorned and your worth lessened because you had forgotten palace ways."

Zeid laughed a little. "If the kind-hearted woodsman cannot lure the thorn bear from the trap, he can at least console him with honey cakes."

Coral Bud grinned. "Yes—and trust he will amble from the trap when he is tired of it. But truly, Zeid, it would hurt me to see you fail to win Fire Lotus because you are too Moonship wise to stoop to tricks that come naturally to a scamp like myself."

"Well, that is most kind of you, little sister. What tricks do you mean?"

"I hardly know until I see who answers the mirror. To begin with, I need but a strip of turban cloth, such as pages wind round their heads and knot over one ear. A page of good birth indicates far more wealth than a mirror-slave—and I warrant Fire Lotus has hired a score from her captains and stewards."

"Wait a moment!" Zeid held up his hand. "Tricks are one thing, but wholesale deceit is another."

"Do you think you're the only suitor the princess has? Of a certainty, they swarm around her. How can she respect you, if you're just another bee in the swarm? Lovesick or not, play the game adroitly.

"Or rather, let me play it for you." Coral Bud jumped up. "Where are the clothing boxes?"

"In our chambers, but—"

Coral Bud was already out of the room.

She returned several minutes later. The new gold scarf was bound and knotted around her head. A second scarf hid the collar of her jacket.

As she sat down, Kalia came into the room, bowed, and handed Zeid a shallow box. She said to Coral Bud, "Moji goes now to the bakeshop."

"Good. When our business is done, we can eat."

Kalia left the room.

Zeid opened the box and lifted a sending mirror from its velvet lining. After a moment he handed the mirror to Coral Bud. "If I don't find out what you intend to do, I'll spend the rest of the day wondering what you would have done!"

Coral Bud laughed and took the mirror. The corner of her mouth quirked, and her eyes grew saucy. She pressed the embossing.

"I call Fire Lotus, princess of the Milk White Quarries."

The mirror hazed, then cleared to show a page's face looking back at her. The boy was scarfed in purple. He was young, fat-faced.

For a moment the pages stared at each other. The young boy said, "I speak for the palace of Fire Lotus."

"If you don't stop eating sweetmeats, moon-face, you'll be too fat to speak at all. My master is the Desert prince, Zeid ben Amfi, with whom Fire Lotus wishes urgently to confer."

"We of the mirror have not heard so."

"You of the mirror are doubtless the last to hear anything, little tub. Lest you find your manhood cut off, give me one who has the princess's confidence."

The boy stuck out his tongue, but his eyes were afraid. The mirror hazed for a longer time and cleared to show a sharp-faced old woman close-coiffed in gray silk. Around her throat was a gorget of pearls. She stared at Coral Bud before saying, "Your master may speak to me if he wishes."

"Most honorable grandmother, we were given to understand that it is Fire Lotus who wishes to speak to *us*. But perhaps the matter can wait. We soon will be arriving in the Marble Lands."

"Arriving? Prince Zeid? I know of no—ben *Amfi*—the Wizard's son?" The old eyes became cunning. "And he's standing beside you? Be most welcome, young prince."

"Save your compliments, grandmother. Zeid is choosing hangings for his ship cabins. However, if the princess will speak with him—"

"Nay, young man. Fire Lotus sails the Quarry Lakes. Tell me—what entertainment pleases your master?"

"Well, grandmother, I have not been long in his service, but I fear he has been made overly sober on the Moonship—or perhaps sated by the great wealth of his father's palace."

"Have your sharp ears heard what the Wizard will pay for Fire Lotus's seed?"

"Nay, grandmother. I hope for all our sakes the princess is as beautiful as rumor says. A disappointed, wrathful prince is no pleasure to serve."

"Fear not, bold page. Are there many in the prince's retinue?"

"So many that we come by private sailing ship with goodly escort. But now, grandmother, by your leave, I must depart. Much remains to be put aboard, and you understand that nothing can be done without me."

The old woman laughed. "I understand you're a charming rascal who gets what he wants from his master. Perhaps we will call when Lord Zeid is on his ship. Farewell."

The mirror blanked, and Zeid took it from Coral Bud's hand. "You do well to fear a wrathful prince," he said wryly. "Tricks!"

"They brought us straight to Fire Lotus's bedchamber lady."

"Yes—an old harridan who thinks more of duplo seed than of her mistress. I daresay it was she who persuaded the princess and bargained with Bulbul."

Coral Bud was silent. The Milk White Quarries were on the same sun-line as Tenfold, and the redhead would not be out of her bedrobes before noon. Sailing the Quarry lakes—nonsense! She had been watching and listening.

Zeid was saying, "The venture has begun ill. The bedchamber beldame spoke of calling my mirror—and I have no receiving mirror."

"Can't you ask a mirror of your Moonship friends? They can deliver it to the *Whizzard* before we sail."

Zeid reddened. "I was educated to bring enlightenment to the planet. I can't demand a lordly trifle like a mirror."

"I don't see that a mirror is a worse trifle than a deadly poniard. Ask the Space Givers."

Zeid shook his head. He replaced the mirror in the box and laid the box aside. "No, little pirate."

"Light-Bearer, you must make up your mind which creature you'll be—a Moonship messenger or a suitor to a haughty princess. If she calls you and sees the mark that means you have no mirror—"

"She'll assume it broke in a sea accident. Never would she

think the Wizard's son lacked a mirror. Thanks to your fine boasts, which convinced almost myself, the beldame will tell her of our call. Her interest will be roused—she'll be awaiting my arrival. That's all I hoped to gain."

Coral Bud bit her lip and lapsed into thought. She came to herself when Zeid suddenly sat up straight and stared out of the window. She asked, "What do you see?"

Zeid gestured to the view before them.

Feelafell, white-suited like a Space Giver, was leaving a white-painted barge and striding across the landing place. His hands were white-gloved. He paused to speak to a porter who pointed to the arcade.

"Aha!" said Coral Bud. "His hands still smart from the pitch-slivers. I suppose we must admit him."

"Yes." Zeid seemed amused. "In fact, he comes opportunely."

"What do you mean?"

But Zeid had already risen from the cushions.

He went to answer Feelafell's knock. Kalia had also come, and he said to her, "Go and sit near the lady Coral Bud, Kalia. I have errands elsewhere and do not want her to be alone."

Kalia hurried into the front room.

Zeid unbarred the door and admitted Feelafell.

"Welcome," Zeid said with more warmth than he had intended. "I regret that chance swerved our course."

Feelafell, who seemed careful of his gloved hands, bowed and said, "Plans often go amiss."

"Please—enter and meet the lady Coral Bud and her free maid Kalia."

The tall, noble-skulled figure preceded Zeid into the front room. "So here we have Hamar's brat," he said in a joking tone. "And once more she has sought her uncle Knarb."

"And glad I was to see him," responded Coral Bud pleasantly.

Zeid said to Feelafell, "As I was just saying to Coral Bud, your visit is opportune. I have business to transact and am glad someone can amuse her while I'm gone."

Glad someone can keep me from following him, thought Coral Bud, and her eyes flashed indignantly at Zeid.

Feelafell was saying to Zeid, "Do you really have business?

Or does my face remind you too strongly of weary hours on the Moonship?"

"Moonship memories are happy ones, in any case," replied Zeid, "but I really have business elsewhere."

He bowed and withdrew. The hallway door opened and slammed shut.

"Well, now, Lord Feelafell," began Coral Bud, "you will think us exasperating customers. My lord Zeid is slow to realize that a man cannot do as he pleases when he acquires a lady. It was I who decided to visit the Weavers Basin."

Feelafell flexed his gloved hands and winced. "I should have known that Hamar's daughter would bring Hamar's tricks."

"Tricks? I'm sure I don't know what you mean. Are you surprised to see us in this costly abode?" she prattled on. "Truly, we should be staying at your hostelry, as the mother Serada ordered. But where's the pleasure in being a prince unless one can live in princely fashion?

"You can call me Hamar's brat," she went on, "but I intend to live like a princess. No horde-ship but a sailing vessel of my own with escort from my father—though *that* part of it you can keep to yourself in Tenfold."

Feelafell smiled. "You're handsomer than you gave promise of being, Coral Bud. Zeid is no proper match for you. Had I known, I would have bid for you myself."

"Your harem has much more beautiful women than I, Lord Feelafell."

"Duplos—my harem has only duplos. Until now, I've been waiting to be matched aboard the Moonship because the planet has no women worthy of Space Giver seed."

"Oh, I'm too dull to be matched to a Space Giver," laughed Coral Bud. "I can't remember any Magic spells at all! Would you believe, I can't even remember how Zeid calls the Moonship."

"How does Zeid begin?" asked Feelafell quickly.

"Now *there* is the worst part. If I could begin aright, I think I could finish. *What* does he say? Was it Moonship—or ship—or—?"

"Satellite?"

Coral Bud wrinkled her nose. "Sat alight? No, I think not."

"I think not, too," smiled Feelafell. "You remember nothing."

"Haven't I just *said* I don't remember? And you laugh because my head churns! It's all very well for you, who inherited a Space Giver mind—but can't you take pity on a lesser creature?"

"If you can't remember what Zeid said, you won't remember what I say, either."

"Oh, I will, I promise! Do please tell me," begged Coral Bud. Feelafell gestured to Kalia. "Is she as dull as she looks?"

"Kalia is very faithful. She was once slave to the mother Serada—"

"And understands no more than food and sleep. Very well. To call the Moonship one says, 'Monitor Board, do you read me?'"

"Monit aboard, do you reed me?"

"Not 'aboard', pirate brat! Monitor board—"

"Monitor board—monitor board—"

A fist banged on the door.

Kalia sprang up. "Oh, lady, it is Moji wanting help with the food baskets!"

"Let him in!" said Coral Bud. "Lord Feelafell, will you join us for a meal? Zeid will soon return."

"You destroy my appetite with those words," said Feelafell, rising to his feet. "Invite me some day when the young lord is elsewhere." As Coral Bud rose also, he added, "You *are* a comely bride, pirate girl—but Zeid will never give you riches."

"Like my father, I'll have to take them for myself, won't I? Fare you well, Space Lord."

She ushered him to the door which was now blocked by food baskets. Moji cleared the baskets aside. Feelafell bowed and descended the staircase, and Moji closed the door.

Coral Bud hugged Kalia and danced around her. "Oh, how well you played the harem slug, dear Kalia! He would have spoken any secret before you!"

"With such a lord, a slave learns to be very quiet," said Kalia ruefully. "I held my breath when I saw the game you were playing."

"But all went well. And now, Kalia—and Moji—if Zeid comes, delay him here. Don't let him into the front room."

She dashed back. Moji smiled at Kalia, "More plots? How can we keep the prince out of his own chambers?"

Kalia glanced at the food baskets. "By spilling soup—or tripping him up—oh, a woman could find a dozen ways, Moji."

CORAL BUD DROPPED ONTO a cushion, and took the sending mirror from its box. She pressed the embossing and said carefully,

"Monitor board, do you *reed* me?"

The mirror hazed. A Space Giver was looking at her. A young Space Giver with a mass of curly brown hair over his broad forehead, a strong jaw, and gentle gray eyes. Surprise and a touch of humor came into the reflection. "Who calls the Monitor board?"

"Oh, please, Space Lord, I am Coral Bud, daughter of the great sea lord Hamar, who has betrothed me to Zeid ben Amfi."

"Lucky Zeid!"

"I wish Zeid thought so. He will not have me."

The Space Lord chuckled, "What's wrong with him?"

"Oh, nothing I can't mend. Do you know him, sir?"

"Sure. We were classmates. I'm Tommy Lund. Hasn't Zeid told you about our hijinks?"

"If a hijinks is akin to a vyu'or or reh-kords—"

"No, it's nothing to do with hardware."

"Good. Zeid always stammers over har-dwayr and says something else. But to return to the matter of my call, sir, Zeid is about to embark for the Marble Lands and sorely needs a receiving mirror but will not ask for one because he says he must not ask for lordly trifles."

"If Zeid needs a mirror, he may have one, of course. How did you learn to call us?"

"Oh, sir, it was not Zeid who taught me! I tricked the words out of Lord Feelafell who thought I already knew them. Can you fashion a mirror and bring it to our sailing vessel at dawn tomorrow?"

"Where sails the sun now, Coral Bud?"

"Alas, I have no az-i-muth measure, Lord Tom-ih-Lund, but the star nears its zenith on the Tenfold sun-line."

"Noon is close enough," smiled the Space Giver. "Yes, we can code a mirror before dawn. Who taught you about azimuths?"

"Well, sir, it is Space Giver lore which was forgotten by all except the sea dwellers. My father Hamar is most cunning about his measures and about the grains in his sand glass.

"But, oh, have I betrayed him with my boasting?" cried Coral Bud. "Such lore has been forbidden since the laming of the horde-ships and barges!"

"Don't worry, Coral Bud. We can't stop guys from navigating by their brains and the seat of their pants."

"You speak strange words, but I think you mean my father is not betrayed. And I hope you will not betray *me*, either—that is, I hope you won't tell Zeid it was I who asked for the mirror."

Tommy Lund smiled, "What do you suggest we tell him?"

"What a question," huffed Coral Bud. "Why would a Space Lord need suggestions as to the words he will say?"

"That's passing the old buck," grinned Tommy Lund. "Where's your sailing vessel?"

"The *Whizzard*, at Knarb's pier, outside Tenfold."

"We'll bring the mirror at dawn, Coral Bud. Thank you. Farewell."

Coral Bud heard a commotion in the hallway. She thrust the sending mirror into its box and ran to see what had happened.

Moji was picking himself off the carpet. An empty basket lay overturned. Zeid was supporting Kalia who had a hand to her head. He explained, "As Moji let me in, Kalia came running from behind the screen, intent on the basket—"

Coral Bud remarked, "I see the basket is empty."

Kalia said, "Oh, yes, lady. I had already put the food in the warming oven."

"Now that was a fortunate chance. But there was no need for haste, my poor Kalia. Zeid won't be ready to dine before he has found out what Feelafell wanted with us."

"I'm ready to dine immediately," said Zeid, "and then to depart. If the *Whizzard* is at the pier, we can live aboard while she is being stowed. I sent a porter to Knarb to request a barge, and

I waited below until the reply came. The barge will arrive at sunset.

"Thus, Moji," he continued, "you and I will cut up our gold chains to satisfy mine host—and to pay Knarb—after we have dined. If we depart before night, perhaps I'll have a few coppers left."

"So!" said Coral Bud sternly, "To save a few links of gold, you doom us to a sleepless night keeping watch against pier ruffians. No lordly retinue boards ship until sailing time. Had I known, I never would have agreed to such folly."

"I know," smiled Zeid. "That's why I waited until you were diverted by Feelafell. To act is better than to argue, little pirate."

After dinner Zeid and Moji left the hostelry. Coral Bud and Kalia stood at the window bars, watching the basin traffic. Suddenly Coral Bud said, "Look, Kalia, here comes a market barge to unload the supper food for the hostelry kitchen. Maybe they will take me along the sound to the sea piers."

"But, lady, Knarb's barge comes for us."

"Not until sunset. And then all the warehouse luggage must be counted and the seal-marks exchanged. I must get to the ship sooner."

"Why? Won't the stowing be done properly?"

"Well, I can probably improve upon it. But the reason I *must* go is to secure a seaman's knife. Lacking escort, I will not board ship unarmed. Knarb's men can find me a tempered blade."

"But the Lord Zeid has Space weapons."

"And what good will they do us when their owner, being human, must sleep? Zeid and I must stand watch-and-watch aboard," explained Coral Bud, winding her hair on her head, "and a knife bests suits my hand."

She pulled her cap over her ears and left the hostelry.

At the landing place the market barge was collecting final seals, which the Bargemaster affixed along a roll of linen cloth. Coral Bud hailed him.

"Bargemaster! The food markets lie near the outer piers. May I ride along with you?"

"Can your master pay me, errand boy?"

"He can but he won't. He's already paying me to use my feet."

The Bargemaster laughed. "Jump aboard, honest boy. Had you tried to deceive me, I would have bade you walk."

Coral Bud leaped aboard and grinned, "You wouldn't have been long deceived. It is the Princess Serada who pays me."

All the bargemen laughed. The Bargemaster said, "Have you gossip from the palace? Pay your way by telling us news. Does the Prince Rustad raid in this season?"

"Raid? Why, gentlemen, he has such battles within his own harem—!"

BY THE TIME THE barge reached the market basin, Coral Bud and the bargemen were like brothers. Delighted by her gossip of palace affairs, they would have invited her to a wineshop, but she cheerfully pleaded haste and skipped away.

The *Whizzard* was the only ship at Knarb's pier. He did not use her often since she was a Fleetmaster's private sloop and could not hold cargo or guards. Her lines were graceful; her mast was tall and strong.

Coral Bud's heart danced as she ran along the pier.

Knarb's men were furnishing and provisioning the ship. No princess could have better accommodations at sea. The *Whizzard* had two cabins forward of the cockpit—a midship cabin for meals and comradeship, a bow cabin for Kalia and Moji.

The Master's cabin was aft of the cockpit. Coral Bud saw that Knarb had furnished it as a bridal chamber. She sighed. How bewitched the Light-Bearer must be, she thought, that he could not imagine her a loving bride!

Then she looked down at her apprentice clothes and laughed aloud.

Knarb's foreman sent to the bazaar for a selection of sea knives, and Coral Bud chose the one that lay most nicely balanced in her hand. When the new leather scabbard was angled into her waistband, she felt fully dressed for the first time since leaving her father's kingdom. With great satisfaction, she bustled among the workmen—directing, shifting, adjusting.

The stowage was finished in the late afternoon. The workmen left the pier. As long as the sun was up, Coral Bud felt safe. She decided to begin supper. The midship cabin held a Space oven as fine as the ovens in the palace kitchens. Soon Coral Bud was slicing vegetables and meats into a stew that could simmer until Zeid and the others arrived.

That task done, she climbed the shorter ladder to the cabin top and sat with her back to the mast. The sun was a white glare in the west. The evening stars hung like Zeid's colored lamps in the darkening east.

She saw a white barge approaching from the city channel. Feelafell! She remained where she was, glad of the knife at her waist.

The Space Bastard steered his barge alongside, rope-moored the barge to the sloop, and climbed aboard. He was still gloved and using his hands with care. When he was in the cockpit, Coral Bud called out,

"Lord Feelafell! Is it tonight that you come to dine? Zeid will be here in a short while."

"Zeid is still embroiled with warehouse details, sea girl," smiled Feelafell. "Come and talk within the cabin."

"Since I may be facing stormy weeks within the cabin, I prefer to watch the evening sky," countered Coral Bud.

Feelafell climbed to the cabin top and sat beside her. "You ever remind me that you are Hamar's daughter, full of guile and treachery—and yet I would have you as my seed-wife."

"Never again will I enter a harem."

"Space Givers are not harem-keepers. Until now, I've amused myself with duplos, yes, but if you left Zeid and married me—"

"Is it Space Giver custom to seduce brides away?"

"When brides are ill-matched and wish to leave their mates, yes."

"What of your hope for a Moonship wife?"

Feelafell smoothed his balding head. "It was never a hope—just a distaste for being a guinea pig."

"I don't understand," said Coral Bud.

Feelafell laughed. "What I meant to say was, this world is only a workshop for the Space Givers. I'm the first of a forbidden breed—but they don't think of destroying me, only of studying what becomes of my seed.

"I've thwarted them by mating with sterile duplos and insisting I would take a seed-wife only from my father's people. They wait patiently—but I continue to disappoint them."

"Which shows commendable determination. Does your father still live?"

"Oh, yes. On another planet. Space Givers are long-lived, you know. He has endowed me with much wealth. As the forbidden child, I think I'm dearest to him."

"A natural feeling, alas!"

"Why 'alas'?"

"Because the seed-mix is not wise, and there was good reason to forbid it. Surely you don't want to breed children who'll suffer the same fate as yourself."

"No. But Space Giver seed and Hamar's seed would result in—"

"Wily, power-driven monsters, probably," smiled Coral Bud.

"With my mind and knowledge—and your shrewdness—they would rule the planet. Hamar forged together a sea kingdom. His grandchildren could rule among the stars."

"Not very likely. Holding others in subjection is a *savage* idea of power. The Space Givers are far beyond it."

"Beyond it? To what?"

"To something I don't understand, Lord Feelafell, since I am a savage, just like your mother's people."

"Your tongue cuts as sharp as your knife—and still I want you, Coral Bud. I should have seized you. Once you were enjoying my wealth and my knowledge, you would have been well-pleased. I've made a mistake, encouraging you to argue. Women never rest until they win the argument."

"That's because we're usually right. But look yonder, Lord Feelafell. Knarb's barge is turning out of the inner channel. Will you stop and share a pirate meal?"

He looked at his gloved hands. "I eat but awkwardly. Another time, sea girl, we will share our love feast."

He descended from the cabin top, climbed over the rail, and dropped into his barge. Before Knarb's barge had arrived at the sloop, Feelafell had proceeded seaward in a turning arc.

As Zeid boarded the sloop, he asked Coral Bud, "What did Feelafell want?"

"To take soundings. Can his underwater boat go as far as a horde-ship?"

"If truly built, it could go farther and swifter."

"Won't you tell the Space Givers? Just telling them wouldn't delay your journey."

"It's not only the delay, Coral Bud. I might be interfering with their plans for Feelafell. It's hard to explain, but they must know he has the boat. I can't see how he can be blocking the power emissions from registering on Moonship hardware. They may be waiting to find out the purpose of his ingenious contriving."

"Do they also wait to find out why a burrow rat sharpens his teeth? *I* think they don't know at all! And if I had my way, I'd chop the Space Bastard's ingenious head from his neck, thus putting an end to the speculations."

Zeid smiled, "Not many people would keep their heads on their necks if *you* had the running of the planet, Rover Bud."

"True. Perhaps it's just as well that I can cut down only the nearest scoundrels, or I would be like Discord's brothers and make the world worse."

"May I hear another legend, Coral Bud?"

"No. We'll help Kalia and Moji with the boxes, and then we'll all go into the midship cabin and eat pirate stew."

"And perhaps sail on the evening tide instead of the morning?"

"Now there speaks a landsman," declared Coral Bud. "There must be not only tide but wind—and proper wind at that if one is not to sit out in the harbor and look foolish. We have enough to do this night. Which watch will you take—sunset to midnight or midnight to sunrise?"

"I don't know. Until you teach me to sail—"

"That a grown man needs to be taught—!" marveled Coral Bud. "Well, it's best that the harbor ruffians see much activity aboard, so after supper we'll raise a Space lamp to the mast top, and I'll instruct you and Moji about the mainsail and jib—the sheets, halyards, and stays—the tacking and reefing—"

"Oh, good," smiled Zeid. "I was afraid you wouldn't find anything for us to do."

The evening saw more hilarity than instruction as Zeid and Moji practiced hauling up the sails and pulling them to one side and the other in the dead-calm night. The heavy steering oar at the stern moved in the opposite direction from the control bar in the cockpit, and Zeid said he could more easily steer a Moonship.

At midnight they hauled down the Space lamp, and all retired except Zeid, whose mind was so crammed with the evening's laughter—and dark perplexity about Feelafell—and star-touched musings in the Space Giver tongue—that he thought no more than once or twice about Fire Lotus.

He had promised to wake Coral Bud when the dawn star rose in the eastern horizon, but she came on deck earlier. Zeid said, surprised, "The tide surges full to the land, and there's not a breath of wind."

"I rise early at sea," said Coral Bud. "The Master's cabin is yours if you want to sleep."

"No, Rover Bud, my mind surges like the tide. I don't need sleep, but diversion. Talk to me."

"About what?"

"Discord's brothers, who made the world worse."

"Well, seamen are not allowed to talk on watch. Ears as well as eyes must warn of hidden shoals and other dangers."

"But we're moored safely at the pier, and soon the night will be too near dawn to shield ruffians."

"Since you wish it—all right, though I have misgivings. Let's sit on the cabin top and keep our eyes open and our voices low."

They sat at the edge of the cockpit, and Coral Bud began, "Now, you can well imagine that the Great Wizard's other children did not like the way their brother Discord's cave was overspreading space.

"The Great Wizard said, 'Why are you complaining? My world is without end, so all of you have as much space as you care to take. It's sad that your brother has made so much trouble for himself, but I'm mending matters as well as I can, and you will do no good by meddling.'"

Coral Bud paused and listened. "Was there not a swell in the surge?"

"Perhaps just the turn of the tide. Go on with the story."

"No. It was the wash of disturbed water. Hark! Did a sling-stone strike our hull?"

"Your fears are fashioning noises. Look and see."

Coral Bud peered restlessly over the rail and into the water.

She settled into her place again. She was thoughtful. Zeid urged, "Well, continue the story. What about Discord's brothers and sisters?"

Coral Bud took a deep breath and resumed the story. "The Great Wizard had five children. The eldest was a daughter named Happiness, and, as we have seen, she married the king of a far country. She was so busy in her own kingdom that she didn't see Discord's world at all.

"But next were two brothers, Justice and Truth. They were very angry because the Great Wizard would not destroy Discord. They consulted their younger sister Harmony, who was very distressed but did not think that further destruction would accomplish anything.

"So Justice and Truth set out by themselves to put an end to Discord's world. However, Truth said, 'We must destroy only evil. In a world where all creatures live by destroying each other, how is one creature more evil than the next?'

"After thinking about it, Justice decided, 'The devouring must not be cowardly or unnecessary or deceitful, and Mankind must be held most accountable because they are most intelligent.'

"The brothers started first with the earth, and rooted out all the strong grasses that would choke out the weak. Then they went to the animals and began killing the fierce that preyed on the gentle.

"But before long, the land was barren, and the grass-eaters, who had increased in number, began to die of starvation. Then Mankind became even more cruel than before, because they, too, were hungry.

"'We're doing something wrong,' said the brothers. 'Perhaps we should have started by destroying Mankind.'

"'You should have minded your own business,' said the Great Wizard. 'Now you've added drought and famine. The weak seedling pine withers if the shade of the encroaching thornbush is removed from it. When the tough, crowding plants are cleared away, the rain washes the more delicate blades from the ground. Thus the pasture land is gone, and the grazers that live too securely become too lazy to find new land, and so they starve.'

"The brothers went home, and the Great Wizard decided to ask his daughters to enter Discord's world to see if they could undo some of the damage caused by Justice and Truth—but that is another story, Light-Bearer, and the eastern sky becomes pale—"

"Look!" said Zeid, pointing upwards.

"A Space Cloud!" exclaimed Coral Bud. "Why can it be descending?"

"A system failure somewhere in Tenfold, perhaps."

The Cloud descended to the sea—slowly approached the sloop—touched the rail—and stopped.

Zeid looked at Coral Bud's face in the glow from the Cloud. He smiled, "Why do you look so anxious, sea urchin?"

"Of course I'm not anxious," scoffed Coral Bud, trying to beat down her guilt. If the Space Givers told Zeid she had ordered the mirror—!

The Cloud opened. A tousle-headed, white-suited figure stepped on the sloop's rail and jumped into the cockpit.

Zeid gave a shout of joy, slid from the cabin top, and held out his hand. "Tommy Lund!"

"Hi, Zeid!" The Space Giver shook Zeid's hand. "What are you doing in Tenfold? Who's your friend?"

"Friend? Oh, this is Coral Bud, Hamar's daughter."

Coral Bud, her guilt reinforced by bashfulness, had remained on the cabin top. The Space Giver smiled at her, "Won't you shake hands with me, Coral Bud? I'm Tommy Lund."

She let herself drop into the cockpit and clasped his hand as Zeid had done. "Greetings, Lord Tom-ih-Lund."

His warm fist gave her hand a squeeze. "You don't have to call me 'Lord', Coral Bud."

"Even among the free companies of my father's fleet, the discipline of rank must be maintained," she responded. "If I stop calling you 'Lord', I might stop calling Zeid 'Prince'—and Moji might stop calling me 'Lady'—and the world would fall apart at an even faster rate!"

Both young men laughed. Coral Bud went on, "But since

you're here, Lord Tom-ih-Lund, come into the cabin and share wine and honeycake, and tell us why you've descended."

"I've brought mirrors—a receiver and a couple of senders. Zeid, why didn't you tell us you'd be doing field work away from the palace?"

"Did the Board try to reach me through my father's mirror?" stammered Zeid. "Thank you! But how did you find me? The palace doesn't know we hired Knarb's ship."

"Have you forgotten that your coding belt beeps your position? Come to the rail—I'll hand you the mirrors."

He sprang to the rail, disappeared into the Cloud, and returned with a large box which Coral Bud thought was of dried sea foam. As he lowered the box to Zeid, he said, "Bio-degradable."

Zeid propped the box carefully against the aft bulkhead. "It's great to see you again, Tommy! If you could stay—"

"I'd better not. You know how Marnadal feels about goofing off. You're welcome on the Moonship anytime." The Space Giver waved his hand to Coral Bud. "Hang in there, kid!"

He stepped back. The Cloud closed, lifted from the sea—and vanished.

Zeid raised his eyebrows at Coral Bud. "And what did that mean?"

"How do you expect me to understand your funny Space Giver talk?" she demanded. "I see nothing to hang except the mirror. Hurry and place it in the midship cabin. The dawn has come—the tide has turned—we must free ourselves from the mooring slot and be on our way."

After breakfast Coral Bud advised Zeid to retire to the Master's cabin and sleep.

"You've been awake all night," she reminded him, "and must take the watch from me at noon. We float peacefully now on the ebb—and soon will have the morning breeze to hurry us northward on the starboard tack. Moji can assist me and practice his sailing lessons."

Zeid smiled, "Your father trained you so well to command, Coral Bud, that only the management of a fleet—or a merchant's realm—or a great palace—would occupy you happily."

"That is indeed so," agreed Coral Bud, "and is why I thought

I could be useful to a prince who was striving to draw the planet nearer to the Moonship. Not that I understand why scoundrelly beggars must be lodged instead of keelhauled—but I would have enough else to do without troubling my head with Moonship ideas.

"And in truth, Light-Bearer, if I were a man instead of a woman, you would be pleased at my competence and would take care to inform me of such things as I had not learned in the Sea Kingdoms."

"A man would not meddle in my personal affairs," Zeid rejoined. "He would serve me without offering opinions."

"Yes, as long as you want to be *served*," smiled Coral Bud, "and I want to be *wed*, we'll never agree on my proper place. However, I can sail the *Whizzard* for you and win favor for you with the princess. A major-domo could not do as much."

Zeid said immediately, "Can you understand, Rover Bud, that *how* I win the princess is important to me? Boastful lies do no harm to palace leeches, but I wish to win Fire Lotus not only for myself but also for my ideas of compassion and learning."

Coral Bud nodded but said nothing.

Zeid complained, "Again, you are wronging the princess."

"As a man would do, O prince, I said nothing."

"When a woman says nothing, that is an opinion," muttered Zeid, striding away.

In the middle of the day the heat-winds blew so strongly toward land that Coral Bud would not let the inexperienced Zeid handle the sloop alone. She sent Moji to nap—in case he would be needed at a later hour—and stayed on deck to instruct Zeid.

He seemed tired. Coral Bud asked, "Couldn't you sleep this morning? A day more, and the sea motion will seem natural to you."

"The sloop rides well, sea urchin. It was my mind that was in motion," he replied. "When I thought I would not have a receiving mirror, I was quite content to wait to see Fire Lotus. But now I'm impatient for her palace to call, and I lay awake imagining what I would say to her."

"Oh, we are as yet far from the princess. But the bedchamber lady has found us a source of diversion and gossip. I think," mused Coral Bud, "we'll place Kalia before the mirror today."

Zeid shook his head. "Do you ever exhaust your supply of tricks and contrivings?"

"If you scorn me for using my wits to help you, the supply will soon run out."

Zeid looked startled again. "I did not speak in scorn. In condescension, perhaps, like an important brother talking to a clever little sister."

Coral Bud laughed. "I suppose I must accept brotherly condescension. Wait until the gale swings more to the west. Then we can ease the sloop off. She'll sail herself, and we can attend to the mirror."

After a quarter hour, Coral Bud eased the sheets and made fast the steering oar. While Zeid paced the cockpit, Coral Bud fetched Kalia and took her into the Master's cabin.

She borrowed a gold gauze robe from Zeid's clothing chest, draped it around Kalia, and dressed Kalia's hair in a loose, wanton fashion. She lifted Kalia's necklace outside the gauze and stepped back to survey the effect.

"You're a sweeter beauty than Fire Lotus," she smiled, "and the rubies attest your worth to your master."

"Oh, lady, is this wise?" asked Kalia timidly. "I love Moji and do not want to incur his displeasure."

"And I love Zeid," returned Coral Bud, "and would not want him to lust after you. But so bitterly do I hate the copper-haired harpy that I would risk anything to defeat her."

Zeid stared as the girls emerged from the cabin. He tugged his beard and said, "You've gone too far, Rover Bud. You've demeaned Kalia into—what? A mirror-slave? A duplo?"

"She becomes whatever the beholder assumes, and my Lord Zeid is to blame if his mirror-friends expect to see slaves or duplos. We go now to unblank the mirror."

The girls settled onto the divans to await the call from Fire Lotus's palace.

A voice woke Coral Bud from a doze. "Calling the Prince Zeid ben Amfi!"

She sat up and looked at the mirror. The fat page's face was staring out of it.

Kalia rose and stood in front of the mirror. She pressed the *speak* embossing and said, "I speak for the noble prince."

"Well, *I* speak for the noble Princess Fire Lotus. Where's the page—the dark-haired arrogant boy?"

"My Lord Zeid has taken him along on a shark hunt."

"One moment. Am summoning."

The mirror hazed. Coral Bud sprang to the cabin hatchway and beckoned Zeid to enter. He scanned the empty horizon quickly, then followed her. When he saw the haze, he gave an exclamation, and Coral Bud said, "Sit quietly and listen. These are just battle feints."

The mirror cleared to show the gray-clad bedchamber lady. Her sharp eyes inspected Kalia. "I can see you are no duplo, my girl. Show me your necklace at closer view."

Kalia quickly unclasped the filagree and held it up to the mirror. "Splendid, isn't it? How can I serve you, grandmother?"

"I would speak with the pert, dark-eyed page. When will he return from the shark hunt?"

"Alas, I cannot say." Kalia reclasped the necklace at her throat. "My Lord Zeid may feast overnight aboard another of the ships. Why do you wish the page, grandmother? He's a spoiled, mischievous lad."

"But knows much of his master. Is he male page or eunuch?"

"He is *not* eunuch, I can assure you!"

"Would the prince beat him if he mirror-spoke without leave?"

"Why, the prince tolerates so much from the lad that a mirror-speaking would go unnoticed."

"Bid him call us when he returns. What's his name?"

"Nay, grandmother, I dare not say. Let the lad himself tell you."

"Well, well. Those are fine rubies and artful goldcraft, my wench. Farewell."

The mirror blanked. Coral Bud jumped up and hugged Kalia. "Oh, you were superb, Kalia. Wasn't she, my noble prince?"

"Moji would have been offended. I don't blame *you*, Kalia," he smiled to the blushing girl, "but please change back to your honest self."

Kalia curtsied and ran out of the cabin.

Coral Bud taunted Zeid, "You fear your own feelings. You know Kalia is much more lovable than Fire Lotus."

Zeid said mildly, "Now there is a scornful opinion of my feelings. To have behaved with discretion on the Moonship—and escaped my mother's matchmaking plots—and then be so weak as to lust after my Counting Master's wife—"

"I wish you could be weak enough to fancy yourself in love with your betrothed bride!"

"There are limits to every man's imagination, little pirate."

CORAL BUD DOZED IN the midship cabin and ate supper before going on deck at sunset to take the watch from Zeid. He said, "The wind is fading with the sun. Let Moji guide the sloop on the star path while you put on your page disguise and call Fire Lotus."

"Why? Do you find the old grandmother so charming?"

"Surely Fire Lotus herself will speak, this time."

"And for that reason you forget your supper? I wish you had been attacked by this love-sickness on the Moonship. They might have had a Magic cure."

Zeid said seriously, "There was no Fire Lotus among the Moonship maidens."

"No. You've said there was no beauty of any kind," retorted Coral Bud. "Blank glass walls and blank white garb like that worn by Tom-ih-Lund. You were a princeling from a palace rich in beauty. Everything you touched as a child, everything you saw and heard and smelled, was rich with beauty. Carved and polished woods, soft rugs, silken robes, mosaic inlays, heaps of sparkling gems, sweet perfumes, lilting music. . . .

"You came home from the Moonship starved for beauty," she continued, "and you saw Fire Lotus in a portrait glass. The shock of so much beauty all at once has made you a little mad."

Zeid considered her words. "What you say might be true, little sister, if I had seen only beauty. But I saw such intelligence in her eyes—!"

"And in *my* eyes, Light-Bearer?"

He looked into her eyes and smiled, "Your thoughts shift so quickly—like night shadows on a deep garden pool. But what use are comparisons? Can a man ever explain why he falls in love? Yes, Coral Bud, you're intelligent. You're comely and graceful. But you're not Fire Lotus."

"I wouldn't be Fire Lotus for all the Wizard's gold! Not even to win Prince Zeid's heart would I be Fire Lotus! You don't know Fire Lotus at all!"

"You have the means to make us acquainted."

"Very true," said Coral Bud. "Eat supper like a sensible man, and I'll call the palace after Kalia has finished her work in the midship cabin."

Half an hour later Coral Bud made herself into the gold-scarfed page and joined Zeid at the mirror. She activated it and called Fire Lotus.

The image of the fat page once more stared from the mirror. "Who calls—oh, is it you, insolence?"

"Do you never leave the mirror, butterball?"

"I like mirror gossip, and I am chief page."

"Well, look you, chief, I grow weary with proxy speeches. Summon your mistress."

"Am summoning."

The mirror hazed. Zeid said to Coral Bud, "Stand aside."

She gave place, remarking, "You're too poorly clad."

"I've been shark hunting."

They waited. The mirror cleared, and the Princess smiled at Zeid. Her copper hair tumbled over her shoulders in springy waves. Her green eyes were lustrous, her mouth wet. Ropes of glowing pearls edged her green gauze robe which lay carelessly off her shoulders, revealing the cleft of her bosom.

Zeid was speechless. Fire Lotus said in an amused, melodious voice. "Lost your tongue, sailor? Where's the handsome page?"

"Princess, I am Zeid."

"How young you are! Scarcely older than your beardless page! I had thought Prince Rustad's brother to be more like him."

"There is difference in our years—and natures."

"You must be the Wizard's favorite since he has heaped such riches upon you. Or does your wealth come from the Moonship?"

"What I wish to share with you comes from the Moonship."

New animation flashed from the green eyes. "Magic in trade for the duplo seed? Start the bidding with a thousand Space Giver lamps, and perhaps we will come to a bargain."

Zeid had stepped back a pace in horror. "Not a copper will I pay in such vile business! What teachers have so miserably mistaught you?"

"Teachers that can think logically, at least. What is vile, young prince? The source of your wealth? Or my demand to be paid? What is miserable? The wise trading that has made me the richest princess on the planet? Why do you make the journey if not to buy?"

"To bring you new ideas. Rich though you are, your mind is as poor as that of a hospice beggar. Beautiful though you are, your mind is as ugly as Bulbul's. I was sent to the planet to teach about wealth that warms a man's inner being while supplying his neighbor. I should have started in palaces, not in bazaars!"

"Don't think you can start droning Moonship precepts in *my* palace, Zeid ben Amfi, unless you pay for the privilege in wealth and wit. We live to entertain each other. Come with your fleet and your Magic and amuse us, and you'll be welcome. And now, call back your saucy page."

"You would rather speak to *him*?"

"With mirrors, one can only speak and look. You wear no interesting gems, shark hunter, and your words are dreary. Let me talk to the witty boy."

"Nay, Princess. Zeid ben Amfi will not be scorned for a page!"

He blanked the mirror. Coral Bud said cheerfully, "Well, that's that. You need not continue to the Marble Lands. I'm glad the affair was so easily settled."

"Settled! How little you know of a man's pride. Am I to slink away because she doesn't want her selfish ignorance disturbed? Besides, she *is* interested—she *would* welcome me!"

"Welcome your fleet and your Magic, fool!" She pulled off the page disguise, threw the scarves at him, and went to resume her watch.

The wind had now died completely. The sloop was vulnerable

to an attack in the eye of the calm. Half a league away, perhaps, the wind could still blow a raider to within sling-stone distance.

Coral Bud scanned the star-blurred, mist-fuzzed horizon. Bright ripples glinted like quicksilver in the rip of opposing currents. Moji was peering over the rail.

"Liquid silver eddies around our hull."

"Liquid life-force, Moji. The brightness occurs when the sea's tiny dust-creatures die in great hordes. They cannot rot—they have less body than a sand grain!—so their life-force winks like a tiny lightning flash before being gathered up by the Great Wizard."

"Where does the Great Wizard take the tiny glitters?"

"I don't think he takes them out of this world which has too little life-force already. Perhaps he re-uses them patiently since he has no reason to hurry. The tale is a sad one—the truth is so often sad—and spoils the beauty of the glitter."

Moji gestured to the bow and smiled, "Spare Kalia such truths, lady. She thinks the brightness is but star-shine."

Coral Bud smiled, climbed from the cockpit, and ran forward. Kalia was at the very stem of the sloop, leaning over the rail. She straightened up at Coral Bud's footsteps. "Oh, lady! How goes the mirror-speaking?"

"Most dreadfully, Kalia. I should have realized that a prince and princess are of the same pith and grain. Fire Lotus has had teachers, even as Zeid, and though they quarrel angrily in the mirror, they are at home with each other in their minds. A poor pirate girl has no entrance to the circle. Even when I help Zeid with all my heart, I seem only to be giving him orders."

"Don't despair, lady," comforted Kalia. "Forget the differences between pirate girl and prince. Use your cleverness on the alikeness of woman and woman. It is there that the princess may be dealt a stinging blow."

Coral Bud recognized the truth of this, but she had been brought up in a man's world. How could she defeat an enemy who was the shrewdest princess on the planet?

FEELAFELL'S PALACE WAS AN island in the chain that formed the outer rim of Tenfold's sound, a fortress that Feelafell's father had secured for his mistress and their son when ill-feeling about the forbidden relationship seemed to threaten their safety.

Feelafell was allowed everything a planetary lord also could enjoy, plus harmless luxuries his exiled father sent him across the light-years. Yet, even as a boy, he knew his planet was intended to be an isolation chamber for a tainted specimen. He had tried working for Moonship approval, but he could not stay on any course long enough. He went into extremes of exhilaration and depression. He imitated the plain white Moonship garb for public appearances but arrayed himself in barbaric splendor within his palace.

His father had told him many Moonship secrets, and Feelafell wanted to know power, not as a barbaric lord but as a great scientist. Deep in his fortress rock he had built a laboratory. But aluminum was not available to him on his Bronze Age planet, and Feelafell could do nothing with uranium ore except curse his own frustration.

However, he could cannibalize the sunken wrecks, and—contrary to Zeid's disbelief—he had succeeded in shielding the reactivated power systems from the Moonship sensors.

Coral Bud's ears had not deceived her as she had sat on the *Whizzard's* cabin top, telling Zeid the story of Discord's two brothers. She *had* heard something strike the *Whizzard's* hull—a tracking sensor that looked like a small silver dart.

Feelafell now dismissed his servants and descended the hidden stairs to his lab. The dart was registering the *Whizzard's* position on the tracking screen. Four other darts also were visible—a cluster further along the Seacoast.

Feelafell smiled and followed an underwater labyrinth to a mooring beneath the palace. He entered the minisub and switched on the repeater screen. The *Whizzard* had made better progress than he had expected—Hamar's daughter knew how to sail—but now she was lying becalmed.

He closed the sub hatch, checked the systems, submerged, and followed the labyrinth to the open sea. He programmed the navigating unit to zero in upon the *Whizzard,* and he pulled the operating rods up to Full Ahead.

The sub arrowed swiftly and silently toward its prey.

Feelafell wondered about the Space weapons he was sure Zeid had been given. The palace purveyor Sejput had brought a remarkable tale to the Seacoast—Rustad's six missing assassins had encountered more than a pirate girl.

The minisub closed in upon the becalmed sloop. Feelafell cut off the propulsion unit and raised the periscope, which contained not a viewing lens but a camera. The star-and-mist obscured sea that was confusing to Coral Bud was as clear as day upon Feelafell's view screen.

He saw the slight figure which was now seated upon the top of the stern cabin. So the pirate girl was standing watch alone! Once she was his hostage, Zeid's Space weapons did not matter.

He reflected that the maneuver would be similar to that for which the minisub had been intended—the capture of sea animals. He would need the mask and air pack and the flexible tail-snare.

But first, he had to program the sub to surface and admit him. He looked at the notches on the timing dial. How did a chronometer express the space of snaring a pirate girl?

Space Age reasoned with Bronze Age—and Feelafell programmed the sub to eject him from the missile tube, wait a span of notches, surface, and open the hatch.

CORAL BUD WAS WATCHING the stars and wondering how to use Fire Lotus' strengths to her own advantage. In her desperate inventing and discarding of plots, she had lapsed from her usual alertness.

When she felt the sloop rise very slightly and fall, she came only vaguely to herself. A swell? Had a large sea creature surfaced beside the sloop?

She remembered Zeid saying that Feelafell's underwater boat could go as fast as a horde-ship. Instinct and training told her not to make herself a target. She threw herself flat—but too late. The strands of a tail-snare had already whipped around her body.

Her arms were lashed tight. She could not reach her knife. Rage and panic seized her, and she screamed. A dripping wet, masked face rose into sight. Long limbs encased in a thick black skin eeled over the cabin top and clutched her in a dank, slimy embrace.

She struggled, but the snare only tightened. The boarder held her easily with one arm, unpeeled the mask from his head, and laughed at her in Feelafell's mocking voice.

Her choked, angry shriek had brought Zeid leaping from the Master's cabin, and Moji emerging more cautiously from the forward hatch. Feelafell called out triumphantly, "Stop! Stop—or the pirate brat dies! Think well before you draw a space weapon, Zeid ben Amfi!"

Zeid paused in the cockpit. He had not even thought about his Combi-shot, so quickly had he answered Coral Bud's cry. He moved nearer the stern ladder and said, "Think well before you take a maiden by force. You are a Space Giver."

"If the girl is still maiden, I'm glad to hear it," mocked Feelafell. "I mean to breed a conquering race from Hamar's seed and my own."

Coral Bud's panic had given way to shame at how easily she had been overpowered. What would her father think of her? Trussed up by an enemy who had no weakness to attack—!

Yes, he had a weakness. His sore hands! She cried out, "What could you breed, you misbegotten son of—"

His hand covered her open mouth. She jerked her head forward and bit down. She could feel his body shudder and double over with pain. At that moment the programmed minisub rose to the surface in a surge that rocked the sloop.

Zeid sprang up the ladder and rushed Feelafell who dropped his captive to the boards.

Coral Bud rolled into the cockpit with a thud.

Kalia crept out of the midship cabin, knelt beside Coral Bud, drew the pirate knife from the tail-snares, and slashed away the strands. Coral Bud jumped to her feet—but Zeid needed no help. He was swarming over Feelafell—keeping under his longer reach—driving his fists into Feelafell's soft body.

Sensing how hate and rage were blinding his opponent, Zeid drew back and swung a powerful blow from the depths of his strength. The force knocked Feelafell clear over the stern. He hit the water with a splash of winking phosphorescence.

Zeid waited for him to come up. Moji, who had seized a fish spear at the bow, leaped across the cockpit to the top of the stern cabin and stood poised to cast the spear.

A scrabbling came from the other side of the surfaced sub. Feelafell was pulling himself upon the ovoid.

Moji cast the spear. It missed Feelafell but jabbed into the mechanism of the raised hatch. The Space Bastard slithered onto the sub, wrenched away the spear, and dove into the hatch.

There was a pause. The damaged hatch mechanism would not lock down. The ovoid gave a jerk and sped away on the top of the water in sparkling lines of foam.

Coral Bud was standing numbly, hardly believing she was free.

Zeid rewound the sash of his night-cloth and hurried down the stern ladder. "Rover Bud! You're a battle comrade without peer!"

"I'm ashamed," said Coral Bud dully. "I was surprised on watch. I didn't even draw my knife."

"But your quick wits remembered how to use your teeth!" Zeid put his arm around her—then gently released her. "What's this? The snare burrs have torn your arms! Kalia, fetch towels and wine into the Master's cabin. Moji, keep the star watch. I'll come when the lady is recovered."

"Zeid, don't make so much of a trifle."

She stepped forward, but her knees and ankles seemed to loosen from their sockets. She crumpled to the deck. Zeid lifted her up and carried her into the Master's cabin.

He laid her on the wide divan that followed the curve of the stern. She quickly revived, but Zeid made her rest against the cushions.

"Now you will laugh at me, Light-Bearer," she said weakly, "but the attack was so sudden. Until that moment, I had not given much thought to what it would be like to be—taken. Or even to being a seed-wife," she blurted, "though there was much talk of such things."

"Talk and experience are far different," smiled Zeid. "For all your fierceness and hard training, you were Hamar's little pet, and no man would have dared disturb your innocence."

"And yet I considered well before agreeing to our betrothal."

"I daresay. But you were considering how fine it would be to command a Space barge and have a merry time selling lamps in the bazaars. You had no idea what the Light-Bearer himself would be like."

"True—but I didn't change my mind after I had met him," smiled Coral Bud, regaining her buoyancy.

Kalia brought towels and a bowl of wine, then left the cabin.

"I should have secured Space Giver balm from Jibbo," said Zeid, sponging her burr-scratched arms with the wine. "How brave you were to outwit Feelafell despite the shock and pain. You would have been a handy shipmate if I had decided upon the barge."

"You will sell no more lamps in the bazaars?" faltered Coral Bud.

"Sea urchin, I was trying to sell compassion—but where is the sense to explaining the real worth of being a giver instead of a taker to poor beggars who have nothing to give? I should have started in the palaces where there is wealth to be given away."

"Fire Lotus said she would not receive you unless you came with Magic and a fleet."

"She challenges me, to see what I will do. But she will listen when I speak."

"Oh, Zeid, do you really believe that after having been indolent and greedy and selfish since birth, she will let you persuade her to give her money to beggars?"

"The whole planet has been ill taught—greedy, careless of another's misfortune. The Moonship gave me an impossible task. Jibbo, I think, begins to understand that in nourishing others he satisfies a need in himself—a fellowship, an accomplishment. But Jibbo is a single hospice host. How much better it would be to teach compassion in a princely palace!"

Especially when the princess is a red-haired beauty, thought Coral Bud. She said nothing. Carping on harsh truths would only make Zeid more stubborn. As Kalia had said, she would have to defeat the woman, not the princess.

THERE WAS A NEW friendliness when Zeid relieved Coral Bud at midnight—and when Coral Bud relieved Zeid at dawn.

The white sun was blinding. Hamar had established himself on islands to the east of the horde-ship route so that he could sail into his prey while they were too sun-blinded to notice his approach.

Coral Bud took a transparent, oiled band of fish skin which all sailcraft hung within their cockpits for quick grasping. She held the band over her eyes and looked at the eastern horizon.

The fish-skin veil dimmed the blinding light. The horizon was a stark line. Four dots seemed to dance on it.

She did not think it could be her father Hamar. His raids were precisely determined by information sent from shore agents by means of trained sea birds. For Hamar to be in that area at dawn, there would have to be immediate prey—and the seas were empty except for the sloop.

Who could the raiders be? Bold pirates, indeed, who chose a course so near to Hamar's islands.

She watched the dots grow. The sloop would be risking impossible odds. It would be wise to flee westward at once.

She loosed the sails and leaned her weight against the steering rod.

Zeid, who had been breakfasting, came out of the midship cabin. "Why are we turning back?"

"Four raiders block our path. We must run before them until stronger winds give us speed to evade northwards."

"More delay! And already we've wasted too many days. We're *not* turning westward."

He seized the steering rod and completed the circle Coral Bud had started. "We'll deal with the raiders if they come upon us."

"Do you have weapons that outrange sling-stones? Our sails will be rags in a breath!"

Zeid made fast the rod and leaped forward to haul the sails tight. The sloop skimmed northeast in a rush of foam.

He returned to where Coral Bud was standing. "What worth to Hamar are captured ships?"

"Why, much gold, of course. Each additional ship increases his striking force—just as each battle beast increases an army's power. A captured ship means replenishment of gear and provisions—cargo to be shared—maybe gold and jewels—maybe crews who would rather raid for Hamar than for the defeated captains."

"And slaves?"

"Sometimes, yes. What else can be done with a harem retinue that would starve if they were freed and thrown into the streets? But ship crews, being reckoned rebellious and treacherous, are not even wanted by the slave dealers.

"There's a knack to all jobs, Light-Bearer, and it's far more profitable for Hamar to free crews than to enslave them because they yield all the more readily the next time.

"And now," she continued, "where are your thoughts tending, that you ask so many questions about Hamar?"

Zeid stroked his beard. "Well, little pirate, I'll need much gold in the Marble Lands. If I capture four ships and sell them to Hamar—"

Coral Bud laughed. "Piracy does not proceed in that fashion. If you capture four ships and approach Hamar, he'll capture you and your booty."

"Rover Bud, where is the fairness in demanding that I escort you to your father—and then letting him capture me? Even for pirates, such dealing is scurvy."

"Not at all, since you can hold me hostage until Hamar either returns your ships or pays their worth."

"But I don't *want* to hold you hostage. A fine mess I'd be in, if Hamar took my ships and left you on my hands."

"A fine mess you'll be in sooner than that, unless you make up your mind to engage the raiders or flee. They alter course to cut us off, and their stone-hurlers are already swarming up the masts."

"Which tack is most favorable?"

"The starboard, as we are, which leaves our battle rail free. But make haste—if their sling-stones reach us, we're lost."

Zeid entered the stern cabin. The minutes hung heavy on Coral Bud's heart. Stones peppered the water as the sling-throwers tested their range.

Coral Bud wrenched open the cabin door. "Zeid!"

The cabin was empty.

INSIDE THE CABIN, ZEID had found his travel rug and unrolled it. He put on his coding belt and Combi-shot, then lay prone on the carpet so that he could peer over the edge. Touching the coding arabesques he recited,

> "One eyeblink from room to air
> Another eastwards, here to there."

Before his mouth had closed, the rug was resting on a small cloud.

"Planetwards ten meters," he ordered.

The rug lowered him out of the cloud and stopped. He looked down. The ships were like toy boats, and he was astern of the raiders. He scrambled to the other end of the rug and drew the Combi-shot.

"Planetwards ten—and ten—"

The raiders, watching the sloop, did not see the strange bird astern of their formation. Zeid triggered his weapon.

Stunned men tumbled from the masts—captains fell upon the quarter-decks—the seamen at the great steering rods collapsed.

Zeid recoded the Combi-shot and aimed at the sheets and halyards. The sails blew free, and the ships began to turn into the wind.

The sloop had already crossed their bows. Moji was now on deck to help Coral Bud. They swung the sloop about in order to bear down upon the wallowing ships.

For the moment, the four captured ships nodded in unison on the waves, but the sea would soon separate them.

Zeid directed the rug to the bow of the nearest ship. He seized the end of a coiled mooring line and drew it to the bow of a second ship. He moored the second to a third—the third to the fourth.

By this time, Coral Bud had turned into the wind yet again to come alongside the ship where Zeid was waiting. He hitched the line which she flung him and helped her aboard.

She ran to the fallen pirates. "Oh, I hope you didn't slay them!"

"What! Has even your bloodthirsty nature become mild?"

"My nature is neither bloodthirsty nor mild—just practical. We need a few of our captives to man the ships."

"They are merely stunned and will remain so for an hour."

"A short time for the two of us to stow them below hatches. Let's inspect this hold."

They threw back a hatch cover and heard human voices. Zeid called down, "Who are you? If not pirates, you have no cause to fear us."

Pale faces crowded into the ray of sunlight. The massed bodies gave way to a broad-shouldered, gray-bearded man wearing an embroidered satin cloak that was chafed and stained.

"Oh, sir, we are from the Crucible Fortress offshore from the Animal Lands. We blend molten earths as the Space Givers taught our ancestors. We fashion all but the evil, heavy earths that dissolve men's bones.

"We thought our Fortress was invincible—not even the great Hamar could conquer our gates—but lo, a monster bored its snout beneath the sea and opened a cave—and we were overrun by masked, frog-footed enemies from the depths. Our treasures were loaded on four ships, and we were taken hostages to ensure that no one would chase after the pirates."

Zeid said, "I am Zeid ben Amfi, also called the Light-Bearer. I would like help from your principal men, if they will make themselves known to me as I release you."

He and Coral Bud uncovered the rest of the hatch and pushed the wooden grid aside. The hostages streamed up the ladder, women and children first. Dazzled by the sunlight, they stumbled to the ship's rail.

Next came the men, eager to know what had occasioned their freedom. The satin-clad spokesman bowed to Zeid and said,

"I am Nevyev, Master of the Bronze Forge. We are grateful for our freedom, Prince Zeid. What help do you require?"

"First, the scoundrels of these four ships must be placed below hatches—"

Nevyev bowed.

"Next, a crew must sail the ships for me."

Nevyev bowed again.

"And next, your treasures must be collected on one ship, because I mean to sell the other three to Hamar the sea rover."

Nevyev's eyes widened. "Hamar? The Light-Bearer—the Moonship Prince—deals with Hamar?"

"I need gold for a venture to the Marble Lands. The lady beside me is Coral Bud, Hamar's daughter."

Coral Bud stepped forward. "Much must be done quickly, before the raiders awake."

It was easy to stow the pirates in the hold of one ship, but not possible to stow the booty of four ships in one.

"Lend me what can't be stowed," said Zeid to Nevyev. "You and my Counting Master will determine the yearly interest due the Crucible Fortress, and you can divide it among yourselves."

"And how can *you* stow cargo on the sloop?" demanded Coral Bud.

Zeid thought a moment. "Why, I intended to sell everything to your father. However, now you put other ideas in my head. If Nevyev agrees, I can arrive in the Marble Lands with a truly princely retinue."

"What is your idea, Lord Zeid?" asked Nevyev.

"At first I meant to demand that Hamar escort you home—and I will still demand it if you wish. But I hope you first will sail with me to the Marble Lands. If I arrive with a rich ship and a retinue, I can persuade lords and princes to listen to a message I bring from the Moonship."

"What of these women and children?" interposed Coral Bud.

"Hamar can sail them home at once along with others who do not wish to accompany me to the Marble Lands."

"Perhaps a man would remain silent, Light-Bearer—but what of your distaste for wholesale deceit?"

Zeid stroked his beard. "In truth, the Space Givers do not believe that the end justifies the means. But I must meet the challenge—and must seize the chance to teach the planet's rulers. And wherein is the deceit? I'm a true-born prince. I'm merely borrowing from Nevyev, on the usual business terms, the means to appear to advantage among others of my station."

Nevyev asked, "Which position would I have in your retinue?"

"Would you like playing major-domo?"

"Chamberlain," amended the Master of the Bronze Forge. "I've always fancied I'd make a superior chamberlain."

Zeid grinned at Coral Bud. "See how fortune favors me! You squandered my gold chains to no purpose."

"Without me, you would not even have thought of the chains. It is truly said, the one gift a prince never bestows is gratitude."

THE NEWEST AND FASTEST of the four captured ships had two masts and a two-deck sterncastle. Her name was *Sulubar*, and she had been stolen from a Preserve Master in the Animal Lands. When the raiders were safely below hatches, Zeid entrusted to Nevyev the stowing of the *Sulubar* and the manning of the ships while he returned to the *Whizzard* with Coral Bud.

"If you let Nevyev himself decide what he will lend you," said the pirate girl, "you'll get only the dregs."

"Perhaps so, yet I don't seem to care," said Zeid. "My head seems heavy and my mouth parched."

"How so? Your parents come of healthy stock."

"And I received regular shots—that is, I was given a warding-off Magic on the Moonship. But the Space Givers say that many maladies come from a troubled mind."

"What troubles you?"

"Need you ask? You heard Nevyev describe how the Fortress was taken."

"The Magic snout that came from under the sea and bored through stone?"

"Yes. Feelafell's underwater boat may have been know-*how*, but the borer was know-*where*."

"Nohow and nowhere? Is that the riddle that troubles you? Will you take it to the Moonship?"

"No. I can endure no more delays. Let the Monitor Board uncover the plots of their kinsman. Is it far now to your father's kingdom?"

"Well, we've lost a morning, and must moderate our speed lest we sail away from your captured prizes. By the way, where is your rug?"

"I directed it back to the cabin—and will rest, myself, before taking the afternoon watch."

"But Kalia will soon serve dinner. Don't you smell the delicious aroma of roasting fish and fruit?"

"My nose seems oddly numbed. I must rest. Truly, I feel ill."

He went into the Master's cabin. Coral Bud raised her eyebrows and leaned thoughtfully on the steering rod.

Shortly afterwards Kalia came into the cockpit to announce the meal. "Will you or the Lord Zeid eat first, lady?"

"Let Moji eat first, and then come and take the watch. The prince is heavy of mind and will rest."

Kalia looked at the horizon. "Do you know where we are, lady?"

"Oh, yes. At any time now, we may sight my father's sea birds. They are the largest of those who have colonies on the islands."

"I've heard that sea birds are scarce, and a rare sight."

"Yes. Their meat and eggs are so good to eat and their feathers so warm that mankind has used them up, except in the areas the Space Givers established near the cold Spirit Lands.

"However, my father has his own Preserve. The large birds may not be touched at all because they are messengers and pets. The lesser birds may be taken in season, and their nests robbed of feathers twice in the spring because they build a third time but not a fourth.

"Except for the messengers, sea birds are silly creatures who chatter and squabble all day long like the ninnies in Rustad's harem."

"Oh, then they must squabble indeed," laughed Kalia. "As a little girl, I was ever glad I served the mother Serada who quickly rids the harem of Amfi's seed-slaves and rules supreme. Three equal wives mean three orders to one poor slave, who is beaten twice no matter what she does."

"Serada is doubtless a great commander," agreed Coral Bud, "and finds the harem a fine battleground."

"And it would have been finer had the lady Coral Bud remained," laughed Kalia.

"Nay, the battle would not have been to my taste," smiled
Coral Bud. "I will build my nest like the messenger bird, having
only one mate, faithful to death. People, too, range from the silly
to the great like the sea birds, and harem treacheries come not
easy to my nature."

ZEID HAD LAIN RESTLESSLY on the divan. He thought a cup of wine
might sooth his parched mouth. He rose and started to open the
cabin door. He heard Kalia's voice. Not wanting to intrude upon
some domestic detail, he held the door ajar a crack and waited—
and listened. . . .

THE FAST LITTLE *Whizzard* could not be held to the plodding speed
of the large, heavier vessels. Under Coral Bud's direction, Moji
turned the sloop back again and again in the afternoon.

The change of tack—the flapping of sails—disturbed Zeid's
fitful nap. Finally he came on deck and complained, "You merely
play games with the wind, Rover Bud."

"The day is glorious," she smiled. "I but play games with the
wind until I can play them with Fire Lotus."

"Don't trouble yourself. The mirror has served its purpose."

"But don't you want to make a grand show of Nevyev's retinue?
While we sail rings around our prizes, we can fetch a mirror-page
from his adventuresome lads. Eat the food we saved for you in
the cookstove, Lord Zeid, while we put back again and run alongside Nevyev."

Zeid nodded. "Yes, I may as well get full use of my borrowed
wealth."

A real mirror-page had been taken as hostage. He had served
the Crucible Counting House and was eager for the fun of going
aboard the *Whizzard*. Nevyev dressed him in jewel-cloth and delivered him to Coral Bud.

When the lad entered the *Whizzard's* midship cabin, Zeid
greeted him kindly, "Ah, here we have genuine ore. Open the
mirror and increase my credit, good lad."

The page unblanked the mirror. Coral Bud, who had followed

him into the cabin, said, "I will call at once, so Sir Page can spend the rest of the afternoon with a fishpole or abacus."

Even as she spoke, the fat page's image appeared in the mirror, saying "I call the prince Zeid ben Amfi."

The lad, aglitter in his jewel-cloth, sprang to the mirror, "Who calls the magnificent prince?"

"The magnificent Princess Fire Lotus. That is, she wishes to talk to the dark-eyed, insolent fellow."

"Pray refer to Masters by name or seal-mark."

"So the prince has insolent shipmasters also! But I'm referring to the mirror-page. Where is he?"

"What matter? I'm the page with whom you are speaking."

"Did Zeid cut off his head?"

"Whose head?"

"The page's, you dolt! Because my princess preferred him!"

"I answer mirrors, not questions. Summon your princess."

"Summon your prince, first."

"Nay. *You* called *us.*"

"Summoning."

The mirror hazed, but did not clear. The boy turned to Zeid for instructions.

"Close the mirror," said Zeid calmly. "You did well. Wait on deck."

The lad bowed and left the cabin.

Zeid said to Coral Bud, "The princess listens, even as I listen, and she seeks to tease me. The mirror game has become too childish—a mere hide-and-seek from boredom."

"Well, what did you expect? The princess and her friends aren't interested in Moonship ideas. If the Space Givers had been able to teach the planet's rulers, they would not have sent you to find a better path."

Zeid stroked his beard. He glanced into Coral Bud's lively dark eyes and smiled a little. "You would have me return to Jibbo."

"Not now, when you have committed yourself to another course," retorted Coral Bud, who was still convinced Zeid's love for Fire Lotus would cool with nearer acquaintance. "Play the palace game yourself. You would not think it childish if you hadn't been schooled on the Moonship."

"I wonder. I can't decide what I would or would not think."

"It's the illness that speaks. A pulse beats at your temple. Your eyes seep tears."

"Do I look as ill as I feel? Then we will put off any more business with the mirror."

He went to talk to Moji and let the sea breeze freshen his countenance.

That evening the *Whizzard* and her four prizes were again becalmed. Coral Bud asked, "Can Feelafell surprise us again with new Magic?"

Zeid, feeling slightly better after his hours in the fresh air, cautioned, "We must keep sharp watch. We don't know what other hardware he may possess."

"Well, we know he has an underwater boat with a wrecked hatch, and a snout that bores through stone. Can either of them be rigged to harm us?"

"The snout is merely a mud slug. The damaged locking mechanism—"

Coral Bud remarked, "Space Magic must indeed be weak if a barbed spear can lame it. And the boat's hull must be as thin as a lily pad. Why didn't Feelafell ram and sink us?"

"We're sheathed in copper," smiled Zeid, "and the boat's nose has sensitive—"

He paused. "Rover Bud, you've given me another riddle. Could the boat shoot missiles? If so—"

"If so, Feelafell is an inept warrior."

"He may have been afraid of overkill. Hamar's seed would end abruptly in a vaporized maiden." After a pause he added, "How strange, Rover Bud, that he would seek you as a seed-wife."

"Well now, even though I'm not comely enough for the Light-Bearer—"

"No, no—you mistake my meaning. Feelafell, like most Sea-coast dwellers, has knowledge of your childhood. You grew up among companies of free men. He could hardly suppose you would want to wed merely to breed like the sluts in Rustad's harem."

"Men seldom suppose anything about why women want to wed—except the Light-Bearer, who is sure Hamar's daughter would wed only to command a Desert barge."

Zeid laughed. "Well, grant me you like to command."

"To forge and shape, like Nevyev—and hustle along the affairs of the moment. Speaking of which, you must make your peace with Fire Lotus. It is all in the game."

Zeid settled back on the divan and said tolerantly, "If it will break the tedium of being becalmed, do as you please."

Coral Bud went into the Master's cabin and rummaged out new scarves. They were only gauze, but when she had added a jeweled brooch and the rare feather, she looked very handsome.

She stood in front of the mirror, pressed the embossing, and called Fire Lotus.

The fat page once more answered. "Who calls—Oh, you still have your head, insolence! Did Zeid beat you?"

"Why would he beat me? He considers me priceless. How goes it with your household? Is the princess all torn with love for my master? Throwing her slippers at her slaves and raging at her Chief Eunuch?"

"See for yourself, insolence. Summoning—"

The mirror hazed and cleared.

Fire Lotus smiled from the mirror. Her copper hair was piled in curls upon her head. Her eyes shone as green as the emeralds dangling from her ears. An emerald-studded breastplate half-concealed her fair bosom. She said softly, "Where have you been, handsome page?"

"Here and there on my lord's ships, beautiful princess. I look to better myself since I grow too old for a page's duties."

"I see no beard-down."

"For that you must come closer, lovely princess."

Fire Lotus laughed, and the emeralds flashed. "What if I tell your master of your boldness?"

"Oh? Shall I summon the prince from his chamberlain?"

"Not for a while, bold page. How did you think to better yourself?"

"Why, today I was aboard four ships, dealing with their commanders. A sea life is a fine life, lady."

"What say you to commanding a pleasure barge on the Quarry lakes?"

"Princess, I'd say it would be merry for a page but no work for a man."

"You aim high, rascal—but I'd assure you of work worthy for a man."

"My lord Zeid, alas, might have something to say to that. Rascal I may be, but he finds me useful."

"He has other pages. Summon the prince. I would parley with him."

Coral Bud pressed the embossing. "Summoning—"

Zeid jumped up and approached the hazed mirror. He said angrily, "Rover rogue, you led the princess on! You enticed her with your wit! I really am tempted to beat you!"

"Why beat *me* because the harem beauty has a taste for page boys?" retorted Coral Bud. She left the mirror.

Zeid cleared the haze and said, "Heedless princess—"

"Sea-clad prince," smiled Fire Lotus, "I have a boon to ask. Give me your handsome, bold page. He can't long continue a page, anyhow."

"No, and for that reason he leaves me to take service with a lord of the sea kingdoms. He will not be with me to the Marble Lands."

"He spoke nothing to me of such service."

"Pray allow me to dispose of my servants as I see fit. If you knew Sir Mischief as I do—"

"I would know him *not* as you do. Now, why do you frown?"

"Because you disgrace your teachers. Wasting your talents in idle pleasure, you forget even logic. What can a mirror image tell?"

The emerald eyes became thoughtful. "Truth, O prince. Bring the page to my palace. Then we will see if the mirror lies. Farewell."

The mirror blanked.

Coral Bud, who was sitting cross-legged on the divan remarked, "And I hope it *is* farewell. I feared she would ask my name, and I haven't had time to make one up."

"It's farewell for *you,* Rover Bud. Tomorrow I'll fetch Nevyev's lad to the sloop, and we'll inform Fire Lotus that the charming page fell overboard and drowned."

"Oh, Light-Bearer, the princess would never forgive you for such an opportune drowning. Rather, let the matter rest. She'll soon forget me for a different whim."

Zeid threw himself on the opposite divan—and began to laugh. "Over the whole planet, lords who are lovesick for Fire Lotus must bide their time while she moons over a dressed-up female."

"You should be grateful, Lord Zeid, because I distract the princess from your rivals. You should keep me with you so that I can amuse her."

"Pirate girl, if I had the strength for it, I'd keep you with me because you amuse *me*. But a man must be tough-fibered indeed to bear up under your embroilings."

He laughed again, but the laugh became a wheeze, and Coral Bud ordered him to rest the whole night. There would be no need for a sea watch until the wind freshened.

THE SHIPS LAY ALL night on a breathless mirror. Coral Bud rose before the dawn. The blinding sun again stirred the air currents. The sails flapped, and the rigging creaked in shifting winds.

Zeid, dressed for the day, came from the stern cabin and asked, "Do we face a storm?"

"I think not," smiled Coral Bud. "It's just that my father's islands lie so near that we feel the disturbance as the sun heats the rocks and draws the air to them.

"Today we'll use our speed and let the prizes lag astern. My father is more likely to recognize the *Whizzard* if she comes toward him alone. Have you thought how you will tell Hamar that you don't want his daughter?"

"Surely he understands a man wishes to choose his own seed-wife. I was never consulted."

"Do you consult a man when you bestow great treasure on him? Of course not. You confidently await his joy and gratitude. If you want to keep your captured ships, if not your head, you'd better let *me* explain why we do not share a marriage couch."

"Oh, no. You'll explain us more tightly entangled."

"You've entangled yourself. The Wizard will be wrathful when he doesn't get Fire Lotus's seed. The Moonship will despise you for not telling them about Feelafell because you were in such haste to court the redhead. I'm not an entanglement. I've saved you, over and over."

"But I wouldn't have needed to be saved, if you—if you—"

Exasperated, Zeid turned his palms upwards and rolled a glance at the heavens.

He saw an enormous circling bird.

"Look!" he cried, pointing.

Coral Bud looked up eagerly. "A messenger! He circles because he recognizes me. Messenger birds can spot a sea worm from a league away."

She put her fingers to her mouth and gave a shrill whistle. The great bird circled lower. Its wingspan was two man-lengths. The body and underwings were pure white. The head, upper wings, and back were dull black. The yellow beak was long and hooked.

"It's old Tem!" cried Coral Bud. "How often Tem guarded me when I was a babe—and picked me up and carried me too!" She called, "Tem!"

The bird glided lower, coming as if to land on top of the stern cabin. It was answering. "Coh—rah! Coh-rah!"

Suddenly Tem swerved drunkenly—flapped his wings—was gaining height—falling—wobbling—

"Oh, what's wrong?" gasped Coral Bud.

Facts clicked together in Zeid's mind. He exclaimed, "Field interference!"

"What fields do you mean?"

The struggling bird slowly fell into the waves.

"He'll drown!" shrieked Coral Bud. "Tem!"

She sprang onto the sloop's rail.

"Wait!" yelled Zeid.

But she already had dived into the water.

Zeid yelled "Moji!" and rushed into the stern cabin. He snatched up his coding belt, buckled it around him, and returned to the cockpit. He pressed the levitation stud and recited,

"All my weight but that degree

Which lets me walk upon the sea."

He jumped over the rail. He saw that the current was sweeping Coral Bud away from the writhing bird.

Zeid was falling too slowly. He reached to the sloop to push himself onto the water. Since the hull had been moving forward, his hand pressed against the stern.

His glance fell on a bright gleam at the waterline just above the copper sheathing.

Space metal imbedded in the wooden hull! So *that* was how Feelafell had tracked them!

He drew his Combi-shot, bent down, and struck the barrel at the gleam, smashing the chip-head of the sensor into the hull.

The blow thrust him outwards. He regained his balance. The water seemed to yield to his feet, yet he did not sink.

He ran toward Coral Bud, each step seeming to bounce him from a deeply piled carpet.

He saw that the bird had regained equilibrium and was rising from the water. He had smashed enough of the Space dart to destroy the distorting field.

Coral Bud seemed to be as far from him as before. A wrench brought sweat to his forehead. Never had he known such fear! To feel so helpless when someone so dear to him was being swept away!

Desperately his feet flailed the wave crests. The increasing distance between Coral Bud and himself was like a gap of loneliness and sorrow opening into his own life. How could he endure losing the brave little sea urchin?

Tem was circling Coral Bud again. He gave a screech, folded his wings, and dived like a plummet.

Zeid saw the black fin of a shark.

Tem hit the water ahead of the fin—and planed out with a shark's eye dripping bloodily from his hooked beak.

The shark thrashed into the air, teeth gaping after its tormenter.

The Combi-shot was still in Zeid's fist. He adjusted the barrel, aimed at the shark, and pressed the trigger.

The gaping jaws were filled with sea. The shark turned on its back.

Tem swooped into the air, hovered over Coral Bud, and flapped down. His talons grasped the girl's woolen jacket—his wings beat mightily—and Coral Bud rose out of the water.

Zeid instinctively lifted the weapon—but did not fire. The bird approached the sloop—rose higher and higher—cleared the mast and increased speed to the east.

Zeid holstered his weapon and ran unsteadily to the sloop. Moji helped him aboard and asked, "Lord Zeid, what shall we do?"

Zeid grasped the rail to keep himself from floating away. "I don't know. The bird is taking her to Hamar. We can only hold course and await Hamar's move."

The bird sped with Coral Bud over the sparkling sea until islands loomed in a silver haze. The haze thinned to reveal gray rocks and green hills. Ships clustered in small bays. Hamar divided his companies to guard the kingdom.

In one harbor, protected by a semicircle of hills, were the dwelling ships. Ashore were gardens and herds. Small boats were plying back and forth.

Tem descended over a large ship with a broad high sterncastle and a lower narrower forecastle. He screeched and then called, "Coh-rah! Coh-rah!"

The lookout in the crow's nest gave a shout, and men ran on deck.

Avoiding the rigging, Tem lowered Coral Bud to the poop. He released her gently and flapped to rest on the poop rail. She picked herself up and brushed her sea-wet tresses from her face.

"Well, well! You leave in a satin-lined barge and swim home," boomed a warm hearty voice. "What mischief have you been causing?"

"Not nearly enough, dear father," laughed Coral Bud, jumping into the arms of the tall stout pirate who was confronting her.

THE GAP OF LONELINESS still haunted Zeid as the sloop continued to lead the four. It was like the stillness of a palace courtyard when the central fountain ceases to gush and spray sparkling freshness into the heavy air. Life and motion and joy depart.

In the early afternoon, when the wind had veered to the west, a glittering fleet seemed to crawl swiftly toward the *Whizzard* over the eastern horizon. Row-galleys, their oar banks flashing rhythmically. Each galley had a mast, but the sails had been lowered because of the adverse wind.

What a superb attack force, thought Zeid. He remarked to Moji, "I wonder why other sea lords don't combine sails and oars."

"Because other sea lords employ slaves, who are indifferent fighting men," replied Moji. "Hamar gives each of a hundred oarsmen one gold piece, each of five captains five gold pieces, and keeps only ten pieces for himself, and he's richer than the despot who keeps a hundred gold pieces for himself and starves slaves."

Kalia also came on deck to watch the galleys. "What a beautiful sight!"

"Not beautiful to their prey," smiled Zeid.

The galleys flashed past the sloop, heading westward to provide escort for the four cargo ships that had lagged far behind. One galley circled the sloop and shipped oars to come alongside.

Zeid saw Coral Bud, pirate-clad in white shirt, blue pantaloons, and black boots, standing on the midship platform with a man whose bulk dwarfed her.

The sea king was not fat, but solid and strong. He was fair-haired, clean-shaven, blue-eyed. A narrow red scarf was bound around his head. His white shirt was ruffled, his pantaloons dark wool, his boots gold-trimmed.

Zeid marveled that they could be father and daughter, yet the resemblance was plain—in the girl's firm chin, in her merry smile so like her father's, in her quick gestures and graceful bearing.

Hamar and Coral Bud stepped from the galley platform to the sloop's rail, and thence into the cockpit.

Conscious of Hamar's keen blue glance, Zeid bowed and said, "Welcome, O sea king. Will you take refreshment within the cabin?"

Hamar nodded, his mouth curved in a grim smile. "We have ships to discuss, Zeid ben Amfi—and a tale my daughter has yet to tell."

Zeid looked at Coral Bud. "You haven't—?"

"How could we have come so quickly if we had stopped to chatter?" said Coral Bud. "No sooner was I on the deck of my father's dwelling than he was giving orders to man the galleys. Could I leave you and Moji to flounder out here with Nevyev and his ore brewers?"

"We were *not* floundering," said Zeid indignantly.

"Already you are one point too high from the course line."

"One point is not a great error, considering that we don't know where the islands lie."

"A course is a course! It doesn't—"

Hamar swept up his daughter and tucked her under his arm like a sea bag. "Which cabin, Lord Zeid?"

Zeid opened the door to the stern cabin. Hamar marched in and dumped his daughter onto the center of the curving divan. She bounced up and settled into the cushions. Hamar sat on one side of the curve, Zeid on the other.

Hamar smiled at Coral Bud, "I will now hear your tale from the beginning before the prince orders a wine that may mellow me."

"The beginning," said Coral Bud, "is that Prince Zeid is a younger son, and his seed-wife will never get a princess's due because his mother dotes upon his brother."

Zeid was startled. "Why, Rover Bud, that's not true!"

"You'll grant it's true that Rustad's three harpies have been so spoiled and indulged that they could invade Serada's apartments and set upon me as if I were a street girl? And, sir pirate," she continued, shaking her finger at her father, "you are to blame. Going in debt to the Wizard for stupid duplos. Did you think Serada would cancel the debt and afterwards squander money on the bargain bride?"

Zeid protested, "But you gave my mother no chance to honor you, Rover Bud. If you had stayed, instead of—"

Hamar held up his broad hand. "Nay, prince. It's fine for a son to defend his mother, but Serada *is* close with her gold. Knarb warned me to be wary of Serada."

Zeid was speechless. Coral Bud continued, "Well, sir pirate, I was angry at the insult to our kingdom. Palace quarters should have been prepared for me with slaves and robes and jewels—"

"But daughter, why didn't you demand those favors when we were consulting with Bulbul? You could talk of nothing but barge travel and lamp selling—"

"Was there any need to *talk* about the natural due of a princess?" asked Coral Bud loftily. "A barge is unusual for a princess—but not robes and jewels."

Hamar rubbed his blond head. "Yet you accompany the prince—"

"Oh, we're still betrothed. I like the prince immensely. But we must live as brother and sister until he makes his fortune."

"As a pirate?" wondered Hamar.

"As anything. His father the Wizard has sent him to the Marble Lands to secure duplo seed, but Serada gave us not even a copper penny for the Seacoast. Knarb let us hire the sloop at little cost. We were coming to beg escort of you when the raiders attacked us. I would have fled, being so outnumbered, but the stalwart prince—"

"Never mind the capture," said Zeid hastily.

Hamar grinned at him. "It's obvious that you captured four raiders only by Magic. If the Space Givers knew, they would be angry."

"Justly angry, sea king. But I'm so desperate for gold—"

"Which is why, dear father," interposed Coral Bud, "you will pay us well for three ships. The fourth ship and some of the hostages will sail with us to the Marble Lands where we need a great retinue."

"In the Marble Lands you can hire retinue," said Hamar. "I'll buy all four ships with crew and hostages. A slow cargo vessel will only delay—"

Coral Bud would have spoken, but Zeid said, "We grow thirsty, little pirate. Tell Kalia to bring us fruit and wine."

"And while I'm gone, you'll lose all our winnings," complained Coral Bud.

"Be easy," smiled Zeid.

Reluctantly Coral Bud left the cabin, and Zeid began, "It's true that the fourth ship will be a hindrance. However, in return for help I needed at the time—since Magic can capture ships but not sail them—I've promised the hostages that they and their treasure may return to the Crucible Fortress. They have loaned me part of the treasure, and I now offer it to you for gold."

"Well, I can't pay too much, you know," said Hamar. "I must resell through agents, which is a costly business."

"Of course, I can hold the treasure and sell it myself in the Marble Lands," said Zeid indifferently. "In offering it to you, I seek only to follow Coral Bud's wishes."

The basis of the bargaining being now established in the leisurely manner of the planet, Hamar turned to another matter.

"I'd like to know how the Fortress was stormed," he mused. "I recognize the ships. They sail with a company of raiders who could not storm a sheep pen."

"The raiders are imprisoned in a hold, but I doubt that they can tell you much about the storming," said Zeid. "Magic undermined the walls—and instead of seeking out the guilty Space lord, as is my Moonship duty, I'm hastening on my desperate journey."

"Hold, young prince," ordered Hamar, once again lifting his broad hand. "Think what you do. In order to please my daughter—and I'm disappointed in the wench, I must say!—you're risking your true wealth in the Moonship. Talk to the Moonship."

"But they would want to speak personally to me. It's a custom called *debriefing*—I could be delayed many days."

"The sea trip will take many days also. Tell the Moonship to fetch you here and set you down in the Marble Lands. Meanwhile Coral Bud can be sailing with your retinue."

Zeid put his aching, feverish head in his hands. He should have realized it would be impossible to leave Coral Bud with her father. How churlish he had been, expecting to return her like unwanted merchandise. She had agreed to a bargain in good faith. He owed her the courtesy of letting her slide out of it without further hurts or disappointments.

Undoubtedly it would be easier for her to continue with him to the Marble Lands. She could return alone with her father's escorting ships, and he could take the blame for their mismating.

But this plan supposed they would be traveling together, and he could counter the mischievous impulses of her lively spirits.

Never could he let her continue alone on the *Whizzard*, mirror-speaking Cosmos-knows-what to Fire Lotus!

Coral Bud was a dear girl, and he was as fond of her as he would have been of a sister, but Fire Lotus—with her pulse-quickening beauty, her tutored intelligence, her power to forward Moonship ideas—held his future in her careless hands. He would have to strain every nerve and resource to win her.

The pirate girl entered the cabin with a tray of fruit, wine bowls, and a flagon. She looked at Zeid and asked her father, "What's the matter?"

"Need you ask, greedy wench?" roared her father. "Will Zeid win a fortune any faster because he hungers for love?"

"Apparently, yes."

"Well, tonight he will feast with my duplos and enjoy the pleasures you deny him."

"Sir pirate, when my mother was alive, you found no pleasure in duplos. But Zeid may do as he pleases."

After partaking of fruit and wine, Hamar returned to his rowgalley. Zeid paced the stern cabin and said to Coral Bud, "Your father reminded me of the folly of letting my impatience lead me into failure and disgrace. How can I teach Moonship ideas while I'm neglecting my own Moonship duties? Yes, I must mirror-speak the Moonship."

"That can't be so difficult, well?"

"What do I say? But first I must withdraw the tracking dart from our hull. Furthermore, if Feelafell tracked *us*, wouldn't he also have tracked the ships carrying the Fortress booty?"

Coral Bud thought a moment. "I'd put the question differently. If the captured ships contain a similar dart, doesn't it prove that Feelafell also stormed the Fortress?

"Although it's unlikely that anyone else on the planet would have an underwater snout," she went on, "it's not impossible since a sea dweller could have grappled up the Magic. However, nobody but Feelafell has knowledge that could distress a bird in flight."

"Well reasoned, little pirate. My head must indeed be heavy, if I didn't come to the same conclusion. I'll now inspect the four ships—"

"Don't reveal too much of your Magic."

"I'll wait until night when we're anchored in your father's harbor."

"But a chill night mist arises from the cooling rocks. None dares breathe the unhealthful miasma, and you're already ill."

"I'm tired, distraught, heavy-headed. Fatigue, not mist, causes illness."

It was dusk before the slow cargo bearers could be herded into the pirate harbor. The *Whizzard* was moored alongside Hamar's dwelling, and Moji went to bargain with Hamar's captains about the worth of Zeid's prizes.

Kalia also had gone aboard Hamar's floating palace, but Coral Bud stayed aboard the *Whizzard* with Zeid who was preparing to look for the tracking darts.

"The dart from our sloop and one other dart from our prizes is enough," she said as he buckled his coding belt. "Take the dart from the *Sulubar,* so Feelafell can't track her further. He's not likely to beard Hamar in his den to get the three ships that will remain here."

Zeid nodded and left the cabin.

The night mist was swirling around the sloop's hull. The beam from Zeid's space lamp barely caught the bright glint of the dart in the woolen fog at the waterline. He dug out the dart, pocketed it, and drifted over to the *Sulubar.*

Here the search went more slowly. He could feel the fog condense on his hair and beard, soak into his clothes, and stuff his nostrils.

Coral Bud was waiting when he returned to the Master's cabin. She cried out when he half fell through the doorway, being supported only by his antigravity belt. With difficulty, he brought his weight to normal and collapsed on the carpet.

Coral Bud toweled his hair and beard dry, tugged and tore his wet outer garments from him, and heaped warm robes around him. She decided that this strange, terrible illness needed Space Giver remedies.

After a moment's thought she searched the pockets of Zeid's discarded jacket, drew out the two darts, and went into the midship cabin.

She stood in front of the mirror and pressed the embossing. "Monitor Board, do you *reed* me?"

A Space Giver face replaced her own—a girl's face, heart-shaped with oval eyes. Fine blonde hair, more silvery than Kalia's, seemed like a cloud puff around her head. Coral Bud stared with such interest that she only half-heard the girl's "Who calls?"

"Oh, Space lady," she said hurriedly, "may I talk to the lord Tom-ih-Lund?"

"Are you Zeid's friend, Coral Bud?" smiled the girl. "You seem upset. What's happened?"

"Nay, lady, forgive me. It is always foolish to blurt great matters to strangers. Lord Tom-ih-Lund is Zeid's friend, and I prefer to speak to him."

"Yes, I understand, but Tommy Lund is off duty. I don't know if I can reach him."

"Oh, lady, please try! Maybe he but slumbers in his bunk!"

The mirror hazed. Coral Bud waited in suspense.

At last the mirror cleared. Tommy Lund was grinning at her. He was not wearing a white Moonship coverall but a colorful shirt with a wide collar. He said, "Hi, Coral Bud. What can I do for you?"

"Much, I hope. Zeid is lying very ill on the carpet of the Master's cabin alongside my father's dwelling ship. I thought it was mist fever, but he's more sick than he ought to be. He has been burdened of late."

"Burdened?"

"He complains of being overwhelmed, and now he lies sense-less."

"Any particular problems?"

Coral Bud held the two tracking darts up to the mirror.

Tommy said, "Wait—hold it—let us focus."

A great shining eye stared through the mirror a moment, then Tommy Lund returned. "What can you tell us, Coral Bud?"

"Well, Space lord, I can tell you it was very foolish to favor Zeid without considering Feelafell the Space Bastard. He naturally feels he, too, should have been given Zeid's Magic, and he has pursued us frightfully in his underwater boat."

"Feelafell has an *underwater* boat?"

"Yes, and we think he owns the underwater snout that broke through the Crucible Fortress and robbed it. Zeid spoke a riddle I don't understand."

"Let's hear it."

"He said the boat was nohow but the snout was nowhere."

"Why hasn't he reported to us?"

"Well, he makes excuses, saying one thing and another, but I think he can't forget that Feelafell was sired by a Space Giver. You in the Moonship are the best of your breed, and Zeid walks in awe of you."

"But you have no awe of us, Coral Bud?"

"No—because you are not all of your breed, and I don't believe mankind on your planet are a bit better than us. Smarter but not better. Thus, to me, Feelafell is no different from any other scoundrel. But about Zeid—he is truly very ill. It would be best if you could lift him to the Moonship."

"And you too, Coral Bud?"

"Well, Space Lord, someone must continue on Zeid's errand to the Marble Lands."

"I thought Zeid was giving you a hard time. Why run his errands for him?"

"Because I must outwit a greedy redheaded harpy who has bedazzled him! Zeid thinks he can persuade her to help him teach Moonship ideas. I must prove to him what a fool she is."

"Which is more important—making a fool out of your rival or winning Zeid? Remember, out of sight can be out of mind. I'll descend presently."

The mirror blanked. Coral Bud rolled the darts slowly in her fingers. She was feeling bashful again. The Space Givers may not have been any *better*, but they certainly were *smarter*.

HAMAR WAS SORRY THAT Zeid was too ill to join in the feasting, but gratified that a Space Cloud would be descending to his kingdom. The Space Givers granted no Magic to the freebooting sea kings.

Hamar was also perplexed because Coral Bud, while refusing

to marry the young prince, sat anxiously beside him and tenderly sponged his fevered brow.

Zeid was still in a fitful sleep when the Cloud descended. Coral Bud saw the glow through the cabin windows and went out to the cockpit. The cloud steadied at the seaward rail, and two forms in white coveralls descended from it.

Coral Bud recognized Tommy Lund. Beside him was the girl who had answered her mirror-call.

"Coral Bud, this is Lovisa," said Tommy. "The Monitor Board gave her permission to come with me. She would like to talk to you while I look at Zeid. Where is he?"

"In the stern cabin—fevered and breathing heavily. Can you save him, Lord Tom-ih-Lund?"

"Oh, I think so. Sounds like he caught one of our ailments. It's not common to white sun planets, and its spores die quickly in your atmosphere."

"The sea mist is unhealthy, and none of us should be lingering in it. Go to Zeid, Space Lord. The lady and I will wait in the midship cabin."

She opened the midship door as she spoke and hastened to turn on the space lamp. Lovisa followed her into the cabin and closed the door. The girls looked at each other.

Or rather Coral Bud looked at the slim, tall Space girl while Lovisa looked at the decorative richness of the cabin's divans, cushions, and carpets.

"Pray sit down, Lady Lovisa," said Coral Bud. "May I fetch you some wine?"

"No, thank you, Coral Bud. We'll soon be ascending."

Lovisa sat uncomfortably upon the edge of a divan, with her legs hanging down. Coral Bud sat opposite her in limber fashion, cross-legged, her hands upon her knees.

After a moment Lovisa pushed herself further back against the cushions and drew up her legs. "My work doesn't take me to the planet, Coral Bud, but when I saw you in the view screen, I wanted to meet you."

"Do you always stand watch at the mirror?"

"All of us who are still students take turns at the Monitor. It's usually a boring job, and it's not fair that some should do it more often than others."

"Zeid has told me that fairness and equality are nearly the same on the Moonship. I can't believe they're the same on your planet, where people are born as chance will have it instead of being hand-picked. Not everybody can be taught, and how can you make a mirror-slave equal when he has no wit to be anything but a mirror-slave?"

"A shrewd remark, Coral Bud. I think you could give much help to the Moonship because you could help us assay what Zeid is doing."

"Oh, Lady Lovisa, I don't understand in the least what Zeid is doing! He wishes to spare assassins and feed beggars and teach princesses to give their gold away, and none of it makes sense."

"Will you come with us to the Moonship?"

"I think not, lady. I am but a pirate girl with rough hands and seaburned cheeks. Already Zeid spurns me because I suffer in comparison to the beautiful Fire Lotus. And when I look at your fine-spun hair and satin skin, I see that Fire Lotus is but a coarse digger of mealy roots. If I am to win Zeid, I must risk no comparisons higher than his brother Rustad's harem ninnies."

Lovisa laughed. "Zeid was never impressed by what a hair style and a bottle of skin lotion could do for a girl. He was brought up with us, you know."

"And never wanted one of you for a seed-wife? But I forgot—the mix is forbidden."

"Oh, it wouldn't have been forbidden in Zeid's case, but he saw the difficulty of bringing a Moonship girl to the planet—and he always felt that his work lay on the planet. If you want to win Zeid, come along and show him you understand Moonship work."

"Well, it would be interesting to hear more than Zeid has told me, but I'd rather go along to be made beautiful, Lady Lovisa."

"No beauty without learning, pirate girl! And your first lesson is that only a barbaric planet calls Space visitors lords and ladies. We tolerate the form of address because it belongs to your present stage of development."

"But even the Moonship has divisions of rank."

"*Earned* rank. Thus you must say Doctor Marnadal and Envoy Rogg. But no more lords and ladies."

"Very well, Lovisa."

MEANWHILE TOMMY LUND WAS reviving Zeid. He took a small box from his coverall, drew out a needle, found the vein in Zeid's arm and inserted the needle.

In a few seconds Zeid awoke. He stared up at the figure standing over him. "Tommy! How did—?" He sat up but the heavy wateriness in his head choked him. He held a robe to his streaming eyes.

"Take it easy," said Tommy. "The shot will work in a minute."

"Who called you?"

"Coral Bud. It seems she tricked the code words from a Seacoast merchant, some time ago."

"Knarb, I suppose. There's nothing that old pirate can't find the secret of."

"Knarb and Coral Bud aren't the only people with secrets. How come you got so close to Feelafell?"

"Feelafell?"

"Coral Bud thought you were overtired and suffering from mists and chill. Overtiredness probably triggered the germs, but you must have caught them from one of us, and Feelafell is the only carrier on the planet. As the saying is, we can cross the galaxy, but we can't cure a cold."

"So this is what you guys were always taking shots for!" moaned Zeid.

"Yeah—and it sure hit you hard. Did you touch Feelafell?"

"I knocked him off the sloop. He came in a damned minisub and tried to snatch Coral Bud. I never expected—! I charged out—forgot even the laser gun—!"

"You'll have to detour to the satellite in order to brief the Board on Feelafell. The incident couldn't have come at a worse time. Marnadal is already on the pan for allowing him—and the planet generally—too much freedom."

"Somebody came out from home base?"

"Yeah. Envoy Rogg. He wants to accelerate the plateau jumps."

"That's how the planet got loused up to begin with—telescoping historical plateaus. Rogg can't force the planet's masses to march to his drum."

"He favors enlightenment by decree, and he thinks Feelafell should have been locked up years ago. Now it looks as if he was right."

"It's never right to assume the worst, Tommy. Feelafell seems to have inherited the worst traits from both parents—but he could just as easily have inherited the best from the genetic grab bag. Rogg is as prejudiced and ruthless as Coral Bud.

"Speaking of which," he added, "we'll have to take the sea urchin with us. Otherwise she'll sabotage all my plans for Fire Lotus."

"Marnadal is interested in seeing Hamar's daughter. Hamar is a new type of man, you know—a despot unconsciously building democratic government through his free ship companies. Lovisa Cox descended with me to persuade Coral Bud to come along."

"Why Lovisa? She's a data analyst, not too skillful with people."

"She was on the Monitor when Coral Bud called."

Zeid got to his feet, draped in robes. "Let me throw on some clothes, and I'll be with you. Climb aboard Hamar's palace and find a servant, Tommy. I'll have to leave instructions for Moji and Nevyev."

CORAL BUD FOLLOWED LOVISA into the Cloud—and stopped with a chill at the alien plainness. She was standing inside a hollow silver sphere—at least, Coral Bud thought the light gray metal was silver. There were six cushioned chairs in a circle facing a low console of operating rods.

She was used to benches and stools in her father's sea kingdom, but her first sight of chairs made her feel restricted, enclosed. She asked, "Where must I sit?"

"Anywhere. Make yourself at home."

"At home would be on a deck cushion," she smiled. She sat primly in a chair as Lovisa had sat on the divan, legs straight down.

Almost immediately she sprang up. "My clothing box!"

"Never mind." Lovisa sat beside her, half turned to face her. "We have plenty of disposables on the Moonship."

Coral Bud sat down again. "What are disposables?"

"Clothing that is worn once and then recycled—shredded, pulped, rolled into sheets, cut into lengths like the cloth sold in the bazaars, and made once more into clothing. Recycling takes less water than washing and rinsing."

"And, of course, water is always a problem aboard a ship, even a Moonship." Coral Bud glanced at Lovisa's white coverall. "Doubtless very fine Magic—but it must cause hardship among the fullers and dyers, the weavers, embroiderers, beaders, and gilders—"

"Decoration for its own sake has no place on the Moonship."

"No place for beauty?"

"There is beauty of line and beauty of function. In its way, the Cloud is very beautiful."

"Do you think so? To me it is very empty and strange. But then, the *Whizzard*'s cabin would have been strange to you."

"Yes, the patterns and rich fabrics seemed what we call *too busy*—too demanding on the eye and mind."

"Any pleasure demands attention, even the pleasure of contemplating beauty. But I forget—the Moonship contemplates other things."

She heard movement at the doorway and turned to see Zeid and Tommy Lund entering. She had to smile at the contrast between the bearded, wool-clad prince, and the taller, white-clad Space Giver. Zeid was wearing his coding belt and Combi-shot, but had left the other hardware on the sloop.

"Lovisa, hello again," he smiled, coming over to Lovisa and taking her hand before joining Tommy Lund across the circle. Coral Bud noticed how easily he dropped into the chair, resting an elbow on the chair arm, and carelessly drawing one leg across the knee of the other.

The Cloud door closed. Tommy Lund touched an operating

rod. Coral Bud could feel the Cloud being lifted swiftly. Zeid smiled at her, "Scared?"

"Of course not! It must be fun to travel to other worlds. I'm sorry I didn't go aloft like the other children."

Lund said, "You may choose a Gift now, Coral Bud."

"The Moonship can have nothing for a pirate."

"What about gold?"

"Oh, we already have gold, and your gold is no different from ours because the Great Wizard seeded all the worlds the same. Even on Discord's world gold is gold, but it isn't pure and has to be dug out of stone or washed from sands."

"Discord?"

Zeid interrupted, "Put us on Hold, Tommy. I see Coral Bud has another story of how the worlds came into being. You may think that a rainbow is light scattered by water, but Coral Bud has convinced me otherwise."

Lund touched the controls again. Coral Bud, not knowing whether or not Zeid was making fun of her, sat stiffly in her chair. Zeid said, "Tell us another story, sea urchin."

"Perhaps it will not amuse the Space Givers as much as it would amuse you."

Lovisa spoke up, "Indeed, Coral Bud, you already have said so many interesting things that I really would like to hear the story."

Coral Bud, who really wanted to tell it, began, "I must explain that Discord was the Great Wizard's youngest son, who snatched seeds for a world of his own, but made it all crooked. His brothers Truth and Justice were angry and tried to right the world, but they only added drought and famine.

"So the Wizard asked his daughters Happiness and Harmony to visit Discord's world. The lovely sisters traveled everywhere, and when all the creatures saw Happiness smile and heard Harmony sing, they forgot that they lived only by devouring each other.

"But after the sisters were gone, the world was bleak again. Happiness and Harmony were very sad that they had not been able to do more good. 'We have our own kingdoms,' said Happiness, 'but perhaps we can take turns walking the world.'

"They talked the matter over, and the first turn came to Harmony. She said to herself, 'One creature alone can't be harmonious. Everyone must be taught to make music together.'

"Not all the creatures listened to her. Because the Great Wizard had gathered the colors together, the plants and trees knew themselves to be perfectly beautiful, and beauty is a silent kind of harmony. That is why a blue flower can grow next to a red one, and both will please the eye.

"Also the fish and lizards and snakes did not think music would make them more harmonious, but the air-breathing sea creatures basked on the water and listened to Harmony. She gave them notes to sing, and when they dived beneath the waves they repeated the notes together and forgot their imperfections and sorrows.

"The birds, too, found enjoyment in exchanging songs—except large, vain birds like the peacocks, who wanted to be alone to admire themselves.

"The animals said, 'We must be silent, for we are either stalking or being stalked, and music could betray us.' So when the tiger screams or the wolf howls, they are not trying to be harmonious. And though cats may *try* to be harmonious when they sing love songs to each other, Harmony closes her ears and runs away.

"Mankind, which had more leisure than the beasts, readily learned the notes Harmony taught them. They sang together and fashioned instruments. But Mankind also had more leisure to be miserable, so when the song was over, they were as hopeless as before.

"Harmony, having done all she could, went home and left to Happiness the task of making Mankind less miserable and discontented. Since Mankind could talk and reason, Happiness said to them, 'You feel my warming glow. Why do you let it fade?' And they said, 'We can't seem to make our own happiness.'

"'Aha, that's the trouble!' she said. 'You can make happiness only for others, never for yourself!'

"This did not suit Mankind, who said, 'If we do someone else a kindness, he may cheat us or even kill us in return. We had better grab what we can and forget others.'

"However, a few people *did* try to make other people happy

and were happy in the reflected glow—until they were cheated or otherwise disappointed, and then they stopped trying.

"So Happiness went to the Great Wizard and said, 'You must send yet another child to Discord's world.' And the Wizard said, 'My dear daughter, you know very well I have no more children. Whom can I send?'

"'That is for you to determine. Mankind *can* create happiness, but he needs a reason to do so, against all he knows and fears.'

"So the Great Wizard sought out Time—but that's another story, and I'm sure we must be at the Moonship."

Lund smiled, "We would have been there in a moment, but I halted us to let you speak. Look here."

A window opened in the Cloud, and Coral Bud saw the Moonship hanging in the spangled sky. She cried out in surprise, "Why, it's a bright ring turning around, with canals leading to the center!"

"It's a *wheel*, Coral Bud. On your planet all your transportation goes by waterway or beast. You use the wheel-principle for grinding grain or molding pottery—but a cartwheel is unknown."

"A wheel!" exclaimed Coral Bud. "Of such simple things is Magic made."

Lund reset the rods. The wheel seemed to rush swiftly toward the Cloud.

Coral Bud watched eagerly. It was more exciting than skimming before the wind in a hard-driving sloop. Nearer—nearer—

She felt a jog. Her mind and heart seemed to leap over a count of time. The window merged into a smooth silver wall. They had arrived.

She gave a little hop of pleasure and was aware of a silence. The others were studying her. She asked, "Have I neglected an arrival rite?"

Lund said, "You weren't afraid of crashing into the wheel."

"Well, it should be plain that a Cloud never crashes since the Space Givers travel without harm. But it was unwise of you to leave the window open, if you expected me to be afraid," she continued with mock gravity. "I could have died of terror!"

"I took a chance," grinned Lund. "I figured you were a feisty kid."

"I see. Now that I'm on the Moonship, everyone will be watching me and wondering what I will do—as a small boy will find a new caterpillar on a leaf and will take it to his friends, and they lay aside their sticks and whirl-tops, and shake the leaf and blow on the little creature and prod him with their fingers to see how he moves."

The others laughed. Zeid's lustrous eyes gleamed so fondly at her for a moment that her heart skipped a beat.

Lund opened the silver wall. Beyond was nothing but a bare chamber. He said, "I thought I'd better bring you to the isolation airlock, Zeid."

Zeid nodded. "Coral Bud touched Feelafell also, and she's had no shots. Maybe she ought to be isolated."

"Well, Zeid, it looks as if the shots we gave you up here backfired and made you susceptible to the virus. Normally the planet's people are immune. There's no reason to isolate Coral Bud."

Zeid's fond but rueful glance touched her again. "You'll find out there's reason enough, Tommy, when it's too late!"

After Zeid had stepped into the small chamber, Lund closed the Cloud. He said to Coral Bud, "I think I can program us into an empty slot alongside the bazaar. It's fun to look at anyhow."

There was a slighter jog, and Lund once more opened the Cloud.

Coral Bud looked out into a bazaar that seemed to stretch endlessly on either hand. It was lit by a steady glow that came from everywhere, yet nowhere. Stalls of rich merchandise, their counters at child-height, were being beseiged by noisy, excited children. The stalls had such heaps of so many things that Coral Bud did not at first see the lamps that illuminated the corners of the larger stalls.

"Come, Coral Bud," said Lovisa. "Don't let the children knock you over. They seem to want to run everywhere at once."

"They're in a hurry to find what their parents have sent them to fetch," said Coral Bud, following Lovisa into the bazaar.

Lovisa stopped. "What do you mean?"

"Well, Lovisa, although my father saved me from your snares, I've spoken to his crewmen, and they all had followed their parents' wishes in their bazaar choices.

"For, you see, it is now many generations since the Space Givers put the Moonship in the sky, and all know what the bazaar contains. If the first ancestor chose a gold belt, his father took it from him and bought land—and then a younger brother was instructed to choose a Space plow—and the daughter a Magic cooking pot.

"And, in their turn, the children directed *their* children, thus— 'I inherited my father's Space plow, so you, my son, must come with the heaviest gold belt, so we may increase our land.'

"Among the lords and wizards, who need nothing from the bazaar, the children perhaps choose as they will. Otherwise the choices merely show which families are wise enough to balance gold with useful objects, for gold is soon spent but a Space plow ever blesses a farm."

Lovisa said, "No one—not even Zeid—has told us that such was the case."

"What would the Wizard Amfi's son know of common needs? And I must say, Lovisa, your home planet must be badly run if all children have their own way."

Lovisa put both hands to her bouffant coiffure and smiled wryly.

Coral Bud's sharp eyes caught a sameness repeated and diminishing. "I see now that the bazaar is not so large. You've enclosed it with mirrors."

"To prevent a panic we call claustrophobia. The children know that a Cloud is enclosed, like the walls of their dwellings, but when they emerge they expect to see open fields or open desert. However, if the bazaar is made to seem vast, they assume the fields lie beyond, and they think no more about it."

The Space girl consulted a bracelet on her left arm. "It is afternoon on the Moonship, but we took you from evening on the planet. We can now go to my dwelling so that you can sleep your usual hours and join our time tomorrow."

"I would be pleased to see your dwelling, Lovisa, but pirates keep long watches and do not have usual hours, so I will join your afternoon at once. I have many things to ask you—and most important is, how can I turn Zeid's love wholly to myself?"

"Alas, Coral Bud," sighed Lovisa, "if I had such knowledge, I would long ago have captured Tommy Lund's heart!"

"Oh? Is he also bedazzled by a harpy?"

"*Harpy* is a bit strong. Tommy never has been serious about any girl. Nowadays, like the rest of the males on the satellite, he's playing around with a hip-wiggler named Ravella who's in Space-coding."

"Hip-wiggler?"

Lovisa minced forward with exaggerated hip swinging.

Coral Bud's merry laugh rang out even over the din of the children. "Yes, thus do the seamen ape the walk of street girls who please them. I don't think Zeid was as quiet on the Moonship as he wants us to believe."

THE MOONSHIP WAS LIKE nothing Coral Bud had ever seen. Behind the bazaar mirrors was a broad street as if a palace landing place stretched forever. In the middle of the street was a broad rail upon which a chain of oval silvery boxes rolled, stopping now and then to let off or take on Space Givers. The buildings which lined the street were walled in opaque glass sheets of various colors and blazoned with lines of seal-marks.

"How busy your Counting Masters must be," marveled Coral Bud. "When Knarb set up shop, all the Counting Guilds on the planet had to be consulted before his seal was approved—a sea hawk clutching a fish.

"I've long contemplated a mark of my own—a coral fan edged with pearls," Coral Bud went on, "but since my father betrothed me to Zeid—"

"Why should a betrothal make a difference?" asked Lovisa. "I'm surprised Zeid would make a fuss about his wife keeping her own seal-mark."

"Oh, he doesn't know of my wish in the matter. We seem to talk around each other." Coral Bud paused, conscious of her shorter stature, her long, untamed tresses. "I'm tired of being a planet girl who never can be as beautiful as Fire Lotus. Would it be forbidden for me to cut off my hair and look like a Space Giver?"

"Of course not. But your hair is so lovely, Coral Bud."

"Fire Lotus's is lovelier. Off with it!"

She pulled her knife from her belt as if about to shear herself at once. Lovisa said, "My goodness, don't do anything rash. We can stop at a hair stylist on the way to my apartment. None of them will be too busy to work with such lovely raw material."

The next two hours were like nothing Coral Bud had ever experienced. The staff of the beauty shop, being given this fine clay from the planet, spun it expertly on their wheels and made it into a matchless vessel. Coral Bud was mist-bathed, lotion-smoothed, clad in white Space Giver garments. Her shorn hair, curling of itself after a foamy shampoo, was styled with a Magic staff so that her forehead seemed higher and her pretty ears, peeking out from under the artful curls, teased the observer's eye.

"How light my head feels!" she exclaimed to Lovisa as they left the shop. "What a useless weight was hanging down my back. Zeid would do more for the planet by building such useful shops, instead of beggars' hostels."

Lovisa lived in a green glass building. She and Coral Bud entered a small glass chamber that moved upwards two decks and stopped.

"I wish we had this Magic on the castle-ships," said Coral Bud.

A door slid aside at Lovisa's bidding. They stepped into a chamber where the front wall was like transparent green water. A "cluttered" chamber, reflected Coral Bud, who thought the scattered chairs and high tables were very ugly.

She set down the bundle of her clothes which she had carried from the shop, moved to the transparent wall, and gazed down at the busy street.

"It's fun to see and not be seen," she smiled. "Imagine, that glass can be solid one way and empty the other."

"Your bedroom and bath are to the left, through the archway," said Lovisa. "You must be tired—planet time would have been nearly midnight. I'll order a meal, and then you can go to bed."

"Oh, I'm not the least tired. Midnight? The princess Fire Lotus will yet be at her revels. And I'm now in truth a crop-haired page. May I mirror-speak her, Lovisa?"

Lovisa looked uncertain, then smiled. "I *am* curious. If you promise not to discuss the Moonship—"

"Be easy. The princess wishes all discussion to center upon herself." Coral Bud took a deep, happy breath. "And now let us set a Moonship stew to simmering in the cookstove."

The room had two glass fronted cabinets. Lovisa went to one which had three buttons beside the window. She pushed the left-hand button. The cabinet lit up, and lines of seal-marks began sliding down the glass, past a red arrow. A second push on the button stopped the seal-marks. Lovisa turned the second button two clicks to the right and pressed it.

The window cleared—and suddenly a rack holding two plates of food, the one above the other, appeared in the cabinet.

"Why doesn't Zeid bring such Magic to the planet instead of a deadly poniard?" wondered Coral Bud.

"Because he'd have to bring the cooks and the kitchen," said Lovisa.

She set the plates on the table, and Coral Bud dutifully sat on a chair. For a moment her eyes sparkled with pleasure. Then she shuddered and jumped away from the table.

Lovisa gave a start of surprise. "What's the matter?"

"'Twas thus that Feelafell tried to poison us," faltered Coral Bud. "Oh, beware of platters that come by themselves!"

"What a planet," smiled Lovisa. "You poor kid. There's nothing to fear. The plates came from a kitchen where poison never enters—and were delivered by Magic that can't tell one box from another."

Coral Bud thought a moment, then sat down again. "I see no bread to eat it with. And I must fetch my knife."

Lovisa unrolled the white napkin clamped to the side of the plate. "Knife—fork—spoon."

"This is all very strange. Show me how to use the pronged weapon."

Lovisa showed her how to use the fork. She began to eat, hesitant at first, then with increasing gusto.

"The fowl meat is indeed delicious, though sparsely doled out," she commented. "The herb-and-bread pudding is new to me, as is your way of crushing the mealy root. I like the little soft green pebbles, but they *are* difficult to chase over the platter. Did it take Zeid a long while to eat with skill?"

"He came to the Moonship as a child, remember. He's really one of us."

But he was also, reflected Coral Bud, very much a Desert prince.

After the plates had been put back in the box and sent away by a push of the third button, the girls set about calling Fire Lotus.

"I'll have to place the call through the Monitor," explained Lovisa, "and it will be recorded and maybe replayed before the Board. Do you understand?"

"I think so. Zeid has already spoken of reh-kords and vyu-ors. I but jest with the princess and care not who sees me. However, say only that the Moonship is calling. Have you a sash I can bind around my head the way pages do?"

Lovisa found a scarf among her off-duty wardrobe. While Coral Bud wound it around her new curls, Lovisa approached the second glassed cabinet, put the call through the Monitor, and stepped aside. Coral Bud sat in the chair that was positioned in front of the console.

The glass cleared. The fat page peered out. "Well, we have Sir Insolence! With Moonship fabric on his shoulders! What the prince's chamberlain told us was true after all."

"You've spoken to Nevyev?"

"But a short while ago. He had just taken the prince's place aboard the command ship. He is most chatty about bronzes, as if he wished to peddle them at the palace."

"Yes, he was robbed in a business deal and has a shipload of Crucible wares on his hands. He bores us with his lamentings—and does not even realize the worth of the wares he wishes to be quit of. I intend to make my own profit from those bronzes, butterball, so keep your sticky fingers from the cargo."

A sly look came and went in the page's eyes, and Coral Bud knew there would be a rush to buy all the bronzes Nevyev wanted to sell in the Marble Lands. She proceeded, "Is your princess at her revels?"

"If you can compose yourself to wait, she would talk with you. Summoning. . . ."

This time the screen hazed for several minutes before Fire Lotus appeared. Her barbaric splendor blazed from the view screen. She was wearing a tiara of diamonds from the blue clay shafts in the Sky Chutes. Diamonds dangled and danced from her ears, and her fair bosom was bound in a net of brilliants.

"Sweet page! At last the prince sends a message I accept."

"Accept himself—and I follow along."

"Why follow, when you could lead?"

"Nay, fair princess—a prince must come first."

"I would rather they didn't come at all since they send me better gifts from a distance. Does Zeid amass more wealth on the Moonship?"

"Since he doesn't need more wealth, he amasses honor—but not as much as myself, you understand."

"What have you done?"

"I tell you only the truth, beautiful lady. On the way here, the Cloud paused in mid-flight solely for my convenience."

"I wonder that you took the prince with you."

"Oh, I have to humor him. It looks better."

"You have a dreary job. He never has anything witty to say."

"I fear he has more wisdom than wit."

"How does he give proof of wisdom?"

"By keeping me to supply the wit."

"He spoke as if he wanted to palm you off on a sea king."

"Well, he has his moods—but a page such as I—"

"Can shape and turn moods as if they were clay bowls. What's your name?"

"Whatever you wish, beautiful one. Tell me, when we meet in the Marble Lands. Until then, think kindly of us."

Coral Bud quickly reached toward the console and turned off the knob she had observed Lovisa turning on. The tube darkened, and Coral Bud got up from the chair.

Lovisa commented, "So that's the enticing bit of flesh Zeid is in love with."

"Infatuated with because of deep conflicts within himself. A prince, he naturally feels more at home with a princess. A man with a message, he dreams of a woman with the power to persuade other rulers. And, of course, Lovisa, the Moonship is rich in Magic and great thoughts—but poor in objects upon which the senses can feed."

"That is why," Coral Bud went on, "I would rather look like a Moonship girl. As a planet girl, I have no chance against the princess."

"Yes, Fire Lotus is gorgeous. Your strategy is very sensible. What will you do next?"

"Sleep. The morrow will bring new battles."

Although Coral Bud had insisted that she was not tired out by the time-lag, she slept late the next morning. When she woke she realized she was listening to the silence of empty chambers. She bathed, dressed in the day's disposable clothing, and went out to the front chamber.

Her first thought was breakfast. She went directly to the food cabinet. Perhaps Lovisa had summoned a plate for her before leaving the apartment.

No. A white square with seal-marks was pasted at the top of the glass door. By itself at the top was BREAKFAST. The line underneath said: FRUIT, MUFFINS, JAM, COFFEE.

A game, thought Coral Bud, a challenge! She remembered Zeid saying that the Space Givers used combinations of unvarying seal-marks. She had to look first for a nine-space seal-mark with the double-bellied hieroglyph.

She pressed the left-hand button on the cabinet and watched the symbols rotate past the arrow. BREAKFAST flashed upon her. Like lightning, her hand stopped the list. But a further line was needed.

She set the list again in slow rotation. She reacted swiftly to FRUIT, BACON . . . FRUIT, HAM . . . FRUIT, POACHED EGG . . . and rejected each in turn. When the correctly matching line rolled into view, she stopped it with a shriek of joy and a little hop.

Her hand reached to press the second button—and stopped.

She remembered the two clicks Lovisa had given the button before turning it. Why? Two clicks—two plates?

She turned the button clockwise one click and pressed it.

A laden tray appeared in the cabinet. She drew it out. A dark liquid still bubbled in a glass carafe. There was a half-round of a yellow fruit, the inside cut into juicy wedges. There were fluffy cakes and a bowl of red berry preserves.

Such a sumptuous meal could not be eaten at a hard, ugly table! Coral Bud started to carry the tray to the front glass wall. As she went past the table she noticed five piles of intricately cut fragments upon it. She set down the tray and peered at this new game.

Each pile had a different number of abacus beads beside it. The smallest pile of thin tongue-and-groove fragments had one bead. The pile of heavy, curiously carved chunks had five. The beads could only indicate the sequence in which the game must be played.

She spread out the thin fragments. They were blank on one side and color patterned on the other. The patterning distracted her from the carved shapes. She turned all the pieces to the blank side and studied them. Surely the long sword hilt fitted here—and the sail corner fitted there.

As fast as her fingers could move, she fitted the puzzle pieces together. But what did the other side look like? Carefully she flopped the puzzle over. A baby animal with long, silky ears and big brown eyes was staring at her.

She laughed with delight. But her breakfast was getting cold. Forgetting her dislike of chairs, she sat at the table and drew the second puzzle toward her so she could study it while she ate.

The puzzle and the breakfast were done at the same time. She returned the tray to the food cabinet and sent it back to the kitchen in order to clear the table for the third puzzle. Why hadn't Zeid brought these fascinating games to the planet?

She was fitting together the last puzzle, a three-dimensional box, when she heard the jingling of chimes. She wondered what Magic they signified. A banging came from the entrance to the chambers. She went out to the hall. Tommy Lund was hammering on the panel.

How to open the door? She gestured, but the Space Giver was on the solid side of the glass and could not see her. She banged back at him. He pointed to a side wall. She stepped to it and looked.

There were two knobs. She seized one and pushed. No. Pull? No. Twist? No. Did it move at all? Yes, it snapped down.

The Space lamp above her head darkened. Really, Magic was very tiring, when on the planet all one had to do was to say, "Ho, slave! Do thus-and-so!"

She snapped the lamp on again and tried the second knob. The door panel slid aside.

Tommy Lund strolled into the chambers. He opened his mouth, took a second look at her, and blurted. "Who cut off your beautiful hair?"

"I did. And I feel so refreshed that I'm like a new person. Bid the door close, and come into the audience chamber. But you must be very quiet while I finish the game Lovisa left for me."

They went into the sitting room. Tommy glanced at the completed puzzles. "Have you masterd all but the last?"

"Oh, I will master *that*!"

She sat down again and seized the last pieces. Tommy sat beside her and watched her assemble the cube. He commented, "You do as well as Zeid."

She fitted the last piece and said, "Then Zeid is much more intelligent than I because he mastered the games without practice."

"How could you practice since the planet has no such puzzles?"

"Space lord, it is easy to see that your cooking pots and flagons never break—or that you throw them away rather than mend them. A ship, too, has earthenware dishes, and when a storm throws them about and breaks them to shards, they must be mended and refired because pirate cooks cannot hasten to a bazaar to buy new.

"So often have I helped the cook with his mending that these puzzles are child's play for me, whereas they were supposed, I think, to test my wits.

"But let us sit comfortably on the carpet," she added. "Chairs are a foolish invention, weakening the spine, stiffening the legs, stopping the circulation of blood to the feet. It's no wonder Space Givers need Magic to keep them alive."

"I don't have time to sit around anywhere, Coral Bud. Marnadal told me to summon you and Lovisa to the Board meeting this afternoon, and I thought I'd come in person to ask how everything is going."

"Each thing goes so differently. Some Moonship ways I like, and some I don't like."

"I don't like your haircut. Instead of a soft waterfall that would cover a man's face with dreams, you have little squeaky bubbles of curls!"

Before she knew what he was doing, his hand gently tugged a curl and let it spring back.

She blushed but could not find words to reproach him since she knew he meant her no harm.

A sound made them look around. Lovisa was standing there. Lund rose immediately. He said, "'Morning, Lovisa. Marnadal wants you girls at the Board meeting today."

"Very well, Tommy. Will Zeid be there?"

"Yes, the Infirmary is releasing him for the afternoon. They want him back for more blood samples though."

Tommy nodded to both girls, said, "Don't work too hard," and left the apartment.

Coral Bud put her hands to her still hot cheeks. "Truly, Lovisa, he was but jesting at my expense."

"No. Girls like you have a quality I lack—*it,* as we say in our language. I guess that's why I became a data analyst. I love Tommy, but I never know what to say to him, least of all how to win him away from the *it*-charmers."

Coral Bud smiled. "I can't advise you about Moonship love— and you can't advise me about planet love. I think, though, I would *do* something. As my father Hamar says, 'if you have the courage to give battle, you have at least the chance of winning.'"

THE ENTIRE SEQUENCE OF events in Lovisa's sitting room had been recorded by the communication console and instantly replayed upon the large wall screen in the Monitor Room. A scattering of Board members sat at the long, semicircular table.

When Tommy Lund disappeared from the screen, the white-haired, calm-faced Space Giver at the center of the table shut off the viewing and said to a younger, bald-headed man,

"I don't like to spy on my own people, Envoy Rogg, but at your insistence I have done so. What have we learned that we didn't already know?"

"Dr. Marnadal, the girl is as intelligent as Zeid ben Amfi."

"The native intelligence generally is of a high order. A planet advances not by intelligence alone but by perception of civilizing goals. Zeid is thinking in terms of ultimate plateaus."

"He's a Utopian!" snapped Rogg.

"He's leaven that will lighten the whole loaf."

"You're criminally lax about everything," complained Rogg. "The planet goes its way—Zeid goes his way—young Lund makes a pass at the pirate girl—"

"Par for Lund's course," smiled Marnadal, and the other Board members laughed.

Rogg glared, and Marnadal said, "We beg young people to come out here and be trained in the monitoring work. Therefore, we must allow them to be young—to have their romances and behave much as they would behave on the planet. Tommy is an engaging rascal—and so was Zeid—but they're dedicated to the project."

"There you go, completely ignoring the danger of mixing planet genes and Moonship genes. Either Lund or the prince could beget another Feelafell."

"Both! Feelafell could happen on any planet."

"Well, he's the result of what your laxness has permitted on this one."

"The true result of letting the planet set its own pace is Hamar, who is evolving a type of democracy within his sea kingdom. Under the restrictive policies you advocate, Envoy Rogg, Hamar would have been suppressed and democracy would have been stillborn. Freedom is the only road to civilization."

"Freedom is an inefficient bumbling from one course to another. Meanwhile, since Prince Zeid seems to have bumbled upon Feelafell's deceptions, what do you intend to do about the Space Bastard?"

"I intend to listen to Zeid this afternoon and perhaps to Hamar's daughter. It's *their* planet. You militant reformers who want to boot me out keeping forgetting that."

CORAL BUD WAS EAGER to live up to her Space Giver appearance. "You must tell me the necessary ceremony for this afternoon's meeting," she said to Lovisa. "The greetings and bowings—"

"There's no ceremony," smiled Lovisa. "We'll be seated in a visitor's arc at the end of the table. When Dr. Marnadal and the day's speakers come to the center arc, we rise briefly, then sit again.

"If you're asked a question," she went on, "remain seated and press down the green square at your place so your voice will be heard. Observe how the others address the Board and use the same terms."

"Thank you. I hope all will approve of me."

Lovisa brought Coral Bud to the Monitor Room early. Coral Bud sat at her place, tried out the green audio squares, giggled at the sound of her own voice, and settled into quiet decorum as the Board Members drifted into the chamber.

She noticed that not all Space Givers were as tall—or as bald—as Feelafell. She looked with interest at Dr. Marnadal who entered with two other Space Givers. One, indeed, was bald as a clam shell and looked cranky. The other was a young man whose clean-shaven jaw seemed pale. As he spoke with Dr. Marnadal, his lustrous dark eyes scanned the table.

Coral Bud's heart jumped. It was Zeid—no longer a bearded Desert prince, but a Space Giver! His chin was blunter than a Space Giver chin, his bone structure was heavier, his brow more defined—but his expression and bearing were no different from those of his colleagues.

His casual glance slid over Coral Bud without recognition. Her short curls and white coverall disguised her completely.

She rose with the others, sat down, and waited eagerly to find out what Zeid would be saying.

Dr. Marnadal called the meeting to order. He smiled toward the visitor's arc and said, "Today let us speak in the planet's tongue. It will be good practice."

Zeid, frowning over written notes, nodded absent-mindedly and did not look up.

Marnadal continued, "Board members, you have been called to this special meeting because Envoy Rogg wishes to address you on a policy matter."

Rogg cleared his throat. He was not as fluent in the planet's language as those who worked on the Moonship. "I protest the indolence and indulgence that has let Feelafell become a menace. He should have been removed from the planet as a child and kept in a far haven. Feelafell is only one matter. If the planet is to go forward, other evils will have to be removed, forcibly if necessary—the parthogen bottles, the assassin bands, the raiders and pirates.

"Dr. Marnadal defends Hamar because he, by chance, is inventing democracy. If we post guards upon the planet and enforce our laws, we can establish democracy without fostering pirates.

"Board members, you've supported Marnadal's indifference long enough. Let's go down to the planet with laws that will refashion it in a generation."

There was a silence. Marnadal said, "Prince Zeid, may we have your opinion?"

Zeid's sober, confident voice began, "Dr. Marnadal, Envoy Rogg, and Board members. Once before, the Space Givers tried to refashion the planet in a generation. I don't need to remind you of the havoc. Since that time, by slow and careful steps, agriculture and basic industries have been brought to the threshold of the Iron Age.

"But social innovations can't come faster than the planet's resources can support them. Yes, Hamar can have independent companies of free men voting how they will share their spoils because each man has been trained to support himself at sea.

"But what of the Desert Cities? Envoy Rogg, I could draw my Combi-shot and enforce equality within my father's palace. With what result? Nobody there has been trained in productive work. Once the palace's wealth was divided and consumed, everybody would starve.

"Don't mistake patient tolerance for weakness. The Moonship must tolerate whatever the planet tolerates—and understand when enforcement is possible. Thus I can order the execution of a child maimer—but cannot destroy the Assassins Guild.

"Dr. Marnadal is allowing me to demonstrate workable improvements—to show that the living standard is raised fastest when people help each other. A prosperous population will police itself because everybody has much to lose by civil disorders.

"To come specifically to Feelafell, Envoy Rogg, all you're saying is that hindsight is better than foresight."

Rogg interrupted, "There has always been a law against Moonship-planet matings."

"Yes—to prevent strife over status and privilege or wars between native sons and Moonship sons. But Feelafell was always judged as an individual. Until now he did not give evidence of serious instability. And we don't really know the extent of his activities. It is unwise to hew down the trunk of a tree before investigating how deep and far the roots have traveled.

"Board members," concluded Zeid, "I speak in favor of caution, tolerance, free planetary growth. Beware of repeating the mistakes that tried to force too much civilization too soon!"

Marnadal said, "Thank you, Zeid. But Hamar's daughter is also here. Let her speak. Coral Bud—?"

Zeid had given a start. His glance flew across the table curve, and his eyes widened.

Coral Bud dared not look at him. She pressed the green speak-square and began bravely, "Dok-tor Marnadal, En-voy Rogg, and Board members. A gathering of this sort is new to me, though all are free to express opinions at my father's supper board. I know nothing of what is best for a planet. Indeed, so ignorant was I that a few days ago I might have agreed with En-voy Rogg."

The irony came as too much of a surprise to provoke laughter. Coral Bud continued, "There is great weight to establish customs as long as people abide in them. No outside force can shake them. But as Lord Zeid says, when people start helping and teaching each other, they live in new customs and think new thoughts. The old customs are emptied and fall of themselves.

"Truly, had I been able to draw my knife, I would have cut Feelafell's throat and gloried in the deed. But now I perceive how hasty and foolish I would have been. The trunk would have been dead, but what of the hidden roots?

"Therefore, having been made so much wiser by this journey to the Marble Lands, I would agree with Lord Zeid. If it is Doktor Marnadal who has so gently watched over the planet, I would thank him and beg him to continue. Board members, you have a great leader!"

Breathless, she released the speak-square. There was applause, and voice after voice voted, "Marnadal—record me for Marnadal—"

The Monitor chief said, "Thank you, members. Meeting dismissed."

The gathering rose, but Coral Bud sat in a kind of shock at her own temerity. Lovisa smiled and patted her hand.

Zeid came over. "Sea urchin! I should have realized you were present when Marnadal conducted the meeting in your language."

She looked up at him. "It's also your language, well?"

"Yes, yes. What mad whim caused you to cut your hair?"

"The same mad whim that made you shave your beard."

"A beard is inconvenient in illness."

"Then why didn't you cut it off aboard the sloop? No, Zeid, a beard is for head scarves and brocaded robes, just as long tresses look best with harem gauze. We're both well quit them. I've decided to live like a Space Giver girl."

"I forbid you to live like a Moonship girl!"

"Aha! I see you are thinking of the hip-wiggling Ravella."

Zeid eyed Lovisa. "What have you been telling her?"

"Nothing about you and Ravella."

"Anyhow," Coral Bud was continuing, "you have no right to forbid me anything since we are no longer betrothed."

"We're betrothed until I can find a place worthy of Hamar's daughter! A Space girl—I never heard such nonsense. Marnadal bids us to supper to discuss how Feelafell can be handled without rousing Rogg again. Lovisa is to come also, and Tommy Lund. Try to stay out of mischief until then."

Zeid strode away.

Coral Bud smiled to herself. Zeid was at last talking directly to her. He was quarreling with her in the same familiar way he quarreled with Fire Lotus.

THE SPACE GIVERS HAD not intended the satellite to be anybody's permanent home. It was a field of foreign service, one of many in the galaxy. The original apartments on the wheel were very much like Lovisa's—similar to those on the home planet with the same furnishings.

However, as researchers and diplomats who were genuinely interested in the Bronze Age planet chose long-term employment on the satellite, the character of their residences began to change. The more comfortable and sensuous divans and cushions replaced the rigid chairs. Except for a wall unit of necessary computerized consoles, Dr. Marnadal's sitting room could have been a chamber in the Wizard's palace.

Marnadal welcomed his four young guests jovially. "I've ordered a mix-and-match feast. You Moonshippers can bring it from the box while Coral Bud and I take our places."

Filling the middle of the dining room carpet was a low round table already laid with plates and utensils. Cushions bought in the planet's bazaars were scattered around it. Coral Bud exclaimed with pleasure and plumped herself down where Marnadal indicated. She noted that the table held a small box with a green speak-square at Marnadal's place.

"What is mix-and-match?" she asked when Marnadal had settled beside her.

"Newcomers to the Moonship think our food box contains infinite variety," he smiled, "but they soon discover that baked ham always comes with sweet potato, and baked fish is tied to spinach. Thus, on special occasions, we order platters in advance, and the diner can mix the selections for themselves."

"And they still match ham and sweet potatoes," said Tommy Lund, setting a large platter of sliced meats on the table.

Lovisa came with a platter mounded high with vegetables. Marnadal courteously motioned her to the cushions on the other side. As she had done on the *Whizzard,* she sat uncomfortably, as if something within her strove against relaxing too much.

Zeid paused with the platter of greens and fruits since the table now had little space left.

Tommy sat beside Coral Bud and pushed dishes out of the way. "Plenty of room, Zeid! Now, Coral Bud, you must try one of everything so you can truly appreciate Dr. Marnadal's feast!"

Zeid hesitated, then set down the platter and sat next to Lovisa. Coral Bud would have been amused by Tommy's maneuver—she sensed that Dr. Marnadal was amused—but she knew it had hurt Lovisa.

During the meal there was merry talk of Zeid's childhood on the Moonship. Tommy had been a "Moonship brat" and had stayed to make the planet his career when his parents had been transferred to another post.

After the feast was eaten and the platters and dishes had been cleared away, Dr. Marnadal became serious. "Zeid, I want to thank you for your support today. And we both owe thanks to Coral Bud."

"Yes," said Zeid immediately. "Though the sea urchin likes to vex me in minor matters, she has her father's directness and good sense."

"The next task needs discretion as well," said Marnadal. "Envoy Rogg intends to exaggerate every unfavorable incident. We must minimize Feelafell, neutralizing his crimes so quietly that no further issue can be made of them."

Zeid, lacking a beard, grasped his chin thoughtfully. "It's difficult to know where to start."

"Start with the riddle," prompted Coral Bud. "The boat that was nohow, and the slug that was nowhere."

Marnadal's expression quickened. Zeid explained, "Feelafell could have constructed the underwater boat from many sources of Space metals. He needed only to know how to do it. But there's no way he could have made the borer head of the mud slug. He had to *know where* the slug lay in a wreck."

Tommy said, "He could have come upon it by accident."

"The wrecks lie too deep. The current drag is too strong. Therefore," continued Zeid, "Feelafell possesses a Moonship chart. All along, I've been trying to figure out what his father might have smuggled down to the planet. I always came up against the fact that hardware is tightly controlled. But a chart could be duplicated and sewn into a jacket.

"Sometimes the simplest things are overlooked. People who store information inside computers tend to forget that the easiest way to steal a chart is to fold it up and put it in a pocket."

Marnadal sighed, "Don't tell Rogg. He'll lambaste me for not salvaging the wrecks."

"Sir, his hindsights are of no value. Nobody could have foreseen Feelafell's twisted ambition, and salvage costs would have been more than the wrecks are worth."

"True." Marnadal thought a moment. "When you speak of the mud slug, you're narrowing the search. I believe there's only one wreck that's crucial—not a horde-ship but an early research Spacecraft. It crashed down in the seas south of the Spirit Lands, and the wreck contains the only mud slug lost on the planet. If Feelafell is using a slug, he must be salvaging that particular wreck. A horde-ship, you know, would not have a great deal of Space hardware. But the research vessel—"

Both Tommy and Zeid looked surprised. Zeid said, "We've never heard, sir, that an early research vessel was wrecked!"

"Well, Zeid, you know we don't restrict any kind of empirical or scientific investigations. But for millennia our own planet was wracked by bloody wars and unspeakable cruelties and tortures because countless sects fought to insist upon their own definitions of the Undefinable and their own knowledge of the Unknowable.

"As we became more civilized, we perceived the tragic futility of this strife. We kept our individual thoughts upon the matter but turned away from the ceaseless arguments that led nowhere. On the Moonship all reference to the Undefinable and Unknowable is strictly forbidden because we don't want to contaminate a planet which, so far, has been spared superstition.

"However, as our mind-knowledge became more sophisticated, the old superstition returned in a more virulent form, having now a scientific base which was called paranormality. And this led to the sabotage of the research Spacecraft—if you have time to hear the story."

"Oh, pray tell it, Dr. Marnadal," begged Coral Bud. "I would so much like to hear a new story!"

"First, I'll alert Oceanography," smiled Marnadal. He picked up the small box on the table, pressed the speak-square, and said, "O-35A."

A voice came from the box. "Oceanography."

"Dr. Marnadal here. Can you pinpoint a wreck for me?"

"I believe so, Dr. Marnadal. Do you have the chart reference?"

"No—but the wreck should be easy to locate. It's the Spacecraft that crashed down off the Spirit Lands."

"Yes, our relay satellites should have it. I'll call you back."

Marnadal laid the box aside and smiled at Coral Bud, "I will now tell you something very true although it happened a long time ago. Isn't that how the old men start the legends?"

"Oh, exactly so!" agreed Coral Bud.

Dr. Marnadal began again, "I will now tell you something very true although it happened when the Space Givers first came to the planet. There was great disagreement as to how to help the inhabitants, and one group worked against another. Of course, we soon discovered that we needed a single policy. Nowadays everyone who comes to work on the Moonship is pledged to carry out the Board's plans. Even Zeid cannot interfere with the planet's law codes.

"But there was no such general agreement in the early days. Every research vessel—every wheel construction team—brought people of varying viewpoints. Some of them felt very strongly and believed themselves justified in using force to get their own way. And, oddly enough, the ones who used violence were the ones who most wanted to bring peace."

"Well, if a warrior kills everyone who disagrees with him, he certainly can live in peace," observed Coral Bud.

"These people were not warriors. They were great wizards— *paranormals*. They had developed their minds until they could achieve Magic without hardware—without *things*. But our own planet had become so accustomed to hardware that it saw no need for paranormality—and indeed, saw much harm in it—so the paranormals wanted to settle a colony elsewhere in a place that would be more attentive to their theories.

"Well, Coral Bud, your planet seemed exactly right. Stone

Age techniques had created few *things*. The paranormals wanted to destroy our technology and keep the planet for themselves.

"So they plotted carefully and became crewmen on a large Spacecraft that was to bring much hardware to the planet. As the Spacecraft descended—"

"They mutinied!" cried Coral Bud. "They drew their daggers and slew the captain and his loyal men! Oh, how the decks ran with blood—!"

Marnadal chuckled. "The truth is duller and paler, pirate girl. Their mental daggers lamed the steering. The crew took to the lifeboats and were rescued by the wheel construction teams. The Spacecraft, though unsteerable, entered the atmosphere under Disaster Checkrein—else it would have become a fiery meteorite and destroyed a large part of the planet. It plunged intact into the sea and has lain there ever since."

"What happened to the mutineers?"

"For many years it was believed they had perished in the fallen ship since the impact would have been far too severe for human beings. And when the paranormals were found, they were so remote in all ways that there was no sense to doing anything about them.

"Because paranormality seems very attractive to strong minds, the subject was at first forbidden, and then forgotten. From time to time, native hunters would venture near the northern pole and encounter these people. Hence they called the region the Spirit Lands."

"Is this information available to researchers?" asked Zeid.

"Oh, yes. We stopped being uptight about the paranormals a long time ago—although, to be frank, I wouldn't want you or Tom getting too deeply into the subject. It's dangerous."

"But Feelafell's father could have realized how much hardware the wreck contained?"

"Yes, that's quite possible."

The little box on the table buzzed. Marnadal answered, "Yes?"

"Dr. Marnadal," came the voice from Oceanography. "We get no readings. The probes pick up no hardware in the probable vicinity of the wreck."

"Thank you." Marnadal clicked off the call.

"Shielded," said Zeid. "Feelafell has shielded the wreck in the same way as he's hidden the other hardware from the sensors."

Lund spoke up. "We still have the wreck's charted position."

"No, you don't!" blurted Coral Bud. "For generations the strong currents off the Spirit Lands have been dragging the wreck along with them, burying it in the sands."

Zeid said hastily, "Rover Bud, the oceanographers know about the planetary currents."

"They know about looms and warps and woofs, but I'd hate to buy a carpet of their weaving. Only a trained seaman can combine the facts of currents and sea bottoms and land contours, and can take hints from how the fish swim and the sea birds fly. If Dr. Marnadal will take me to the charted position of the wreck, I warrant I'll find the Spacecraft in a hurry."

Zeid was silent. Lund pointed out, "If we're trying to sweep Feelafell under the rug, the fewer Moonship departments we bring into the project, the better."

"Very good reasoning, Tom," nodded Dr. Marnadal. "You and Zeid always made a good team. You can take Coral Bud out there in a Cloud and let her try her luck."

Zeid said, "The project will take some thought. If Feelafell is out there—"

"You'll need a large transport Cloud and investigative equipment. You're looking tired, Zeid. You caught a mean virus. Go back to the Infirmary and get another day's rest. Tom can stay here a few minutes and help me plan the logistics."

He rose, and his guests did likewise. He turned to Lovisa, "Thank you for coming along, my dear. I can see you're making Coral Bud feel welcome. Zeid, take it easy tomorrow—"

Zeid escorted Lovisa and Coral Bud from the apartment. "You do look tired, Zeid," commented Lovisa. "Harrassed, somehow."

"I didn't want to get involved. I've got plans of my own to worry about."

"Don't bother to escort us home. We won't get lost."

"Okay, thanks. See you later."

He sprang to board a chain of vehicles.

The girls walked along the broad street. Lovisa said, "Hopeless, isn't it? I begged this assignment from Dr. Marnadal in order to be working with Tommy. But I'm not included in the Cloud project."

"I fear you need some lessons from Zeid's mother, Serada. I myself am not expert in palace intrigue, but I'm sure Serada would know how to be included."

"I can't importune Dr. Marnadal again."

"Talk to Zeid. Tell him he must let you come, or you'll reveal a dark secret from his past."

Lovisa laughed. "I don't believe Zeid has any dark secrets. At least, I don't know of any."

"He was very uneasy about Ravella."

"Coral Bud, you certainly are an intriguer!" Lovisa laughed again, but her intelligent eyes became thoughtful.

DR. MARNADAL WAS SMILING at Tom, "Well?"

"She's a cute little fireball, isn't she? Like Zeid, an impressive IQ. But a differently oriented brain. An engineering brain—'let's take what we've got and see what we can do with it.' Zeid is more a visionary—a creative philosopher."

"Visionaries *are* the creators." Dr. Marnadal was silent a moment, then added, "You realize the importance of keeping Zeid away from the paranormals. He's their kind of scientific brain, and we don't want to lose him."

ZEID MADE NO PROTESTS against being held another day in the Infirmary. He felt he had earned a day off. Since returning to his planet and founding his hospice, he had been constantly at work, assembling lamps by night and selling them in the bazaars by day. The hospice ate up what the lamps earned and more besides.

Then there was the labor of finding teachers and employment for the beggars who wanted to work or finding apprenticeships for the children. Jibbo was taking hold in a fine manner, but still—

The morning after the supper with Dr. Marnadal, Zeid allowed himself the luxury of reading a book. He was seated in the Infirmary library when an orderly approached his chair and whispered that a visitor was waiting in a reception alcove. Thinking it was

Tommy or Dr. Marnadal, Zeid put down the book, rose, and followed the orderly to an alcove overlooking a garden.

Lovisa Cox was seated at the table.

He slid the door panel shut and sat down opposite her. "Good morning, Lovisa. Where have you moored the sea urchin?"

"In the official printing office, waiting for her seal-mark to be photo-processed."

"Her seal-mark?"

"Her most cherished wish, or so she told me."

"What design? A skull crossed by two daggers?"

"Not at all. A sea fan with a gold monogram, a *C* like a cargo hook holding the loop of a *B*. And a rope of pearls at the base of the fan. Very lovely. She stayed up all night drawing and coloring it."

"You've taught her the alphabet?"

"She's teaching herself. Zeid, how serious are you about Coral Bud?"

"Our betrothal was a harem farce, but I definitely feel a responsibility for her. Why do you ask?"

"Tommy likes her—a little too much, I think. And Coral Bud is taking to the Moonship like a duck to water. They're a natural pair."

"But a planet-Moonship marriage—!"

"If Coral Bud remained on the Moonship, there would be no planetary repercussions. The marriage is so possible and probable that it makes me sick."

"Tommy will never settle down, Lovisa."

"Of course he will. And I want to be the nearest girl when he makes the decision. Zeid, take me along on this Cloud trip. You can clear it with Marnadal. You can say you'll need another person in the Cloud when you and Tommy descend to the wreck."

"Yes, I hadn't thought—with only three of us, Coral Bud would be alone with Tommy while I was inside the wreck. Not that I really believe there's any danger—but a fourth would be an advantage. Okay, I'll requisition you from Marnadal."

"Thanks, Zeid."

"Oh, you're quite welcome, Lovisa. I hadn't noticed—that is,

I had noticed, but—" Zeid straightened in the chair. "Tommy is a nice guy, but he's not the man for Coral Bud."

Lovisa felt relief and a secret elation. She had always thought conniving was beneath her, but maybe it was about time she learned a few harem lessons.

THE LARGE TRANSPORT CLOUD had two decks—high-ceilinged spaces connected by a spiral ladder. The upper deck contained the circle of the bunk compartments and other service rooms. The lower hold was for vehicles and hardware.

While Moonship workers stowed the lower deck, Coral Bud twirled up and down the spiral ladder and poked her nose into all the nooks and crannies.

However, the Cloud was stowed at last, and she had to join the others in the circle of chairs. Tommy touched an operating rod—and grinned at Coral Bud.

"The wreck site is now on the dark side of the planet. We'll have to wait in orbit."

"And which of you mighty Space lords planned so foolishly," smiled Coral Bud.

"I did," said Tommy, "so that you could tell us a story from Discord's world."

Lovisa and Zeid exclaimed, "Yes, a story!" Coral Bud, well-pleased, settled back in the chair and tucked her legs under her. She began.

"The Wizard's first children were given him by Eternity, a very serene lady he loved above all else. She enjoyed his company and that of her children, but she could not understand why they couldn't live with her all the time.

"As long as they lived in their own kingdoms, she felt near to them because the Wizard's world-without-end extended into her own domain, but when Discord seeded his own world, she felt deserted. First Discord left her, then his brothers and sisters tried so hard to help him that they were in Discord's world more often than they were in her own.

"Thus, when the Great Wizard went to her for another child,

she said, 'I think not, my dear Wizard. Discord has spoiled everything. You know that Happiness, Truth, Justice, and Harmony are eternal, yet they wear themselves to shadows trying to enclose infinity in Discord's wretched cave. I will give you no more children until the ones we have are restored to me.'

"The Great Wizard knew that Eternity was right. No matter how hard he tried to help Discord's world, it was only a wretched cave that could not hold Eternity's children.

"But could he perhaps find a womb within the cave? He looked and saw that Discord was now battling a new enemy whom Discord himself had created—an impatient, imperious girl named Time.

"Discord complained to the Wizard, 'How can I improve my world when Time is always against me? Make her kinder, and I can get more done!'

"So the Great Wizard went to Time and said, 'What would you want of me, in return for giving me a child?'

"'The jewels of Eternity,' she answered at once. 'I rule Discord and his cave the same way Eternity rules you and your worlds-without-end. Yet she is serene and has everything while I must rush and shove and devour to make Discord's cave aware of my existence.'

"'You ask a hard gift,' said the Wizard. 'I cannot give you serenity, but I can endow you with a stately step. Men will keep you in their heartbeats. Your law will determine all seasons and procedures, and whatever you do cannot be altered.'

"As he spoke, Time's pace became regular and majestic—not hurried but unchanging. Seasons and procedures provided countless jewels. In Discord's cave she totally eclipsed Eternity and was very happy. She nurtured the Great Wizard's seed in her womb, and the Great Wizard suddenly realized he would need a nurse for the child.

"He called his five children from their kingdoms and said, 'All of you must understand that I cannot bring Time's child home to Eternity. You must take turns living in Discord's world and rearing the babe.'

"Truth and Justice immediately protested, 'We never mean to be cruel, but sometimes we might have to deal harshly. Truth must always be spoken, and Justice must be meted out. So you must see why we can watch over Time's child only now and then. For the child's sake, don't expect more of us.'

"But Happiness and Harmony said, 'We're continually in Discord's cave anyhow, and a child will be a pleasure to us. When will it be born?'

"'Alas,' said the Wizard, 'whenever Time decrees, for such is the wish I have granted her.'

"So the child appeared in the mother's good time—and lo, it was twins—a boy and a girl.

"The Great Wizard brought the twins to his older children, and the girl captivated Truth and Justice so that they could scarcely bear to be parted from her. On the other hand, Happiness and Harmony, who had long yearned for a sympathetic brother, took instantly to the boy.

"The twins loved their brothers and sisters, of course. They also were proud of their mother Time, who had become quite rhythmic and graceful, rivaling Harmony in the pleasure she bestowed.

"With the fine rearing they had, the twins were eager to help the creatures in Discord's cave. The girl would coax leniency from the brothers who adored her and who unbent their stern rules whenever she begged them. So Mankind called her Mercy because she is the only creature who can soften Truth and ward off Justice.

"The boy never needed to coax Happiness and Harmony who already were doing what they could for Mankind, but he often appealed to his mother Time to let her steps go in different paths. Therefore, he encouraged Mankind to look to the future where another path might open up. Mankind called the boy Hope and loved him even more than Happiness and Harmony because, after he was born, no situation was unendurable.

"However, the twins grew at different rates because Mankind wanted Hope and helped him grow strong, but a man with Truth and Justice on his side seldom wants Mercy so that she is weak and fragile to this day.

"And now I have done my part to make the company merry," finished Coral Bud. "I want to hear what another shipmate will add."

"My contribution is very short," said Tommy. "Let's order a round of beer!"

WHEN THE NIGHT-SHADOW MOVED away from that side of the planet, the Cloud descended and hovered over the ice-shell of the northern sea. Through the wide viewing window, Coral Bud could see thick fog.

"Now here is a strange thing," she exclaimed. "And most unnatural. The temperature has been separated like oil and water. All the cold has been put into the sea, and all the heat has been driven into the air. The sea dwellers do right when they avoid Magic that can change a planet's nature."

"How near are we to land?" asked Zeid.

Tommy touched a control. The window became a screen upon which headlands and coves appeared.

"Can we rise and view downward?" asked Coral Bud.

The screen became a relief map.

"Aha!" said Coral Bud. "The wreck now lies within yonder sickle-cove."

"But Rover Bud," protested Zeid, "the steady current flows at right angles to the headlands."

"And did you never float sticks in brooks as a child, land crab? But, of course," she added, "you had no brooks in the Desert or on the Moonship. So I will say only that the cove arms cause a scouring along the land that would pull the wreck toward itself over many generations, especially if the hull remained whole or nearly so.

"Magic can tell us no more," she went on. "We must leave the Cloud, enter a boat—"

"We brought a two-man submersible," said Tommy. "I can run a grid of the area."

Zeid said quickly, "Now that we're here, I'm the one to go after Feelafell. I'm the one with a score to settle."

"But, Zeid, you've never handled this latest submersible," said Tommy.

"And neither of you know what to look for when you once are in the water," insisted Coral Bud. "I must be the searcher—and my helper must be a Moonship pilot whose skills have not become dusty with disuse."

"Over my dead body do you squeeze into a two-man submersible with Tommy Lund," protested Zeid.

"If you wish it that way, we'll give you a splendid funeral," shrugged Coral Bud.

Lovisa interposed, "Tommy is right, Zeid—and so is Coral Bud. They're the experts. For the safety of us all, let them do the job."

Zeid said gruffly, "All right. The job comes first, of course."

Tommy let the Cloud descend onto the ice-shell over the cove. When it had been positioned to Coral Bud's satisfaction, he led her below, to the air lock that already held the submersible.

Zeid took Tommy's place at the console. At Tommy's signal he dispersed the ice beneath the air lock and released the two-man craft. He remarked, "I could have handled the submersible, Lovisa. There can't have been so many design changes since I was on the Moonship."

"Perhaps not. But I suddenly decided I couldn't endure waiting here with a Tommy who'd be grumbling and fretting and wishing he was with Coral Bud."

"If that's all the reason you had for stopping me—"

"I didn't want to seem to oppose Tommy when he was, in fact, right about being more qualified. I want Tommy to like me, not to think of me as a stumbling block."

"Lovisa, when will you learn not to keep giving in to other people? You hide away in the data banks and are so afraid of offending somebody. Look at Coral Bud—she's done nothing but put roadblocks in this trip to the Marble Lands."

"And you love her?"

"Well, I'll be damned if I'll let her marry Tommy Lund!"

"Oh, Zeid, you used a forbidden phrase!" laughed Lovisa.

BEYOND THE ICE-RIMMED COAST, the hot fog rose from the land and became high, puffy clouds that massed over the pole and obscured the lush gardens beneath. The piercing white sun turned the clouds to glowing lamps that spread such even illumination that nothing threw shadows.

The Spirit Lands were only gardens. No dwellings disturbed the long vistas of greensward—the flower-bright borders—the tall groves.

And yet there were people who strolled through the vistas like walking flowers. They, too, did not throw shadows—but perhaps they would not have thrown shadows in ordinary light.

They were the galaxy's supreme wizards. They had begun by contemplating a box—and making it move. Then they had contemplated the molecules in the box—and had made it into sawdust. So they contemplated the atoms in the sawdust—and turned them into gold—into blood—into vapor—

"*Things* are not necessary," they said. "A primitive planet becomes civilized quickest by destroying *things*. Stop shipping hardware. When Mankind cannot move a box any other way, he will learn to contemplate it."

But, of course, it's much easier for Mankind to let hardware do his contemplating for him. Primitive man had his muscles, which are a kind of hardware. His muscles fashioned tools, which fashioned machines, which fashioned robots, which fashioned more robots, and nobody needed the supreme wizards.

On the other hand, the wizards did not need the rest of the galaxy either. So they settled on remote planets and continued to contemplate. And to recruit—which is why the Moonship kept very quiet about the colony under the polar clouds.

As Coral Bud and Tommy disengaged from the Cloud and began to probe the cove, a group of Contemplators were lounging around a garden pool—ghost-limbed figures clad in color-shimmers.

"I see that the satellite is at last remembering our shipwreck," said a smoke-robed ghost.

"Is that so, Quintus?" said another. "Where is Feelafell the thief?"

"Don't ask me. Querota is supposed to be contemplating the thief."

"Querota is contemplating her substance today. She was becoming wispy. What do you see at the shipwreck? How many descended?"

"Four. Two couples. It's a long time since we hunted in couples, isn't it?"

"Still complaining, Quintus? What do you lack, being immortal?"

"If you've forgotten, forget it."

"What sort of brain power among the four?"

"I'm a visualizer, not an analyzer. Where's Quist?"

"Here I am, visualizer, right beside you. Oh, the satellite sent brains—no doubt about it. And two of them are in native skulls."

"Like the thief?"

"The thief is only half native, Quimmeron. You know, as I contemplate the one native, I see a largeness of concept—an idealistic yearning. Do you suppose he would join us, Quimmeron?"

"If we approached him subtly, Quist."

"And if he also happens to be plumb outta his gourd."

"Quintus!"

CORAL BUD THOUGHT THE two-man sub was very cozy. She wished she could see out a window, but the only view was of Magic *tubes*. She watched their lines, dots, and sweeps as Tommy talked with Zeid in the Cloud.

"As far as I can tell, just a hundred meters of nothing," said Tommy after a swoop through the middle of the cove.

"Are you speaking of depth, Tommy?" asked Coral Bud. "How many fathoms would that be?"

"Fifty fathoms."

"Oh, no. I saw that the headlands had sheer vertical walls which usually mean a chasm twice as deep."

"Usually is not *always."*

"If we are to search by logic, we'll go away empty-handed. Here we have the cove where a wreck must lie. The cove is too shallow. Therefore, somebody has placed a barrier that stops your Magic. *That* is the truth of it, if you will descend fifty fathoms."

"The barrier might incinerate us—blow us up—"

"Feelafell does not seem to me to be a person who would set fatal barriers where he too must descend. How does he know that his makeshift Magic will always work? O that we could simply drop a stone."

Tommy asked Zeid, "Got anything you can jettison through the airlock?"

"All sorts of hardware," replied Zeid, "if you'll write out the explanation in six copies for three departments."

"Whatever *that* means," said Coral Bud. "I perceive the Space lords are unable to do what a child could encompass. Put me ashore and let me cast a rock into the cove."

"A rock isn't a conductor."

"Did you expect it to usher you down? Oh, look! Why did the line jump up the glass?"

"It's registering fish three fathoms below our keel."

"What good is a line on a glass? I want to *see* the fish. Tommy, where are the water masks and frog feet?"

"We don't have any."

"You lie. Feelafell wore a mask when he surprised us on the *Whizzard*. And the Crucible Fortress was stormed by men in masks and frog feet." Coral Bud twisted in her bucket chair. "What do those lockers contain?"

"Nothing. Flotation jackets. Sit down."

"I only want to reach—"

The side of Coral Bud's hand grazed under Tommy's ear. He slumped in his chair. Coral Bud scrambled aft and opened a locker. Yes, there were the masks and feet.

Zeid was saying, "Tommy? Tommy!"

Coral Bud did not answer. She was trying to find a mask that fit.

Zeid said, in a different tone, "You are meddling with Magic that will kill you, Rover Bud. The masks are only for shallow water. If you go deep and come up fast, your blood will bubble."

Coral Bud paused. Zeid went on, "Think a moment, sea urchin. What happens when your father's fishermen drag a great fish from the deeps to the surface?"

"He bursts inside," said Coral Bud. "Yes, you are right. I acted hastily, I was so impatient—"

"What did you do to Tommy in your haste?"

"Nothing. . . ."

"I'll explain how to bring the sub back to the Cloud."

Coral Bud wriggled back to her chair. "Can the boat go up and down without bubbling my blood?"

"Yes, the boat is safe. You're just below the surface, aren't you? Now, grasp the red rod—"

"Oh, I have observed, Light-Bearer. Thus."

Coral Bud pulled up the rod. The sub began to descend.

Tommy stirred and groaned. "What happened?"

"I bumped against you when I turned around."

He rubbed his neck. His glance fell on the screens. "Holy Cats!" He grabbed the rod and stopped the descent.

"How far are we?" asked Coral Bud.

"One hundred five meters."

"So, after all, the barrier didn't incinerate us. Let's continue."

"Let's see where we are." Tommy clicked more switches. "I'm activating the camera, Zeid. Are you reading me on the Monitor?"

Coral Bud was staring at a bright picture, that suddenly came to life on the control panel. A wall was in front of them—Space metal gleaming in the strong lamps the boat had switched on.

Tommy turned the sub. The wall became a corner—became another wall—another corner—another wall—

"Zeid!" exclaimed Tommy. "We've fallen into a lifeboat bay. We're still settling."

"That's because the water is being bailed out," observed Coral Bud. "We've nothing to float in."

At that moment the sub came to rest. The picture on the control panel showed the water draining away. Tommy asked, "Still reading me?"

"The signal isn't good, but I can see you're in a lock," said Zeid. "Better stay there—Feelafell might be home."

The wall in front of them began to slide downward. A lighted chamber seemed to be beyond. Tommy shut off the sub's lamps. Girders angled in emptiness.

"The spaceship is on its side," Tommy remarked.

When the wall had finally slid out of sight, there was movement at one corner of the opening.

Coral Bud gasped, "Oh, Tommy! What if Feelafell seeks to kill us? Do you have a Space poniard?"

"Neither of us can risk a Space weapon. We'll just have to sit tight."

"We could not possibly be any tighter. Look! He moves again!"

They watched. The white figure slowly crept into view and stood up.

A child-sized, white-smocked figure was gazing wide-eyed at the sub.

Coral Bud exclaimed aloud. She reached past Tommy, activated the hatch mechanism, and poked her head out of the sub.

"Thoughtless breaker of a mother's heart," she chided the boy. "Why did you leave the Weavers Basin without a word?"

"The Lord Feelafell said there was a great haste, honored lady. He hid me in a box in his underwater boat—and lo! I was here in a twinkling. There is much to eat, as the Lord Feelafell promised, but I *was* getting rather lonely," said the boy who had brought the platter of poisoned cakes to the barge.

ZEID AND LOVISA, WATCHING on the repeater in the Cloud, saw Tommy and Coral Bud leave the submarine and enter the spacecraft. The air-lock door slid shut.

"A little boy!" said Lovisa. "Who is he?"

"A defense for logical thinking," smiled Zeid. "I didn't realize Feelafell had a portation system. He must have found it in the wreck. It was easier for him to port the boy than to kill him and dispose of his body."

"He might have ported him out of the galaxy."

"Not unless the terminal was out of the galaxy. If you start in a box, you have to end in a box."

"What should we do now? Try to get down to the wreck?"

"Since the hull seems to be intact, I think it would be easier to bring the wreck up. The vessel specifications must still be somewhere in the archives. The Moonship can direct Tommy in repairing the sabotage that distorted the steering."

"And Feelafell—and possibly his father before him—has been

using the ship," marveled Lovisa, turning from the repeater screen. "That he could keep the work a secret—*eeek*!"

Zeid swung around to find the reason for the girl's terrified yell.

A being was standing there, as if molded in pearly vapor and clad in folds of iridescent dew. He was tall, and his face was young—a broad, high, Space Giver forehead and narrow chin. He smiled and spoke in pure sound frequencies.

"Greetings, Zeid ben Amfi. I am Quimmeron, of the Quanta who live in the Spirit Lands. May I assist you?"

WHEN THE SPACESHIP HAD tumbled from orbit—slowed by the emergency braking of the reciprocal gravity field—all loose furnishings had been thrown around, coming to rest finally at right angles from their normal positions. Feelafell had cleared only a small section of this enormous jumble.

The boy from the Weavers Basin led Coral Bud and Tommy over the side wall of a gymnasium, along a corridor where they trod on closed door hatches, and into a suite of rooms—an officer's quarters that had been put in workable orientation. Scars remained where Feelafell had removed fixed furniture from the bulkhead that originally had been the deck. As on the planet, cushions and footed trays replaced chairs and tables.

"Behold, how I entered," explained the boy, opening a narrow locker in the corner. "Pray be seated. Will you dine?"

"We will hear your story, scallawag," said Coral Bud, sinking onto a cushion. "Lord Tom-ih-Lund will have much to say to your master."

The boy looked uncertain at her brusque tone. Tommy sat down, motioned the boy to join them, and said, "What's your name? Where did you find the messman's jacket which fits you with rather too much space left over?"

"My name is Muff. I am well-known to the bargemen who come to the Weavers Basin because I am reliable in errands and have applied to them all to be taken as apprentice.

"One day recently—at least, it will seem recent to yourselves but has been a long time for me—a bargeman named Grodd came and asked me if I would like to serve a Space lord.

"Honored lady, you and the Prince Zeid ben Amfi had newly arrived, and I thought Grodd would take me to the prince. But instead he took me to a riverbank outside the town. A boat rose from the water, and the Space Lord Feelafell emerged and spoke to me."

Tommy asked, "Had you heard of Feelafell before?"

"Oh, yes, he is the great merchant of the Seacoast, the owner of the horde-ships, close kin to the Space Givers. I was overjoyed at being in his service. He showed me Magic from his pockets—boxes that played music and spoke and showed little mirror pictures. I was to run an errand for Grodd and then meet him again at the riverbank.

"There was a great wedding feast in the town, and Grodd had procured a platter of cakes for the Desert prince. He gave me several cakes to eat while he arranged the platter, and then I delivered it—as you remember, lady."

"Yes, I call it to mind," said Coral Bud.

"I then ran to the riverbank and went aboard the underwater boat. The lord Feelafell said there was much haste—and, indeed, I understood what he meant because there had been much haste and excitement in town all day.

"He gave me thin little boxes to put inside the player box and said they would instruct me. He told me to lie on a narrow pallet in the boat—and be prepared to stand up when the Magic carried me to his workshop.

"I lay as he instructed me, though a little afraid when the lid closed on the pallet. And in a moment I was tumbling out of another box into the chamber. The little boxes were safely in my pockets. One after the other I have put them into the player box, and so have found how to eat and sleep and bathe and tend the workshop. One box told me of the alarm that would ring when he arrived. It was *that* alarm I was answering—and was amazed to see yourself, lady, pop up and reproach me."

"Well, you are not so much to blame, after all, for not telling your mother that you were leaving."

"She should know better than to worry," said Muff stoutly. "I have always taken care of myself in any scrap."

"But I think your present situation leaves much to be desired," returned Coral Bud. "You've apprenticed yourself to a wicked master."

"Oh, no, lady! The Space Givers have always shown honor to Lord Feelafell. Tell me, Lord Tom-ih-Lund, does the Moonship not treat my master with respect?"

"With leniency, Master Muff," said Tom, "and the chief Moonship lord will be in trouble because of it."

"Well, he is not in trouble *yet*," said Coral Bud, "and we're trying to help him, little Muff, because it is a dreadful thing for a kind chief to be punished for his kindness."

Muff looked downcast. "I had hoped to be a Space apprentice. Lord Feelafell said he was going to put this workshop in the sky to be another Moonship, and I would be apprenticed to him the same way the prince Zeid was apprenticed. And then we would travel to other worlds."

Tommy and Coral Bud looked at each other.

"Yes, Feelafell has a Space Giver mind," she said, "and he told me he wanted his grandchildren to conquer the galaxy."

Muff had worked hard during his lonely days. He had cleared clothing and loose objects out of another suite, though he was unable to do anything about the furniture still jutting out from what was now a wall.

"I can take you to the center of all Magic, Lord Tom-ih-Lund," he said. "I've been following trails."

"Trails?"

"When a palace has fallen on its side, and one walks on the walls, one leaves trails because even Space walls are not to be walked on. So I came to many halls and rooms—and felt very lonely at the emptiness—until I came to a place where Magic winked in colors and spoke to itself."

"Yes, let's go there, Muff," said Tommy.

They rose from the cushions and climbed through misplaced hatches. Light and air and heat purred through the craft that had been made to last a thousand years. Coral Bud thought the desolation was due as much to the monotonous plainness of design as to the emptiness.

Tommy stopped them at a panel that lay at floor level. He pushed a button. Seal-marks lit up and traveled from one end of the panel to the other. The panel slid into the floor, revealing a lighted chamber.

"Come on," he smiled and stepped into the chamber. Muff and Coral Bud jumped after him. He pressed another button. The door closed and the chamber moved sideways with increasing speed—then stopped with a suddenness that sent Coral Bud and Muff clutching each other.

The opposite side of the chamber slid away. This time they were in the middle of a great wall, looking into a chamber of Magic consoles that showed light and made noise, although some of them hung strangely.

"Stay here—don't jump," said Tommy as Coral Bud stepped to the edge of the chamber. He pushed a button that kept the panel from coming into place. "It's just the control room—the command platform—"

"It's all very wonderful," said Coral Bud, "but it makes my head feel all wrong."

"Wrong?"

"Yes. I've used it to become clever about things that can be observed and touched and comprehended whole. But these things must be comprehended in a deep part of my head I've never used. As I stand here I feel the great gulf of time between the planet and the Moonship."

"You're just imagining the gulf," said Tommy easily. But he closed the panel and sent the chamber back to where they had entered.

"I shall remember what you did," Muff said to him, "so I can visit the Magic as befits a Space apprentice. For even if Feelafell be removed, the next master of the palace will need an apprentice, won't he?"

"Fear not, little Muff," said Coral Bud. "If we can't find you a Space master, I will take you as apprentice myself. I now have my seal-mark ready to register with the Counting Guild and am thinking of entering the lamp trade.

"But I grow thirsty," she continued, "and would return to your master's comfortable cushions. Can you summon wine?"

"The little box tells me much—but apprentices are not told where the masters keep their wine, lady. Perhaps the Lord Tom-ih-Lund—"

"Nay—bring us as you've been instructed, Master Muff."

The boy skipped off. Tommy said, "So you're thinking of going into the lamp trade?"

"I shall discuss it with Dr. Marnadal. Zeid isn't the only one who can sell lamps and build hospices, well?"

Muff served bubbly drinks and fresh honey cakes to his guests and left them by themselves while he returned to work. Coral Bud sighed, "Muff is a dear lad. I forgive Feelafell much because he spared him."

"Well, he needs agents, and young ones are easiest to train."

"Even in his ambition and resentment, he must have yearnings for love. And now I'm going to tell you a terrible thing, Tommy Lund. Perhaps Zeid has been right all along."

"Why is that terrible?"

"Because it weakens action—and our planet devours weakness. But as I said at the meeting, I would have slit Feelafell's throat—and what would have become of poor Muff? The lad would have lived weeks—months—years—and gone mad waiting for a master who never came.

"In wanting to destroy Feelafell, I was thinking only of the moment. It was Zeid who thought not only of the visible trunk, but of the hidden roots. I so nearly doomed Muff. What a horrible thought."

She shuddered, and Tommy quickly moved to put his arm around her. She rested against his shoulder a moment. "When I knew only the planet, I thought our way of life was brave and right. I thought only of striking the first blow and glorying in victory. But now I'm confused—and afraid."

"And I'm weary of sampling loves that never satisfy. You know, Coral Bud, I think the Moonship would allow us to be truly wed."

Coral Bud gently moved aside from him. "And then we would become another project to be watched—and our children—and our children's children. No, dear Tommy. You can find a faithful love much better than mine.

"But we can't continue to sit on fine cushions and eat honey cake! You must find a way we can speak to Zeid or the Moonship. This craft is vast. How did the captain give everybody orders at once?"

"Do you see the little box that is next to the doorway we climbed down from? One was placed in every room, and when there was danger the captain spoke, 'Now hear *this*!'"

"Good. You must connect the vessel's boxes to the Cloud Magic, so when Zeid calls us, we can hear him wherever we are."

"That's a tall order, Coral Bud."

"Well, you are a tall man. And after you splice the voice channels together, you must find a way to keep Feelafell from boarding us. And after that—"

Tommy got to his feet. "You must have been a top sergeant in your last incarn—"

He stopped abruptly. She asked with a smile, "Is it so hard to find planet words for Space Giver ideas?"

"Sometimes it's very hard. And I pray to God—that is, I hope the planet never finds all the words we know."

ZEID, REMEMBERING DR. MARNADAL'S story, assumed Quimmeron was one of the controversial paranormals but decided it would be discourteous to ask. Instead he indicated the circle of chairs.

"Assistance would be welcome, Quimmeron. Will you—that is, do you—sit down?"

"Yes. Old customs persist." Quimmeron drifted to a chair, smoothed his iridescent robes, and sat down. "After all, as long as one has a body, one must place it somewhere."

Zeid gestured Lovisa to sit down. She chose the chair across the circle and said nervously to Quimmeron, "Is that all the body you've got?"

"It's enough body to keep intelligence functioning within the structure of an atomic universe. We Quanta generally believe Mankind's duty is to keep intelligence functioning."

"That's only half a duty," said Zeid, also sitting in the circle.

"That's simply keeping the motor running. What do you do with it?"

"We contemplate. Have you never heard of the Contemplators?"

"Yes—if you also are called paranormals."

"An ugly clinical term. We prefer Contemplators."

"I deduce you're a descendant of the mutineers who sabotaged the research craft."

"We *are* the mutineers. Having become thought structures, we are free of fleshly processes. We are immortal."

"And thus all your imperfections and limitations live forever," mused Zeid. "No wonder this knowledge has been forbidden." He smiled across the circle at Lovisa. "If Coral Bud were here, she'd say the Contemplators tie the Great Wizard's hands, making it impossible for him to improve Discord's world."

Lovisa smiled back, "Tommy would say they're living in Instant Entropy."

Quimmeron did not seem to resent the comments. He waved his ghostly hand. "You perceive why there has been a truce between us and the Moonship. Immortals and Mortals simply live on different continua. Nevertheless, we've become interested in the thief Feelafell and in yourselves. We really would like to help you."

"And I'm sincerely grateful for your offer," said Zeid. "When you came in, we were contempl—discussing—how the Spacecraft could be raised if the steering malfunction were put right."

"Oh, it could be raised since the power systems are undamaged. But the physical displacements involved would be considerable because of the mass and thrust. There would be a flood tide and topographical upheavals—"

"To say nothing of the Moonship upheavals if Envoy Rogg got word of it. I had not thought out the physical problems," admitted Zeid. "I guess all we can do is to retrieve our friends."

"Not quite all. If we Quanta contemplate the ship, the mass will dissolve and there will be no thrust. However, in such case we would like—"

At this moment a pert burst of native language spurted out of the console. "Now hear this, O deck swabbers! It is I, your captain who will have the gizzards of all who do not obey!"

Tommy's voice overrode with, "Hey, pipe down, captain, until I find out if the sending channels—"

"Which pipe down? This?"

A voice blared, "...good backhand return...a forehand lob...Fritz kills it...game, set, and match...."

"Shut it off, will you?" Tommy was saying.

A silence. Coral Bud's small voice. "But somebody said *kills* in Space Giver tongue, and I want to know who was slain. Why are you climbing the wall?"

"A question with a couple good answers," came Tommy's mutter. "For one thing, the ship is on her beam ends, and the sending board is up here. Now, let me take a look—oh, jeesh—!"

Abrupt silence.

Zeid sat back in his chair and roared with laughter. Lovisa's smile was wistful.

Quimmeron said, "When your friend reopens the channel, tell him to stay away from the control board. He and the girl and the little boy are to board the sub. When they're inside, I'll release the lock."

"Thank you, Quimmeron."

"And if you wish the Spacecraft to be moved out of Feelafell's reach, allow me to contemplate this Cloud to the Spirit Lands. We would need to confer with you about deranging the Spacecraft molecules."

"Don't you mean *disarranging*?" asked Lovisa.

"Why no. I mean *deranging* since atoms are electrically bound thought patterns and disturbed thoughts are said to be *deranged*."

"But hardware isn't thoughts."

"Hardware is *only* thoughts. Take the logic in steps, Moonship girl. The human brain and the computer are effective only because they are electrically bound patterns. Solidified thought, if you will. But computer components and decks and bulkheads are only atoms—again, only electrically bound patterns."

"As are blood, bone, and nerves," remarked Zeid.

"Precisely. The world is only thought patterns made visible—audible—tactile—"

Quimmeron faded—became transparent—vanished.

"Well!" said Lovisa. "You won't let them move the Cloud to the Spirit Lands, will you, Zeid?"

"Moving the ship out of Feelafell's reach—quietly with no dislocations that Rogg could complain about—would be a tremendous advantage, Lovisa."

"But Dr. Marnadal didn't want you or Tom learning too much about paranormality."

"He didn't want us attracted by it. But I'm not attracted—I'm repelled by the whole idea. To spend an eternity as a static ghost— However, I certainly think we should accept the help the paranormals offer. It's a shortcut that will remove the source of Feelafell's Space equipment."

"Well, it will doubtless lengthen the time I'm on assignment with Tommy, so I guess I ought to be in favor of it," said Lovisa.

Half an hour later the released submersible surfaced in the Cloud's opened lock and was drawn onto the lower deck. Coral Bud popped out of the hatch, and Tommy emerged, carrying Muff.

"It was fortunate that Muff and I are so slender," Coral Bud said to Zeid, "because there was not much place."

Zeid smiled at Muff, whom Tommy had set on the deck. "Have we a new mirror-page?"

The lock sealed with a thud. The Cloud seemed to rise. Zeid leaped up the spiral ladder, the others straggling after him.

The upper deck was empty, but a window was showing the polar cumulus cover. The Cloud slid downward through the cumuli and hovered over a beautiful green meadow edged by masses of golden flowers.

"What the hell?" wondered Tommy.

"It's a long story," said Zeid.

A dull pounding came from the lower deck. Tommy gasped and ran down the ladder.

"What the hell?" wondered Zeid.

"It's another story, but short," said Coral Bud. "Muff had thought that Feelafell would come to the wreck in his underwater boat, merely because he had been told that an alarm would sound if the boat arrived.

"But Tommy and I saw that there was a second and much

better way for Feelafell to visit the wreck—the Magic box in which Muff had arrived. Indeed, as busy as Feelafell is every day at the Seacoast, how could he find time for sea journeys?

"So Tommy brought the box with us, taking the sections apart and fitting them together within the boat since they lay easier in that manner. However, the door lay bottommost, so I assume the pounding is that Feelafell chose this moment to use the box—and cannot get out."

Voices were heard from the ladder well. Muff ran, jumped into a chair, crouched on the seat, and looked over the chair back.

Feelafell's balding head, noble brow, and Space Giver face rose into view. His height loomed into the chamber. He was white-clad and still white-gloved.

"What have you done with my Moonship?" he demanded of Zeid. "My life's work! What have you done with it?"

"I don't know," said Zeid. "I honestly don't know."

"THIS IS VERY IRKSOME," said Coral Bud. "Zeid, you and Lovisa should not have agreed in your thoughts to come here."

"Now who's second-guessing?" growled Zeid. "I saw a chance for a quick end to Feelafell's power, and I took it."

Zeid, Tommy, Lovisa, and Coral Bud were conferring within the circle of chairs. Feelafell had been ushered to a compartment, and little Muff was sitting outside the door to make sure he stayed there. Since Feelafell had always wanted to visit the satellite, he was pleased to be aboard the Cloud and had no intention of making trouble.

The Contemplators had opened a hatch in the lower deck. The Cloud crew could have walked out into the gardens, but they had stayed within the Cloud.

Lovisa sighed, "I wish they'd communicate. It's frustrating to be dumped into Paradise and not dare step across the threshold."

Suddenly a young, brightly robed man was sitting among them. Like Quimmeron he was broad-browed with noble features, but he seemed more solid. His hands were more like alabaster than smoke, and his robes more like Space cloth.

"Greetings," he smiled, "I am Quintus."

A breath of relief went around the circle. Zeid said, "I'm glad you got in touch. Where's Quimmeron?"

"Contemplating on your behalf. You wanted the ship moved, didn't you? That requires a combined colony effort."

"But you're here?"

"I'm the goldbricker in the crowd. How come you're not out playing softball or having a picnic? A picnic!" he groaned. "Why do I remind myself?"

"You don't eat?" smiled Coral Bud.

"No. I just spend an eternity thinking about fried chicken and potato salad. But honestly, folks," he added, "we don't try to hijack recruits. What good would it do? You can lead a horse to water, but you can't make him contemplate.

"Of course, if any of you liked it here, Quimmeron would be tickled pink. Like this," said Quintus, his robes becoming a rose petal tint. "But we're strictly soft sell. Quimmeron wanted to bring you here to show you our layout—but you don't have to buy.

"He's doing you a favor—how about obliging him by taking a look? We have our shortcomings, but we contemplate gardens very well. The gardens are what keep me hanging around. I wouldn't give two cents for the rest of the package."

It was impossible to dislike or mistrust this genial ghost. Zeid smiled, "I really have to stay aboard with my prisoner, Quintus. The others may leave the Cloud if they wish."

"Nobly said, captain," approved Coral Bud. "I will take Muff for a romp, and Quintus may show us his favorite flowers."

Lovisa said to Tommy, "Will you go ashore with us? Muff is no great protection."

"Neither am I, against a paranormal. But I don't like the idea of you girls going ashore alone."

Muff, given permission to leave the Cloud, dashed across the meadow like a stone from a slingshot. Tommy would have run after him to bring him back, but Coral Bud laughed and said, "Pirates best know the art of overtaking. I claim Muff as my prize."

Tommy nodded and smiled agreement. With a grateful look at Coral Bud, Lovisa drew him away to the edge of the meadow where a hillock overlooked a sparkling stream.

Quintus had vanished, but when he saw Coral Bud crossing the meadow alone, he reappeared and strolled beside her. They continued in silence until they came to a deep pool in a little glade. They sat down at the edge of the pool, and Muff came to run and tumble beside them.

Quintus remarked to Coral Bud, "I think you grow bored with the beauty."

"Perhaps I'm too accustomed to the sea where no two days are the same," said Coral Bud. "Perfection leads nowhere, really. If, among all your beautiful flowers, I could see an impudent little weed—"

"How strange you should mention it! Only this morning I found an intruder among the purple cluster plants. Would you like to come and look at it?"

"Indeed I would!" said Coral Bud, jumping up. "But I would not stray too far from the Cloud, lest we be given word that the Spacecraft is moved and we can go."

"Oh, the Spacecraft is moved," said Quintus, rising also. "I was suppose to impart the fact when I came, but I wanted a few moments alone with you."

"With me?" exclaimed Coral Bud, astonished.

"Yes, you've been enchanting to watch, you know."

"I fear you haven't watched very many girls."

"Not for years—centuries—" sighed Quintus. "When I was a man—a physical man—I saw no girl I wanted to fall in love with. I thought there never would be such a girl. And then I saw you, watched you. Can you think what it's like—after centuries—to fall in love?"

"I think, after centuries, a man could fall in love with anybody. I have observed that my father's crews, after mere weeks at sea, are not too particular about the girls they embrace in the first port."

"Oh, Coral Bud, it is not thus I love!"

"Yes, so they also say. Where did Quimmeron place the ship?"

"Elsewhere under the sea, too deep for salvage. But we were speaking of love—"

"No. We were speaking of the impudent weed. Don't you want to show it to me?"

"Very well," sighed Quintus, "very well."

They began to walk back to the Cloud, Muff frolicking after them. Quintus paused at a hollow filled with purple blossoms. Coral Bud looked until she found a vine twining a flower stem and shooting into the air.

"Yes, that is a fine weed, Quintus," she said gravely.

"I'm rather good with solid thoughts. Do I seem substantial?"

"Alarmingly so, Quintus."

"May I—just once—embrace you, Coral Bud?"

"Dearest Quintus, please consider me as the memory of an embrace. You might die if you experience mortal emotion, and I don't wish to kill you."

"I would die supremely happy."

"But what about *me,* dear Quintus? The rest of my short life would be filled with self-reproach and sorrow. Make me happy by continuing to live in your gardens. Many, many times the thought of your beautiful flowers and impudent weeds will give me great joy. It is all I will ever know of immortality—please grant it."

"Of course, my darling—my darling—"

Quintus became like smoke—like mist—and vanished.

Coral Bud cried a few moments, then went to tell Tommy and Lovisa that the Cloud was free to lift off.

WHEN THEY WERE AGAIN in orbit, Zeid said, "We can't take Feelafell to the Moonship while Envoy Rogg is there. We must return him and his box to Tenfold."

"Destroy the box," said Coral Bud and Tommy together.

"I don't think that would be wise," said Zeid. "Whenever Feelafell has to repair hardware, he seems to improve upon it. The waterlock was not, I think, in the original Spacecraft and took considerable contriving. And when Feelafell needed to hide from Moonship trackers, he found new hardware we don't yet understand."

Tommy said thoughtfully, "We'll have to overpower Feelafell in order to force him off the Cloud at Tenfold since he expects to strut ashore on the Moonship."

"Nonsense, Tommy," said Coral Bud. "We will do as my father does with hostages when returning them after ransom has been paid. We will blindfold Feelafell, telling him he must not gaze on certain Moonship mysteries—and quickly push him out the door."

"And then what, little captain?" smiled Tommy.

"Why, then we must let Muff's mother see that he is alive and well. And *then* you and Lovisa must return Zeid, Muff, and me to the *Whizzard*."

"Muff can be left with his mother," said Zeid.

"No. Under the laws of the planet, an apprentice who has been taken from his master must be given an equal apprenticeship. I shall register my new seal-mark and take Muff with me."

"That would not be an *equal* apprenticeship," retorted Zeid. "I will take Muff with me."

Lovisa looked timidly at Tommy, and he smiled and took her hand.

They were rid of Feelafell as quickly as Coral Bud had foretold. The Cloud descended to a terrace of Feelafell's island fortress at Tenfold. Zeid and Tommy carried the portation box onto the terrace. They blindfolded Feelafell within his compartment, wrapping the ends of the scarf loosely around his face so that the sea breezes would not give the trick away too soon.

Believing himself to be on the Moonship, he followed them willingly to the opened hatch, walked ahead five steps as they had instructed him—and then sensed the planet's air through the scarf.

He tore the scarf away—and became dizzy with rage at seeing his own terraces.

He sprang around—but the Cloud was already ascending through the skies.

THE MARBLE LANDS, BEING the source of most of the planet's gold, were the wealthiest areas. Yet the population ebbed and flowed. Except for the mine owners and forest owners and merchants, all agreed that the Marble Lands were nice places to visit, if one did not have to live there.

Craftsmen in particular felt their talents frozen by the demands of gold and preferred to live elsewhere on the planet, where nobody cared if they spent a week studying a stone or a gem or a loom before starting to work on it.

This meant a great shipping trade to and from the Marble Lands. The main port was named the Gold-and-Silver Pier—the Pier, for short. A roofed and colonnaded landing place stretched far out into the sea. Smaller colonnades jutted from the central pier, all of them built of the same veined white marble which glittered rivulets of gold and silver in the sunlight.

Along the colonnades were the stalls of the bazaar sellers, and the marble floor was worn down where generations of sandaled feet had hurried on the shortest paths.

The Pier swarmed with buyers, sellers, seamen, travelers, and heavily burdened porters carrying cargo to lines of cargo beasts waiting at the shore end of the Pier.

Knowing they would be observed, Hamar's captains had chosen to appear on the horizon when the noon sun could blaze fully on their bright sails and on the bronze shields they had hung along the rails of the oared galleys.

The rich glintings had brought the port's inhabitants thronging to the breakwater. First vessel to arrive was the fast little *Whizzard,* which darted and swooped outside the breakwater while the escort brought up the slower *Sulubar.* At the entrance to the breakwater, the escorting fleet turned back, to seek a haven further along the coast where none would enquire too closely as to their allegiance. The turning maneuver was executed with a precise flashing of oars and interweaving of vessels that brought cheers from the onlookers.

Fire Lotus's agents had been among the throng. Convinced that Nevyev indeed had rich wares on the *Sulubar,* they hastened to board—and were jostled aside by other agents who had been spying on them. Nevyev soon sold out his stock of wares and was using the *Whizzard's* mirror to speak with the Crucible Fortress and order more.

The "retinue" had made such an excellent first impression that Zeid decided not to let it be marred by time and familiarity. He sent the *Sulubar* to rejoin the escort, along a coast which had been so cowed by the show of strength that no raider dared venture out against Nevyev.

Zeid had remained clean-shaven. He explained to Moji, "The lady Coral Bud would have me thus. Not that I do it for her sake—but if she likes me better without a beard, perhaps the princess also will like me better."

"Well-reasoned, Lord Zeid," said Moji with a straight face.

After the *Sulubar* sailed, there was a conference aboard the *Whizzard*. Zeid was surprised at Coral Bud's apparent indifference to the palace visit.

"I dare not approach the princess, anyhow," she said. "I can stay at the Pier and begin sending my seal-mark to the Counting Guilds. It's time I called the Moonship and ordered the wares for my barge."

"Rover Bud, I welcome any help in setting up hospices," said Zeid. "I know you're sincere because you've been intent on a barge from the very first. But you don't have the training to assemble Space lamps—and can't learn the craft overnight."

"Perhaps not—but I can borrow gold from Knarb and buy other wares from the Moonship. The Desert harems will pay well for Space Giver hair foam and the Magic styling staff. I think also to bargain for the softening lotion. Then there are things my hospice beggars can learn to make—the game puzzles and maybe even the food prongs.

"And Zeid, if you're really taking Muff as an apprentice, order his apprentice clothes. He yearns for a leathern apron, important with loops and pockets."

"Yes, yes—tell Moji," said Zeid impatiently. "But can't you understand I'm most concerned about winning Fire Lotus? To arrive properly at the palace—"

"Is no great problem, well? Be assured the princess will let you know what tribute she expects."

They were sitting on the curved divan in the Master's cabin. Before Zeid could find words for the reproaches in his mind, Moji knocked at the door and entered.

"Lord Zeid," he said, "a gem seller has arrived whom I dare not send away since he is purveyor to the princess and, I surmise, comes at her bidding."

"Well, show him in and stay to hear the business."

Moji ushered a well-clad Guildsman into the Master's cabin. The man bowed deeply to Zeid and, after a moment's thought, to Coral Bud.

"Prince Zeid—and princeling," he began. "I bring the planet's largest and most exquisite gems—an emerald and a pearl. Either would enchant the princess—both would ensure her highest favor."

He reached into a large pouch belted to his waist, drew out two smaller pouches, and handed them to Zeid.

Zeid shook first the pearl, then the emerald, into his palm, and studied them in the sunlight streaming through the portholes.

He repouched the gems and returned them to the Guildsman. "I buy no wares made dull by greasy commerce," he said calmly. "The pearl's lustre is clouded, the emerald's bezel is worn smooth, so often has the princess sold and resold them to aspiring suitors. I will not have her think me such a fool that I don't see her game."

"She certainly will think you a fool if you see the game and don't play it!" retorted the Guildsman.

Zeid nodded to Moji, who opened the door and ushered the gem seller out of the cabin.

Coral Bud said, "Zeid, don't break your heart because beauty has ensnared you. Like Discord, you're battling Time. Fire Lotus is a child of her generation and can't understand future ideas."

"Weren't you also a child of your generation? Yet, as I look at you, I think you belong more to the Moonship than the planet. Indeed, I think you'll be very unhappy unless you can get back to your hair stylist and bargain with Moonship agents for the latest imports. Time has been no barrier. In one leap you've gone from pirate girl to Space Age commuter."

"But, of course, I am Hamar's daughter, and you've heard the esteem in which my father is held. Don't expect the same wit from a mere princess."

"What I expect, Rover Bud, is that you'll mastermind our visit to the palace. I'm too intent on forming persuasions and arguments to give thought to robes and jewels. The gem seller mistook you for a young prince with your short hair and slim figure. You can still play my page if you're adroit about it."

"I daresay being a Master Mind will leave my lustre clouded

and my bezel worn," smiled Coral Bud. "What boon will you grant me in return? Will you speak to Dr. Marnadal on behalf of my plan?"

"Yes, I'll secure the Space barge you want," promised Zeid. "Now call Moji back and order whatever will win the respect of Fire Lotus and her courtiers."

"Like it or not, you must come with a gift. Buy a golden girdle, stud it with brilliants, and needle it into filagree as you did for Kalia's necklace. The princess will welcome it, I promise you."

THE MILK WHITE QUARRIES were inland. The little party from the *Whizzard*, followed by their porters, met their caravan beasts at the shore plaza. Each person sat sideways on a beast in a satin-lined, plump-cushioned, sandalwood chair. When the bundles and parcels had been stowed on other beasts, the caravan set out through the town.

Coral Bud felt very small, winding past the polished marble terraces and castle-like marble buildings. Here was massive wealth, each object twice as high as it needed to be. Statues on the terrace walls seemed man-sized at a distance, only to grow and grow until they towered over her head as she rode past them.

They left the town and started up the winding road into the mountains. On either side were tall, dark green, comb-toothed trees, fragrant but casting heavy, deep shadows. A cold, sparkling brook leapt and foamed, running first on one side, then crossing under the road in a deep chasm and running on the other.

After a two-hour ride, they paused at the top of a rise. Below lay a forested valley where clear blue lakes were chained by a canal. White splotches in the green hills showed where marble was being cut from the underlying rock.

At the end of the valley was a narrow abyss leading into the next valley. It was there, on either side of the abyss, the halves connected by a bridge, that the many-towered palace of Fire Lotus gleamed in the sun.

After the pause they continued down to the first Quarry lake where richly draped pleasure barges were waiting to take them aboard. The transfer from beast to boat was done speedily and courteously by well-trained servants.

As they proceeded along the chain of lakes, they saw other barges and skiffs.

"The princess must have many guests," said Zeid. "I'll have many listeners for my ideas."

"Yes, Fire Lotus holds magnificent court. Poor little Muff. He hasn't blinked his eyes or shut his mouth the whole journey, so overawed he feels. I must rehearse him in the arrival ceremony we arranged, else he will stand and gape for breath like a goldfish."

"I'm in danger of gaping myself," smiled Zeid.

"Take heart," said Coral Bud. "Remember, Fire Lotus doesn't know you as well as I do."

"You're a great comforter, sea urchin."

The barges arrived at a marble landing beneath the abyss. The cargo was hoisted on ropes. The people followed a winding marble staircase that had landings with benches where guests could sit and rest awhile before resuming the climb.

"Well, it's one way to ensure having only young, healthy suitors," commented Coral Bud.

At the top of the staircase the major-domo greeted them and conducted them to the guest suite that had been prepared for them. The wide-silled windows looked out over the next valley. The suite's rugs, tapestries, mosaics, and cushions were of the finest artistry.

"And yet," said Zeid, "my father has furnishings as fine."

"And well he might," said Coral Bud. "Duplos certainly sell for higher prices than marble blocks."

After they had bathed and costumed themselves, the major-domo led the small party through the high-vaulted marble halls to the chamber where the princess was holding her afternoon audience. At the gold-leafed double doors they paused to regroup. Kalia and Moji, accustomed to palace routine, were at ease. Muff was icy-fingered and white-faced.

"Dear Muff," Coral Bud whispered to him. "A short speech is nothing to trouble a Space apprentice. Be brave and courteous, and all will be well."

The slaves flung open the doors. A buzz of sound came from the crowd in the chamber.

The major-domo strutted ahead down the gold-edged carpet. After him came Kalia and Moji, attired like a peasant bridal pair. Then came three richly clad look alikes—Muff followed by Sir Page followed by Prince Zeid.

Coral Bud had decided that identical costumes would best distract Fire Lotus from herself.

Zeid was an impressive figure from two worlds—clad like a planet prince, yet clean-shaven like a Space Giver and wearing his coding belt and Magic poniard.

Surprise and wonder silenced the crowd. How would Fire Lotus respond?

The princess was seated on a purple-draped divan, which was raised atop a three-step dais. Her most favored guests lounged on the wide marble steps around the divan.

Her beauty was more vital, more intense, in the flesh: the sheen of her rich copper hair—her pearly skin—her bright green eyes. Rare, flashing crystals pinned back her hair, dangled from her ears, looped her bosom, edged her gossamer gown which had been made in panels that revealed her fair limbs as she moved.

The major-domo stopped before the dais, tapped the end of his staff on the marble floor, and announced, "The Prince Zeid ben Amfi!"

The courtiers murmured at the name.

Kalia and Moji stepped aside, made low bows, and proceeded to kneel, one on either side of the dais.

Muff stepped forward and bowed; Sir Page and the prince bowing at the same instant.

They straightened up, and Muff recited,

> "Fair one, we could not hope our plea
> —that you love us as we love thee—
> Could all at once a true joy be."

Sir Page continued the verses,

> "So hope we, if your love start small,
> the shoot will grow to middles tall
> And at the last embrace us all."

Muff and Sir Page also stepped aside and knelt. Zeid advanced, drew the gem-sparkling, gold filagree girdle from his robes, and began,

"I bring homage to beauty with gold—"

He hesitated. Fire Lotus's green eyes were staring at the golden girdle with feral joy. He went on, with serious emphasis,

"Homage to wit with thoughts—"

Nothing stirred the predatory joy in the princess's countenance.

Zeid looked around. Everywhere he saw the mindless lusts of a planet just beginning to know its strength—eager for sensuous pleasures, greedy for toys, trinkets.

He lowered the golden gift and said, "This is ridiculous! It's not even a ceremony or a game—it's a nightmare!"

At last the princess glanced from the dangling gold to Zeid's wrathful, bemused expression.

She smiled, "Have your wits been turned by our magnificence?"

"What do you know about magnificence?" demanded Zeid. "A starship blasting off and outrunning light so fast that light seems to stand still—*that* is magnificence! A galaxy of worlds trading with and enriching each other—*that* is magnificence!

"I stand here like a time traveler," he went on, "knowing what course the planet will take, and yet working to direct it to another destination. Bronze Ages have a changeless tenor that makes them seem golden ages. No one disputes the right of princes to amass treasure. Beggars are content to beg.

"But know, O princess, the Iron Age will overturn and destroy princes. What does a tide of beggars understand—except revenge and destruction?"

He held the glittering girdle up again. "You can choose, princess. Will you transform the worth of this bauble into food and learning? Will you share and educate, so that future ages will have less need to avenge and destroy?

"Or will you have the bauble for itself, to wear a few days and cast aside? Will you linger like a stupid grazing beast on a doomed plateau—or will you climb with me to a further plateau where Mankind is more important than baubles and learning is more powerful than gold?"

The princess had been listening with amused interest. She smiled, "The planet can take what course it likes. My course runs briefly now—and stops forever. I'd be a stupid grazer indeed to share my lush pastures with a trampling herd.

"Nor would you be doing so, either, Light-Bearer, if your father's lush pastures were all you had. But you have the Magic of the Moonship, so you lose nothing when you squander your patrimony on beggars."

"But enrichment is the whole sum of the message I bring you, princess!" urged Zeid. "I gain more true wealth from my hospice than I lose from the gold I spend on it. I gain the warmth of another's happiness, the pride of new learning, the wisdom of new experiences. I gain a power within myself that is more nourishing than fine food—more sublime than thoughts."

"Well, Light-Bearer, I don't know how thoughts can be sublime. Sublimity is only an emotional degree of pleasure. Obviously you take pleasure in strange labors. Yes, of course, I accept the princely gift for itself and will wear it to enhance my beauty."

Zeid sighed deeply. "I thought I loved you, princess. If you were real, your foolishness would break my heart. But you're only a dream from a thousand years in my own past. Enjoy your lush grazing, Bronze Age beauty."

He tossed the girdle at her feet. She snatched it up and held it aloft for the courtiers to admire.

Zeid said, "Rise, Kalia and Moji, my dear friends. Rise, little Muff. This has been a sad beginning for your Space apprenticeship. And you, sea urchin. Woe to me if Hamar finds his daughter has knelt to greed and ignorance."

"What!" The princess flung the golden girdle to her divan and stared at Coral Bud as she got up from the carpet. "The page is a girl!"

She leaped like a tigress upon Coral Bud. "You'll pay for

playing games with me, sea king's daughter!"

A fistful of red hair just suited Coral Bud. Her strong pull jerked Fire Lotus off her feet, and Coral Bud swung her by her hair into the nearest courtiers.

Guards were converging from the edges of the chamber. Zeid drew his Combi-shot and mowed a clear swath toward the double doors. "Run!" he ordered. "Moji—the portation rug!"

Muff, Kalia, and Moji made a successful break for the double doors, jumping over the stunned bodies.

Coral Bud was again entangled with the furious princess. Zeid mowed another swath, catching Fire Lotus's upraised arm in his beam. She cried out and ceased to fight. Coral Bud gave her hair another twist for good measure and sprang free.

Zeid finished stunning the princess, covered Coral Bud's escape, and followed her out of the doorway. He stunned the corridor guards, slammed the chamber doors shut, and melted them together with another programming of his weapon.

When he got to their suite, he found that Moji had already unrolled the portation rug, and Kalia was hastily assembling bags of gems upon it.

Coral Bud had lost her headscarf and half a sleeve. She had a claw scratch along one cheek, but was in merry spirits. "A splendid fight, O prince!"

"I must have been mad, calling you by name," muttered Zeid. "Now we must flee or be torn apart. We are too many to port, so we must levitate. Kalia, Coral Bud, Moji—sit on the rug."

They scrambled upon the sacks of jewels. Zeid pressed a stud on his coding belt and ordered, "One meter—and half again."

The rug rose into the air and hovered. Zeid stooped down and said, "Climb upon my shoulders, Muff."

The apprentice clambered quickly upon Zeid's shoulders, and Zeid rose to full height. He pressed another belt stud and recited,

> "All my weight, and half again,
> To lift us from pursuers' ken."

He floated, and Muff gave a little cry and clutched his hair. Zeid smiled, "Hang on tight, Space boy."

Muff eased his frantic grip. Zeid grasped the fringe of the hovering rug and ordered, "East ten meters."

The rug moved through the open window and stopped over the terraces. Zeid said, "Are my passengers ready to rise into the sky and fly directly? Kalia?"

"Indeed, prince, I have shut my eyes tight, so it makes no difference whether I fly or crawl."

"Muff?"

"I observe there is nothing to fear, sir, so I'm ready to soar like the eagle."

"Here we go," smiled Zeid. He ordered the rug, "A hundred meters up—and south by southwest."

The rug rose and started off, now grazing hilltops, now soaring over valleys, seeming to fly ever higher and higher as the land sloped toward the coast. So high had they been in the mountains that they were far, far above the city and the sea.

The rug halted over the Gold-and-Silver Pier, and Zeid gradually lowered it. Spectators rushed to watch, but the Pier guards kept them from spilling onto the *Whizzard.*

Finally the rug rested on the top of the stern cabin. Zeid deactivated the coding and said, "We can't stop to provision the sloop. As soon as the princess regains her senses, she'll mirror-speak her city agents. We must hasten along the coast to rejoin the *Sulubar* and the escort."

"The tide is unfavorable," said Coral Bud, "and the wind will soon die to the evening calm."

"I will tow us out to sea."

"With what?"

"You're sitting on it. Clear away the jewels. We can also use the hovercraft if you'll rig lines for us."

"A job after my own heart," said Coral Bud. "But first, let's all rid ourselves of our palace finery and change to honest wool. We came so quickly that we need not haste for the sake of the princess."

"Perhaps not, Rover Bud," said Zeid with a strained smile, "but I would like to do all the necessary work and get the sloop to sea at once. After that, I can retire to mourn a lost dream."

"Did it hurt that much to reject her?" asked Coral Bud slowly.

"She was very beautiful. I yearned mightily to possess her. Don't ask me more, sea urchin. I must close my mind until no harm will come to others from my outpouring of grief."

MUFF HAD NO KNOWLEDGE of his master's broken heart. He had run at once to change into his new apprentice clothes. A few minutes later he again stood in front of Zeid, so proud and happy that Zeid had to smile,

"Why, you can be a walking workbench, Muff."

"I asked Moji for the very best apron, master. I know Space tools must be well-kept, the work they do is so delicate and fine. What job do you have for me?"

There was no real job. Both the portation rug and the hover pallet could be controlled by the coding belt. But Zeid said solemnly, "Yes, Apprentice Muff, you must help me tow the sloop out to sea."

The lines were now rigged, and the towing could begin. Coral Bud remained aboard the sloop to direct Moji at the steering oar. Zeid sat on the air-jet-lifted pallet, and Muff sat on the rug.

Zeid coded the Magic from the belt. Pallet and rug moved forward, slowly drawing the sloop out of her end-slot position.

Muff was in constant motion, scrambling from one end of the rug to the other—now peering ahead and calling the course excitedly, as they moved between pier and breakwater, now frowning aft at the tautness of the towing line.

As long as he had Muff under his eye, Zeid's face held a soft brightness like a sunshine behind a cloud. When the towing job was finished and Muff had helped him stow the hardware once more on the sloop, the brightness went away.

"Now I wish to be alone," he said to Coral Bud.

"For a reasonable time, if you will," retorted Coral Bud, "but you must not overburden your shipmates. The tide has turned and runs outward—we are catching the sunset winds. The sloop must be sailed and steered, and Moji and I are just as fatigued as you. Kalia is making supper. Eat and rest."

"I will not eat. Call me for the next watch."

He entered the Master's cabin and shut her out.

AFTER SUPPER MUFF TOOK his robe and cushion to the forward deck to sleep soundly under the lee of the rail. Moji went to the cockpit to steer the sloop. Coral Bud and Kalia sat in the midship cabin.

"Kalia, when we rejoin the *Sulubar*," Coral Bud said, "Moji must come to a business arrangement with Nevyev. Nevyev has created a market for his bronzes in the Marble Lands. He needs a Counting Office there to serve his interest—and to offer other Crucible wares."

"Oh, lady, the Marble Lands are far from the Seacoast and Uncle Tind!" cried Kalia.

"Yes, but a new beginning should be *new*. I admit the Pier city is grand and cold—but then will your own hearth seem warmer and cozier. Moji will have more opportunity in work that he likes. And, best of all, your children need never know that either of you were Desert slaves. Not that captivity is a shame to the captives, but it puts a shadow over young lives that should know only joy."

Kalia considered and said, "Yes, lady. No residence can have all that one would wish—and, as you say, the coldness of the city need never enter our own home. But it will be hard to say farewell to you and the prince—and dear Muff."

"Well, as to that, Moonshippers seem to be much on the go, as if the planet were a small village. I don't doubt we'll meet often."

After a pause Kalia said, "Is it wise for you to leave the prince alone with his sorrow?"

"I can't make up my mind. When a man has been wrong about something, he doesn't like being fussed over by a woman who was in the right about it. In an hour or so, I'll venture to interrupt him."

Shortly before midnight, Coral Bud took her courage in both hands and entered the stern cabin. To her surprise, Zeid was not sitting in darkness. He had drawn the curtains and lit a Space lamp. A carved box was beside him on the divan, and he was staring at it.

He looked up at her approach. "Is it my watch?"

"Soon, yes. May I sit and talk to you?"

"Sit on the other side of the box if you like. Behold."

He continued to stare at the box. It lifted up—moved several inches—dropped down.

"What's the meaning of this?" demanded Coral Bud.

"I'm contemplating. I recalled something Quimmeron had said," Zeid went on, "about Mortals being on another continuum from Immortals."

"If you'll now explain a *continuum*, Light-Bearer."

Zeid thought a moment. "It's like a parallel course, as if one barge canal ran beside another—"

"You don't have to explain parallel courses to a pirate," said Coral Bud with some asperity. "Continue with the continuums."

"Well, it occurred to me that Fire Lotus and I, though existing at the same moment of time, were likewise removed from each other. And I thought, if I removed myself to the paranormal continuum my heartache would cease.

"I don't think paranormality is the healthy way for a civilization to go," he added. "In fact, paranormals don't go, they stop. But somehow, Rover Bud, I must damp down my disappointments and sorrows—"

"If *damp down* means *forget*," said Coral Bud, "I imagine the Spirit Lands would be the worst place to forget sorrow because it's empty of everything else. You'd be surprised how quickly a hurricane or a pirate attack can distract the mind. For that matter, the sight of little Muff in his new smock and apron would so fill my heart as to drive all sorrow out of it.

"You saw how Quintus regretted his immortality," she went on. "Even remembering good food was painful to him. How tragic it would be to contemplate people, as if seeing them in a speech mirror or tube. Why, I even had to refuse poor Quintus a farewell embrace because it might have killed him."

"What!" Zeid sprang from the divan, knocking the box to the carpet. "Can't I keep my eye off you five minutes without finding you entangled with another man? No sooner are you separated from Tommy Lund than you're saying tender farewells to a rascal like Quintus! I wish I could find a way—"

He paused, then exclaimed, "The barge! O sea urchin, I promised you a barge and forgot my promise."

"Sit down, dear prince." Coral Bud took his hand and drew him to the divan. Still clasping his hand, she sat close beside him. She could sense his proud reserve and said, "I but hold you in the continuum while we talk sense."

He smiled a little, and she went on, "I wanted the barge only when it seemed you would leave Mus-al-ram and your hospice work. But now that you'll return, it's best that you keep the barge for yourself."

"Your idea of selling wares to build more hospices was very good, Rover Bud. We'll order two barges."

"No, Light-Bearer. Even on the Moonship, har-dwayr does not grow on trees. It's better to have one barge that is well-planned and fully equipped than two that have been skimped.

"When you have sent your order," she added, "perhaps you'll be kind enough to have the Moonship include my wares which I can market through my Uncle Knarb."

"Which wares?"

"Tomorrow I'll mirror-speak with Lovisa and find out quantity and price."

"Yes, tomorrow we both can speak to Dr. Marnadal, and I can give him the barge specifications I would like."

"Good. And now, dear Zeid, you must take the watch from Moji."

She released his hand. He laid it gently on her arm and said, "You are very dear to me, Rover Bud. I'm sorry that my heart can't rebound from my love for Fire Lotus as fast as—as those of other Space Givers I know."

Coral Bud laughed. He put his arm around her, gave her a little hug, and a quick kiss on her curly head. Then he let her go and strode from the cabin.

MUCH BUSINESS HAD TO be transacted when they rejoined the *Sulubar* and the escort in the coastal harbor. Moji also had been thinking about the business possibilities in the Pier city. He had dealt with several Counting Houses in the course of buying robes and jewels for the palace visit, and he had wondered if Kalia's gold might be invested to buy shares in one of the older, more prosperous Houses.

"For if I come as an intruder," he explained to Zeid and Coral Bud, "I have everyone against me. But if I ally myself to one already prospering, I have immediate profit."

As soon as Nevyev agreed to give Moji the exclusive agency of the Crucible wares, he and Kalia hesitated no longer. There was much mirror-speaking from the *Whizzard*, with a week of negotiations among Counting Houses, Uncle Tind, and the Crucible Fortress, but at last Moji was confirmed as partner in an established Counting House with temporary residence quarters also secured.

"Now for coastal transport," said Coral Bud.

"If Kalia can shut her eyes another time," smiled Zeid, "she and Moji and I can levitate in a half hour, and set down on the very terrace of the Counting House."

"And what about their clothing boxes?"

"We'll tie bales to our shoulders like the Pier porters—and small bales they will be since we left so much when we fled from the palace."

Thus it was arranged. One fine morning the laden trio lifted off to the cheers and waves of the assembled fleet. Coral Bud watched them sail into the fleecy clouds and thought how lonely the *Whizzard* would be without them.

"But, lady, why can't you and I and the prince return to Mus-al-ram on the rug?" asked Muff.

"The sea can't be crossed on an open rug," said Coral Bud, "unless the crossers want to be drenched by storms."

She paced the *Whizzard's* deck, estimating when Zeid would be at the Pier city.

"Now, certainly," she murmured, cocking a practiced eye at the sun's height, "he has started his return journey."

The door to the stern cabin opened, and Zeid said, "You pace the deck to splinters, Rover Bud."

She jumped around and put a hand to her fluttering heart. "Oh, how you startled me! You ported home!"

"Yes, when I was alone I could reach the portation patterns.

Moji has chosen a fine Counting House, I'm sure. I liked the old merchant who commands it."

"Zeid, can't we leave the *Whizzard* with my father's escort and port to Mus-al-ram? We have very little cargo."

"And will have less when I give Nevyev the sacks of gems and such lamps as I have left as part-payment for the debt I owe him. Yes, Coral Bud, I can port the boxes by themselves, but three people are too many to lie within the patterns. So I will port Muff with myself and return for you."

"Tell me the Magic and just send back the rug. I can port myself."

Zeid looked apprehensive. "It's too risky—"

"One continuum has no more risks than another. I learned to sail. I can also learn to port. I like this new continuum," she said, patting her Moonship curls, "and will travel in it with ease."

"Yes, I think you will," agreed Zeid.

When they were ready to depart, Zeid ported their boxes. He rehearsed Coral Bud in the workshop code and ported with Muff.

After a moment, the empty rug reappeared. Fearful but determined, Coral Bud lay on it, carefully touched the patterns and repeated,

> "Would I were where work is done
> For-to-see if-I've-won."

A jog like a skipped heartbeat. She was lying on Zeid's workroom tiles amid the hastily piled cargo. She looked up and saw that Zeid was alabaster pale, almost like Quintus.

She rolled off the rug. Zeid caught her up and stood her on her feet, keeping his arms around her. "My dear brave little pirate! No man ever had a finer sister!"

"We progress, don't we?" smiled Coral Bud. "I don't know which makes me more dizzy—the portation or your approval. But now let's put your workshop in order and see what lies beyond the door."

The door had to be opened so that the cargo could be cleared away. Coral Bud said to Zeid, "Draw your weapon. An assassin may lurk—or a burrow rat or fang snake—"

Zeid smiled and pressed his thumb in a certain slot upon the door which then opened. A murmur of voices came from the sleep chamber. Now he *did* draw his weapon as he preceded Coral Bud to the source of the voices.

Two hired cabinet makers were measuring a wall. As if that were not surprising enough in itself, the Princess Serada, gossamer-swathed and veiled, was standing gracefully at the foot of a ladder which had been placed under the open window.

"Mother!" exclaimed Zeid. "How came you here?"

She gestured to the ladder. "The way everyone must come since you bar your doors by Magic."

"Are you renewing palace furnishings?"

"Preparing a surprise gift for you, which you do not deserve. Nor do you, Coral Bud, for attacking the Princess Fire Lotus tooth and nail."

"She attacked me first," grinned Coral Bud. "How did she complain to the Wizard?"

"Oh, she mirror-spoke at some length. If you wish more gold from the Wizard," she continued to her son, "you must have a good story for him this evening. He means to cut you off because you didn't get the duplo seed, and I can't help you, you know, because I have very little gold of my own."

"Yes, Mother, your poverty is the talk of the bazaars," returned Zeid ironically. "How can you afford a surprise gift for me?"

"Oh, it's being given by somebody else. And very beautiful it is. All the Wizard's customers wish to keep on good terms with him, so we *do* get lovely craftsmanship. May we continue to work?"

"Certainly. I'll unlock my chamber door. Coral Bud and I will visit Jibbo. I have a new apprentice named Muff whom I will place at your disposal before we leave."

Zeid returned to the workshop where Muff was on tiptoe, eyeing the Space tools on the workbench. Zeid said, "You must busy yourself elsewhere in my chambers, Muff, because I always seal the workshop when I'm not inside it."

"May I—may I have something for my apron pockets?"

"Let me see." Zeid moved to his drafting board. "You may have pencils—and a drawing compass—and the little straightedge—

and the right angle—and the triangle—and the arc—and the little abacus box—and the magnifier—"

When his apron bristled impressively with bright Space metals, Muff marched beaming into the other chamber and bowed low to the Princess Serada.

Zeid and Coral Bud set off to the hospice. Coral Bud asked thoughtfully, "What did your mother Serada mean about a gift?"

"Oh, I suppose she has received an ugly mirror or cabinet and has decided to place it in my quarters. It will not lessen the price of a duplo for the giver though such is usually the intent."

CORAL BUD'S little feet skipped for joy as she hurried alongside the Light-Bearer through the narrow streets.

All at once Zeid stopped so short that she almost tumbled as she stopped beside him. He was staring at a pair of door lintels that might have been twins in the row of dwellings. Each had a large *O* carved as a seal-mark.

Outside the thresholds, beggars squatted with their gruel bowls. Children's voices came from under the farther lintel.

A stocky, leather-aproned man emerged, scolding the beggars but walking softly nonetheless. When he saw Zeid he lifted his arms in surprise, then bowed and smiled, "Light-Bearer!"

"Jibbo!" Zeid stepped forward and embraced his host. "It seems that both the gold and the hospice have calved. I left you with one hospice and have found two."

Jibbo bowed again. "My prince—and lady—come inside and hear my tale, for one thing led to another—"

He escorted them up a narrow, steep stairway immediately inside the first lintel. It rose to a plain, clean chamber. A divan edged the inner wall. Zeid and Coral Bud sat down. Jibbo paced before them.

"Now I must say, Lord Zeid," he began, "I was not pleased at having your gold thrust upon me. However, I told myself, 'You were quick to criticize the prince—now do everything you had been wanting him to do.'

"So I did not rush out to the merchants of Mus-al-ram and

place the gold. The real business is done at Tenfold. But how could I take time for the journey? Who would feed the beggars?

"And then I understood what you had said, Light-Bearer, about the hospice satisfying a need I had not even known existed. For when I thought about the hospice being shut, I realized I would feel hungrier and more anxious than the beggars! Being a source of food had fed my self-esteem, and I would feel woefully starved if I deserted the beggars."

He paused, "Do you remember, Lord Zeid, the babes that were lamed—and the mother who was widowed when you punished the father?"

"Yes," nodded Zeid. "How are they doing?"

"The babes are almost healed by the balm leaves. You said I was to find honest work for the mother, and it occurred to me that I myself might employ her to keep the hospice going. She agreed, and I showed her how to infuse the leaves and how to summon healing Magic from the box.

"She then thought to gather cloth scraps and catch the Magic fluid—and found that the scraps also healed. So she sold them to the merchants' wives and thus increased the amount I had left with her.

"Meanwhile at Tenfold I was trying to place my gold at the best interest and went from one merchant to the next, and at last came to the old pirate Knarb. He had immediate business to push forward and needed gold desperately enough to give me a splendid return for the loan."

Zeid laughed helplessly. Coral Bud explained to Jibbo, "I fear it is Zeid's own gold that financed my father's escort to the Marble Lands—and now calves to itself, as if it had been put in a parthogen bottle. But continue with your tale."

"Well, lady, when I returned to the hospice, I found the mother taking coppers to mind the children of the bazaar sellers, who would rather have their children being taught simple crafts instead of wandering the streets. Their coppers have leased the next dwelling.

"Moreover, among the beggars I find are old men of learning who have been discarded for younger men and who are glad to teach the children in return for hospice care. Thus one thing has led to the next—"

Zeid said, "You've done splendidly, Jibbo—but we're not supposed to sell the healing Magic."

"Nor do we! What we catch and sell is merely what the Space Givers waste. If people wish to keep such Magic on hand in their homes instead of begging from our box, what's wrong with letting them buy?"

Zeid considered. "Nothing, as long as the hospice box continues to be free. Also, the new infusings must be pure and full strength. We cannot sell watered-down Magic."

Coral Bud suggested, "Now here is a job for your new apprentice. Take a jar of fluid to your workshop and teach Muff how to cut scraps of the same size and soak them in measured amounts of the Magic. For if the scraps are too wet, a scoundrel may wring them out and sell them yet again—and the Moonship would forbid the whole traffic."

"A good idea, Coral Bud. I must keep Muff employed, but he is far too young to understand even the tools with which he has stuffed his apron's loops and pockets."

AFTER ZEID HAD UNLOCKED his chamber door for his mother's servants, it did not take them long to install the cabinet that was to be the new gift. When it was in place, Serada and the workmen went away, and Muff was alone.

The servants had carried the ladder away. The white-hot midday heat was billowing through the open window. Muff placed a hassock on a chest so that he could climb up and draw the shutters together.

In the dimmer, cooler light, he stood in front of the cabinet and wondered what his master would place inside. It was indeed beautifully carved—and tall and broad.

As Muff stood there, he heard a thud. The bronze latch of the cabinet door lifted—the door opened—

Muff's former master, the Space Lord Feelafell, walked out of the cabinet.

Muff was too shocked to move. He believed his death had come.

Feelafell was wearing lordly satin robes. A drawn sword was in his ungloved hand. The blade was iron—a novelty from the new smelters of armorers who formerly had worked with blends of copper, tin, and zinc.

From his Space Giver height Feelafell looked coldly at the boy. "Where's the prince?"

"G-gone into the city," stammered Muff.

"And what do you imagine I now will do with *you*, false Muff?"

"No harm," said Muff steadily, "because Space Givers harm none. Didn't I work hard for you—and keep watch alone on your Moonship? You are too wise to blame a poor boy for matters far beyond his sphere."

"I have a grievance against all who think Zeid ben Amfi is nobler—or more learned—or cleverer than myself."

"But he can be none of those things," said the wily Muff. "He is not a born Space Giver. There's no limit to your cleverness, Lord Feelafell. Who else would send a travel box as a gift to his enemy?"

"The prince has such contempt for me that he discarded the portation box when he tricked me out of the Cloud. I'm returning the compliment," said Feelafell with a sweep of the iron sword. "What has he done with my Moonship?"

"Alas, Space Lord, the Spirit people have your Moonship, and the prince has no idea where they have placed it. Do you know the Spirit people? I think they once were Space Givers themselves—"

Muff's ear caught the sound of the chamber door. He broke off his tale and yelled, "Beware, O prince!"

Feelafell raised his sword and slashed at the boy, knocking him to the tiles. A red streak spurted across the apron.

The primitive iron sword met Space Age steel and snapped. The broken edge flew up and pierced deep into Feelafell's heart.

At the moment Feelafell had raised the sword, Zeid had dropped the jar he had carried from Jibbo. He sprang into the room, seized a cooper lamp from its niche near the door, and hurled it at Feelafell.

Having completed his slash at Muff, Feelafell crumpled to the tiles—to Zeid's puzzlement. He had not seen or heard the blade snap. All his attention was on Muff, lying on the tiles with an ugly red streak part way across his apron.

Zeid rushed to him and fell to his knees. Muff opened his eyes, "Am I dead, Master?"

"Muff!" said Zeid almost fearfully. "Such a cruel slash did not slice you in two?"

Coral Bud, standing over the dead Feelafell said, "The sword broke—and killed the wielder. And Muff is so thickly armored with Space tools that the blade went no deeper than flesh."

"Don't lift him!" ordered Zeid. "The regeneration fluid—"

He rose and went to the dropped jar. The pieces lay scattered, but the fluid had drained into worn hollows in the tiles. Zeid fetched a clean scarf from a clothing chest, blotted up the precious Magic with the scarf, and brought the scarf to Muff.

Coral Bud had carefully removed the apron that had saved the boy's life. She lifted aside his torn clothing. The cuts welled blood.

Zeid drew the Combi-shot he had not thought to use against Feelafell, adjusted it to a needle, and made a zigzag along the cut which pulled the edges together. A crossing zigzag—and Muff was stitched as neatly as fine embroidery.

They bound the Magic-soaked scarf against the cut and lifted Muff to the divan. He murmured, "I begin to be sleepy."

"Then the Magic has entered your blood," said Zeid. "Sleep happily, Muff—all is well."

Muff gave them a drowsy smile and drifted into healing slumber.

Zeid finally turned to look at his dead enemy. Unbelieving, he put his fingers on the edge of the blade protruding from Feelafell's body. "The damnedest kind of accident—!"

Coral Bud said, "He chose to kill from the wrong continuum. His weapon came from a doomed plateau."

"What am I going to do about him?"

"Put him in the box, port him back to where he came from,

and lame the box. You are a very learned man, Zeid ben Amfi, but if you had once sailed before the mast, you would know when trouble is to be bundled up and left for another man to explain."

"We'll never know how Feelafell shielded his hardware."

"Why, that's simple. He removed portions of the planet's atmosphere that guide birds and fish. He removed *direction*. That's why poor Tem could not fly or keep his balance. But talking idly about Magic does not remove Feelafell's body."

"True. Lift his feet, Rover Bud, and I'll take the shoulders. Somehow we must stow him in the box."

With much effort they fitted the tall body and the broken sword into the cabinet. Zeid ported Feelafell away. He then lamed the portation element so that the box was only a cabinet.

When a slave came to enquire if they wished refreshment, they were busy clearing the bundles from the Space workshop as if nothing had happened.

"But we'll hear from the Moonship," sighed Zeid.

"And you must act very surprised, and thank them for telling you."

"My fingerprints are on the blade end."

"I wiped them off. Too many times as a child did my floury little fingers give a trail for the cook to follow. Dr. Marnadal is a kind man, but I think he's probably as shrewd as a sea cook."

They kept within Zeid's chambers the rest of the afternoon. Neither of them wanted to leave the sleeping Muff. They fetched the mirror, which Zeid had brought from the *Whizzard*, and hung it on the chamber wall. Later in the afternoon it began emitting a beep—beep and showed the seal-marks CALL MOONSHIP.

Zeid stepped to the mirror and called the Monitor Board.

Dr. Marnadal's somber face looked out. "Your weapons code you as being in Mus-al-ram, Zeid. How did you get there so fast?"

"We ported earlier today, Dr. Marnadal. Is there something wrong?"

"Yes—and very strange it is. A native named Grodd called us. He had been employed by Feelafell, and he found his master's body slumping out of a portation box. We sent a Cloud for it immediately."

"And?" queried Zeid as Marnadal paused.

"There's no doubt Feelafell was killed by the iron sword he apparently was wearing or carrying. Only his fingerprints are on the grip. The blade had snapped off against harder metal and plunged into his heart."

"Harder metal? The planet has no harder metal than iron."

"Space machines are everywhere. I don't know why Feelafell would strike against steel—in rage, perhaps, or just to test the blade. Whoever witnessed the accident ported him back to Tenfold and cancelled further portation. Understandable, of course, but—"

"Didn't Grodd know where Feelafell had been porting?"

"He says not, and I believe him. The Tenfold castle is in great confusion. The horde-ships now revert back to us—the castle reverts to the city defenses—the personal property reverts to next-of-kin, siblings and a father on other planets. And what use have they for duplos and barbaric splendor? I daresay we'll have to hold a public auction."

"Who are you sending to sort out the mess?"

"Our choice may surprise you, Zeid. What we need is a person capable of unscrambling a mass of data and keeping the horde-ships running. We're sending Lovisa Cox. She's a data specialist, and you and Coral Bud can help her with the human relationships. Through old Knarb, Coral Bud can keep the Seacoast merchants in line."

"Lovisa is an excellent choice, Dr. Marnadal. I trust Envoy Rogg isn't making trouble."

"How can he? The Moonship had no way of stopping Feelafell from dressing up like Hammurabi and shattering his own sword. By the way, Zeid, Tom Lund will be delivering your barge. Sorry we can't let him stop off awhile. Good luck with the hospices!"

The mirror blanked. Zeid said, "I don't know why I feel guilty. I haven't done anything."

"You lived. It's nothing to apologize for, but it was enough for Feelafell."

AT SUNSET A SLAVE came to summon Zeid to supper in his mother's apartments where the Wizard would be joining them. Zeid sighed,

"I hope Tom delivers the barge soon, or I'll be sharing a pallet at the hospice."

"You'll defend yourself against the Wizard's tirades, well?"

"Defend, how? I didn't get Fire Lotus for him. Besides, I don't care."

"Oh? How are you to repay your debt to Nevyev unless you get your share of your father's wealth?"

Zeid's face darkened. "Yes, I borrowed unwisely—and futilely. The cost of the golden girdle alone—"

"And the skill wasted in the exquisite filagree! But stop brooding over losses and think how to make them up. We must answer your father and win his favor."

"We? You haven't been summoned."

"A mere oversight, which your mother will remedy when you tell her of it. What! After helping you so faithfully, I'm to stand aside and see you brought to disgrace?"

Zeid began to laugh. "You just want to match wits with the Wizard. Very well. I'll send word to my mother that I wish you to dine with us."

"While you're about it, send also for a nice grandmother to look after Muff. I don't want him to be alone when he awakens."

THE PRINCESS SERADA'S APARTMENTS were the same whirl of activity—duplos being instructed—slaves and eunuchs hurrying with cushions and jewels. There was perhaps more of a bustle on this evening since the Wizard was favoring his seed-wife with a visit.

A slave ushered Zeid and Coral Bud into the audience chamber. A table had been placed among the cushions, but the chamber was empty.

"Will you sit?" asked Zeid.

"No, since we must rise when your parents enter," said Coral Bud. "At least Rustad and his three ninnies will not be present."

The panel to the bedchamber slid aside. Serada appeared, richly gowned in embroidered rose satin and hung with ropes of delicately carved apple-green jade. Her cinnamon hair was held back by jade pins. Her youthful cheeks were as rosy as her gown.

Behind her sauntered the Wizard, a darkly bearded pleasure-lover clad in gold brocade. He looked satisfied—even satiated—and Coral Bud guessed that Serada had been using the wiles of the marriage couch to win forgiveness for her younger son.

Zeid and Coral Bud bowed deeply, and the two couples sat on the cushions around the table. The Wizard clapped his hands, and slaves hurried into the chamber with food and wine.

"Enjoy your meal, Prince Zeid," said the Wizard sarcastically, "since it's likely to be the last under my roof."

"As you wish. But you really have no reason to be angry with me, father."

"You lost me a chance at prime duplo seed!"

"True. But as we say on the Moonship, what would you have done for an encore?"

"So the answer is to be a flaunting of Moonship power—the beardless Space Giver face and the incomprehensible tongue?"

"Your pardon, Wizard," spoke up Coral Bud. "I think Zeid means you were creating a market you never would be able to supply—and destroying the market you already have."

"How so, lady Coral Bud?"

"Who would be content with a nameless duplo if his neighbor had a Fire Lotus doll? Your customers would hold back buying duplos until you had found a still more beautiful princess—which would have been impossible. Fire Lotus's seed would have wrecked your business. You're angry because Zeid failed—but you would have been far angrier if he had succeeded."

The Wizard eyed his son. "I hope you didn't trouble yourself overmuch, failing to such purpose."

"Well, it *was* trouble, father," said Zeid gravely. "I could more easily have succeeded, to your ruination."

"And about depriving me of Moji? And your mother of Kalia?"

"Father, serfdom and slavery are not economically viable."

"Your pardon again, Wizard," said Coral Bud. "Zeid is speaking only to tease us both. What he means is that Moji was a freeman who knew his worth. Soon you would have to displace a palace official to accommodate him. Having freed him to retain him, you would have had to promote him or let him go.

"And promotions are expensive, Wizard. You received the best of Moji's services at a minimum price—and are now quit him at an opportune time for you both."

Serada smiled, "And what did Zeid's words mean about Kalia?"

"Kalia, having grown from child to woman, would have become a worry and expense. She would have mated and would have paid more attention to her family than to her palace duties. But now, grateful for freedom, she speaks with praise of the Princess Serada's gentle supervision—of the wise teaching and fine clothes she enjoyed."

"So you see, father," grinned Zeid, "I don't fail—I merely translate very poorly."

"You have an excellent interpreter," replied the Wizard, "but you know, I feel distaste for an heir who enriches me only incidentally while pursuing other goals."

"Would you have Zeid ignore the greater for the lesser?" retorted Coral Bud swiftly. "Until now, Zeid has been known as the Wizard Amfi's son. But hereafter will your own fame rest upon being the Light-Bearer's father!"

The Wizard laughed. "Poor Hamar! Soon to be reduced to Coral Bud's sire."

A white glow briefly lit the darkness of the opened window. Coral Bud cried, "A Cloud descends!"

Zeid jumped to his feet. "My new barge! Come, father! See what the Moonship has granted me!"

The Wizard rose and followed his son from the chamber.

The princess smiled at Coral Bud. "You may leave me if you wish. You must be eager to see the barge."

Coral Bud slowly rose to her feet. "Eager—but I'm playing for high stakes, Mother Serada. The barge is the final throw of the dice—the last move on the board. Now I must await the outcome alone, where Zeid knows he can find me."

THE PALACE LANDING PLACE was thronged with warriors and officials. Bulbul was completely agog, jiggling and flashing as he hastened to bow before the Wizard and Zeid.

The Cloud was still hovering over a mooring slot. It released the barge from its lower cargo hatch, winked a green light rapidly—G-O-O-D L-U-C-K P-A-L—and lifted away.

The barge was no wider or longer than those of lords like Bulbul since such barges were the maximum allowed by canal dimensions. It was, however, built with Space efficiency. The lower midship cabin had not only a workshop but a comfortable apprentice nook. The upper cabin was enclosed with windows of two-way Moonship glass. There were double-decked forward and aft cabins and enclosed lockers instead of the provision chests.

Zeid saw his brother Rustad haughtily sulking among his warriors, and he called out, "Come hither, elder prince! Honor me by being the first, after our father the Wizard, to step aboard the new craft."

Rustad immediately regained his arrogance. Zeid bowed his father aboard. Rustad swaggered after. Zeid stepped behind his brother, thus blocking out Bulbul to the glee of the other officials, who did not mind being excluded themselves as long as Bulbul had been set in his place.

Rustad soon tired of the inspection. "There is no roistering or gaming space here," he complained, "nor any duplo chamber. My own quarters are far finer."

Satisfied about his own superiority, he ambled ashore.

The Wizard said to Zeid, "I don't understand—or care to understand—Moonship teachings, but I *do* understand power when I see it. I would be very foolish indeed to show you less favor than the Moonship.

"Thus your share of my gold will continue. I wish I could increase it, but Rustad costs me much, and your mother—"

"Yes, yes, father. Whatever you can spare me, I accept with gratitude—and will try to spend wisely."

The Wizard left the barge, pleased at still being able to manage cheaply as regards his younger son.

Zeid toured the barge alone, smiling to himself. Something was missing. He had expected it to be missing, but he wanted to be sure. As long as he was alone on the barge, it would be empty, hollow. There would be no coziness. Coziness was Coral Bud.

He hurried ashore and said to the major-domo, "Provision the barge at once—and send slaves to my quarters."

He paused. Having made his decision, how could he tell it to Coral Bud? The planetary bethrothal words and forms were inappropriate for a Moonship girl. Not only her pretty curls but also the shrewd thoughts inside her head were Moonship-oriented. She had never heard the words *economically viable*, but she knew slave labor did not produce.

To say, "Coral Bud, wilt thou espouse me and be my true seed-wife" was—ridiculous. It was from the wrong world. On the other hand, she knew only scraps of Space Giver tongue.

A happy solution occurred to him. They were already be-throthed. They could move aboard and let mutual love speak its own language.

CORAL BUD HAD FOUND Muff propped up on cushions and being fed by a motherly nurse. He explained, "I was hungry—I hope my master approves of a meal for me."

"Well, since you're tightly sewn and lashed fast, none of it will dribble out," smiled Coral Bud.

The nurse left with the empty dishes. Coral Bud once more sat at Muff's feet and recounted how the Cloud had descended.

Zeid entered with slaves. Coral Bud could not help but notice how his face glowed with happiness. Was she a part of it?

Zeid came over to the divan. "The slaves can pack and bear the cargo, but the apprentice must be carried more gently."

He pressed a stud on his belt and the hovercraft pallet hissed to life from the corner where it had been stowed. Zeid guided it alongside the divan and said, "Now, sea urchin, sit on the pallet and support Muff."

He was taking her aboard the barge! Coral Bud's heart swelled with such gladness that she nearly fainted. But she sat on the pallet. Zeid lifted Muff and his cushions, and laid the boy on the pallet so that Coral Bud was holding his head and shoulders.

When all was comfortably arranged, Zeid sprang upon the chest beneath the window, opened the shutters, and pulled himself to the sill. The pallet gushed like a whirlwind and rose to follow him.

He let himself drop to the shadowy, night-fragrant garden, and the pallet skimmed through the window and descended to *shush* in pace with him.

Zeid did not speak, but Coral Bud sensed his carefully restrained excitement.

The landing place was still crowded with spectators. The stowing of the barge had only begun, so there was much confusion aboard. Zeid guided the pallet into the new workshop only he could unlock. He halted the pallet before the aft panel.

It opened into a cabin with a full-sized divan, a small workbench, and a clothing chest agape to show Moonship coveralls. Zeid lifted Muff from the pallet and laid him on the divan while Coral Bud unkinked her limbs and scrambled to join them.

"Everything here you must grow into, Muff," smiled Zeid, "but this button dims or brightens the lamps—and that button speaks to the cabin above—and here is the box that plays music—"

They left Muff dazedly trying all buttons at once. In the workshop, Zeid deactivated the pallet and slid it behind the workbench. "Let's wait in the upper cabin, Rover Bud, until the barge is stowed."

Feeling as dazed as Muff, Coral Bud climbed the ladder and entered the midship chamber. It looked like a tent because the large windows were draped with flowing curtains and the ceiling was also cloth-draped. There were the usual cushions and small chests and trays. The speech-mirror had already been hung between two windows.

They sat on cushions in their usual places. Zeid said, "I seek for language to explain my feelings for you, Rover Bud. I can't live without you."

"Dear prince, are you sure," smiled Coral Bud, "after the merry chase I've led you?"

"It *has* been merry, and your heart is kind and loyal. I overheard you telling Kalia that you would mate for life like a sea bird. Such is my wish also, and I saw no reason to wait beyond tonight to begin our travels."

"Very sensible. And no reason to wait to begin our mating either."

Zeid blushed red. "You tease me, little pirate—and I feel shy. The idea is so new to me—and so exciting—and so solemn—"

"Oh, I daresay you'll get used to it."

"Yes, we have the whole night ahead of us after we clear the city watergrid. How the slaves dawdle! I'll die of impatience! Tell me a story to make the time go faster."

"What shall I speak of?"

"The Great Wizard's worlds-without-end. You've spoken of Happiness and Harmony, Truth and Justice, Mercy and Hope— but where is Love?"

"Why, the Great Wizard is Love, of course—and shows it in so many ways. Now, because Hope was always hastening after his mother Time to bid her take new paths, he tended to be always on the horizon and not as much comfort as he could be if he were inside Discord's cave to protect the poor creatures from Doubt and Despair.

"So the Great Wizard took his own cloak off his back. It was very warm because it had two linings. One was called Faith, and the other was called Patience—"

Zeid settled back into his cushions and smiled. When he watched and listened to the sea urchin, he was transported out of Discord's cave and the tyranny of Time—and into the Great Wizard's worlds-without-end—without end—without end—

Berkley's
Finest Science Fiction!

ROBERT A. HEINLEIN

____ GLORY ROAD   (04349-5–$2.25)
____ I WILL FEAR NO EVIL   (04386-X–$2.50)
____ THE MOON IS A HARSH MISTRESS
                                           (04348-7–$2.25)
____ THE PAST THROUGH TOMORROW
                                           (03785-1–$2.95)
____ STARSHIP TROOPERS   (04331-2–$1.95)
____ STRANGER IN A STRANGE LAND
                                           (04688-5–$2.75)
____ TIME ENOUGH FOR LOVE
                                           (04684-2–$2.75)

ROBERT SILVERBERG

____ BORN WITH THE DEAD (04156-5–$1.95)
____ THE MASKS OF TIME   (03871-8–$1.95)
____ TO LIVE AGAIN   (03774-6–$1.95)
____ TO OPEN THE SKY   (03810-6–$1.95)
____ UNFAMILIAR TERRITORY
                                           (03882-3–$1.95)
____ A TIME OF CHANGES (With a new
Introduction)   (04051-8–$1.95)

Available at your local bookstore or return this form to:

B **Berkley Book Mailing Service**
       P.O. Box 690
       Rockville Centre, NY 11570

Please send me the above titles. I am enclosing $_____
(Please add 50¢ per copy to cover postage and handling). Send check or
money order—no cash or C.O.D.'s. Allow six weeks for delivery.

NAME_____

ADDRESS_____

CITY_____STATE/ZIP_____ 26J